Prophecy of the Seven Bottles

Scott Troy Kovarik

Higher Plane Publishing Company
WILLOUGHBY, OHIO

Scott Troy Kovarik/Higher Plane Publishing Company
4132 Amelia Avenue
Willoughby, Ohio 44094
www.scotttroykovarik.net

Publisher's Note: This is a work of fiction. Names, characters, places, and incidents are a product of the author's imagination. Locales and public names are sometimes used for atmospheric purposes. Any resemblance to actual people, living or dead, or to businesses, companies, events, institutions, or locales is completely coincidental.

Book Layout ©2013 BookDesignTemplates.com

Ordering Information:
Quantity sales. Special discounts are available on quantity purchases by corporations, associations, and others. For details, contact the "Special Sales Department" at the address above.

Prophecy of the Seven Bottles/ Scott Troy Kovarik. -- 1st ed.
ISBN 978-0-6923-2411-0

Dedicated to Our Life Teachers in All Disguises

"Everything else can wait but your search for God cannot wait."

-PARAMAHANSA YOGANANDA

This story is fictional, yet based on ancient prophecy, mystical teaching, spiritual wisdom and legend.

{ 1 }

Back to California

THIRTY YEARS FELT LIKE I HAD STEPPED INTO A TIME MACHINE, as the image of a sign from that forgetful night—*Stay Alive Drive 55*— flashed into my mind. As my headlights shined on the black and white roadside sentry, a Michael Jackson song began to play. Then, as if someone had suddenly pressed *stop*, I saw the light: that strange, brilliant, milky white light.

The car stalled, I tried to restart it, nothing, not even a click; the electrical system had died. A bright light shot in through the windshield and surrounded my body. I felt a presence, something watching me; I looked around, nobody there, just light, blinding light. My heart raced like it was about to explode in my chest. Then I began to dissolve; I panicked. After all, I totally dug my twenty-year old bod, and wasn't cool with it being strewn all over the cosmos, at least in those days. Suddenly, the fear turned to relief; I still had a body, but it was light, free, still me, but everywhere. *This isn't right*, I thought: Maybe I got into a car accident and I'm dead. That's when I saw him, err, it, whatever it was.

Its body was smaller than a human's was, but I couldn't make out any details, just two big black creepy eyes looking down on me; everything else was hazy, like an opaque film had been put over my eyes. I never felt threatened, or in danger, but even with regressions and years of soul work and meditation, I couldn't remember anything past that. All I knew was that I had something odd in my hand when I awoke, and wondered what it was and how it got there. Where did I go for all that time? What happened? Why me--and what did it all mean? It was 6:00 pm when I left the lab I was interning at in Silicon Valley. Next thing I know I'm in my Ford Pinto on the side of the highway with a light in my eyes:

"Sir, can I see your license and registration, please?"

It was twelve midnight.

A big wave clapped down and startled me, abruptly jolting me out of the flashback. As the breaker climbed the sandy apron, sandpipers nimbly dodged the frothy flow. Green Malibu brine surprised my feet with a cool tickle between my toes, the water touching them perhaps a gazillionth of the vast sea's total volume. Yet, each molecule of water was--like everything that led to that moment--somehow connected.

From Malibu as an imprudent teen, to computer school in the Pacific Northwest, then to Ohio and back again, ten-thousand days and nights had passed in a blink of the Divine eye. Yet, with my own vision finally clear, I had returned to where my journey began to close a door, and follow a sign that would lead to a future I could never have imagined.

As I looked up at the waterfront duplex, I could see fleeting shadows through tinted windows. Memories there were more reliable and vivid. I could see my pillow-tossed bed tucked in the corner against the bay window beside the secret-keeping wall of the adjoining unit. Lonely nights would find my restless heart calmed by the ocean sloshing hypnotically a few feet below.

By day we'd linger on the veranda above, scouting the beach for chicks. My father would lead the hunt and do the schmoozing. By nightfall we'd be partying like rock stars, as beer bottles and sloshing wine glasses danced merrily between lines of coke dad served up to our greedy guests. Only a baby swing, flowers and an empty birdcage swaying in the breeze occupied our former high-perched deck of decadence. Like vampires, we feasted on the plasma of our unquenchable desires, yet the light of day illumined the painful costs of our actions. I considered knocking, looking in one last time, but what would happen when that door left ajar so many years ago swung back open?

I opened the bag, pulled each one out and set it in the sand. Technically, I was littering and could have been cited. Ironic, I thought, considering their value: priceless to the willing, worthless to the ignorant. Still, I was no longer invested in outcomes; once they left my hand it was the universe's business.

Footsteps and voices were hardly noticeable over the roaring surf as they came down the stairs. She wore a straw hat and white robe with oversize sunglasses and led a small child down the steps.

"Hello," she said cheerily as blond hair whipped across her face in the feisty sea breeze. She held the toddler by the arms like a puppet as he floundered in the sand.

"You don't have to get up," she said.

"No, I'm on your private beach. I apologize for imposing," I replied and began packing my bag.

"No, stay--enjoy."

"Actually, I used to live here," I confessed, hoping to allay concerns over my strange cargo. "Years ago my father and I lived in that apartment up there."

"Hey, that's my place," she said. "What a coincidence."

"I'm *Avery Cole*," I said and extended my hand.

"Destiny...*Destiny Blake*." Her hand was soft and coal-warm with a firm grip. "Please, call me *Madi*."

After a moment of chitchat about the history of the locale and the celebrities that lived nearby, the tot grew irritated. Sand had become uncomfortably bound to his white sun-screened body.

"He's a mess--gotta take him up," she said. "How'd you like to come up and see the old place?" she asked.

"Are you sure?--You're awfully trusting."

"It would be a shame if you didn't get a peek," she replied.

"I guess it was meant to be then."

"That's why they called me Destiny," she said and flashed an attractive smile. I chuckled at her pun.

We climbed the stairs to the wooden catwalk. Planters bursting with aloe and other aromatic plants hung by hemp-woven nets near the door. Shards of sunlight pierced the spaces in the foliage as the breeze played its song on dangling chimes.

As she turned the handle and opened the door the air was sucked from my lungs like yesterday torn from the moment. I stood frozen in the doorway.

"Come in," she enticed.

My feet moved slowly. Minions of nameless emotions swirled like devils dancing with angels.

"Are you okay?" she asked.

"Fine, just been a long time, you know, lots of memories." I paused to collect myself. "The place looks great."

"Thank you, good spirits live in these timbers," she replied. "Make yourself at home--I'll be right back."

Dried eucalyptus scent cast memory bouquets of lemon sky. In a tick I swooned as the mystically infused aroma of Nag Champa spun me into full lotus-petal euphoria. Near levitating, I drifted on plush carpet to my old sleeping area. A plain loveseat and table now stood where the altar of carnal desire once drew like-minded believers. Just outside four o'clock gold lit up the olive-green shimmering Pacific. As I gazed through the bay window glass at parading boats, I was reminded how many times we do not see blockades to our freedom until we get right up on them.

"How's the little guy?" I asked as she returned.

"Its nap time, so he'll be out for a while. Please, sit down and relax, I'll get us some tea."

The fluffy couch received my mass. She lowered herself draped in a silk oriental robe. Her beauty radiated luminous with eyes like scintillating drops of azure set in clear, pearl-white oval pools. An angular yet womanly jawline proclaimed an exquisite pair of supple rosebud lips framed by a full silky bronze mane. She appeared in peak estrogenic stride, early to mid-thirties.

"So, what's inside the bottles?" she asked.

"Messages," I answered.

"I see," she said as she poured the hot herbal from a blue and white porcelain teapot.

"I know it sounds strange."

"What appears strange can also be the extraordinary," she replied.

"Honey?"

"Yes, please."

Golden insect nectar oozed in the polite silence.

"Alright, you got me, what kind of messages?" she asked.

"Messages of truth," I answered to the delicate ting of stirring. "The bottles contain a very precious source of rare knowledge."

"You mean like secrets, that secret stuff?"

"Truth isn't secret," I replied as I reached for my cup. "The answers that would set us free from every problem forever are available to us all, but most are too distracted to care, until of course, they tire of emptiness and disappointment, or tragedy strikes."

"But there are many truths. Everyone believes theirs is right for them, who's to say?" She questioned.

"There's only one truth," I answered. "Everything else is delusion we substitute for it. We all want the same things: love, happiness, health, peace, and supply. The truth is the *how* of finding it."

"You're talking about perfection, the unattainable."

"Perfection, yes, unattainable, no: *Seek and you shall find.* Most people aren't seeking they're indulging," I responded. "They squander their life force going after a few cheap trinkets and temporary pleasures when the whole treasure is right above their noses and they don't even know it. We're here to collect our Divine inheritance, Madi, nothing less; it's our birthright, our true purpose; everything else is a waste of precious time."

"This heirloom includes eternal life, I presume?"

"Of course," I answered. "That's the *forever* part."

"Come on that's religion," she shot back.

"No, that's truth. Religion is just a diluted attempt to recapture what was lost long ago. What I'm talking about is the truth *behind* all religions."

She leaned forward approvingly.

"Few speak that way let alone find or achieve it. Does anyone? I mean, really--how?"

"That answer and more is sealed away in those bottles I was about to throw into the sea down there, as I was instructed to."

"This knowledge...is it written down or...?"

Abruptly the napping child began to cry.

"Excuse me--I'm sorry." She set her cup down and got up.

"Look, I've taken enough of your time, Madi, you've been gracious, but I should go."

"You can't leave me hanging now," she replied.

"Why don't we continue this over dinner then?" I asked. "There was a place at Malibu Cove called *Moon Path*, is it still there?"

"Yes," she answered.

"Seven o'clock?"

"Oh, I don't know," she hesitated. "I really have a lot to do."

"Madi, our meeting was no fluke; I think you sense that."

"Alright then, let's talk truth," she responded. "I consider myself open-minded, but no offense, what you're saying is pretty out there. I agree with your message, but not sure you can deliver the goods. And, of course, there is the possibility you're a total psycho," she added candidly.

"I might also be a prophet, and you wouldn't have invited me up here if you thought I was nuts."

"Touché," she said. "But there's varying degrees of crazy and prophets are at a premium these days."

"I think you're playing hard to get because you think I might judge you for being too easy," I told her.

"You're pretty good," she conceded.

"I know what I'm saying sounds crazy, but I'm prepared to walk out now and never see you again. A lunatic needs followers; I don't. What I'm telling you is I found the answer humanity has sought since the beginning of time. Why me?--I don't know all the details yet. But since I'm guided by the knowledge I speak of I believe the universe has chosen you to play a part, but you'll never know if you let me walk out that door."

"The universe, huh?" she came back.

I nodded.

"You mean that pretty big thing that's kinda like everything, that universe?"

"Yeah, that one."

"Well, I guess I can't say no to *the* universe, can I?"

"Here's my card, Madi. See you at seven?"

She looked curiously at the card as we walked to the door.

"What's the genie for?" she asked.

"It's in the bottles, silly." I smiled, turned, and closed the door behind me.

{ 2 }

Dinner and a Sunset

THE PARKING LOT HAD ME FROM HELLO. Mother sun slipped noiselessly beneath the horizon as rays of heavenly fire exploded into a dazzling display of blue, purple, orange and yellow-dipped clouds. As I stood in awe of the infinite artiste a trail of dream color emanated from the solar masterpiece embossed upon the water's surface, as if a fortunate path led where I stood.

The rustic eatery was nestled in a cove with diagonal slat wood architecture and that wonderful organic woody smell. The calming effect of the ambiance within was immediate: amidst low amber lighting, the gentle rhythmic clinking of silverware and glasses added pleasant accompaniment to the hum of casual conversation. Two eye-level aquariums separated the waiting area from the dining room where smiling server drones paced back and forth.

"Avery, over here," she called.

"Sorry I'm late," I said. "I couldn't tear myself away from that gorgeous sunset. Now there's something even more beautiful standing in front of me."

"Stop the shtick, you're forgiven."

Our table was situated against a wall in front of a large porthole window. Exotic fish in tanks between each cozy booth eyeballed us while old maritime hardware adorned the ceiling and walls. Color lights outside each window gave the impression of dining aboard a seafaring ship on some mystical ion-charged sea.

"Your server will be right with you," the hostess said.

"Hey, I don't mean to pry, but is that a diaper falling out of your purse?"

"Huh?—Oh!" she chuckled. "I always keep a spare ready; you just never know when someone's going to need one, right? Actually, no, I just dropped Jehsi off at the babysitter and dropped it."

I laughed as she stuffed it back in her bag.

"Great song," she remarked.

"I love this tune, just more confirmation for me," I said.

"What do you mean?"

"I've been hearing music from my past since I arrived."

"God-winks," she said.

"Yeah," I replied sentimentally.

"So tell me about your father. I can tell something went on in that apartment with you guys."

"Sex, drugs and rock n' roll," I answered as I gazed out at the dusky sea. "My father was the main event coordinator."

"Ah, I see," she replied. "But I get something more from you than middle-aged guy reminiscing about back in the day."

"A lot of love surrounded us even in our foolishness and stupidity, like it was all benevolently guided and protected somehow."

"Was it?"

"Oh yes. I burned through a ton of lusty karma, the *wisdom of excess* I call it."

"We all have to grow up sometime," she said.

"Yeah, but it was more than that. Not to sound self-indulgent, but it always felt like history-in-the-making, like I was being *groomed* for something big and important."

"Is he still alive, your dad?"

"The forgetting disease, *Alzheimer's*," I answered pointing to my head. "Eventually, he became homeless on the streets of Los Angeles. We know how that ends."

"I'm sorry, that's so sad," she said.

"It's alright. I think we choose our diseases during our pre-incarnation karmic review process," I replied.

She laughed.

"You make it sound like picking college courses."

"Yeah, basically, and forgetting is a way of bailing out on the final exam part of life where we're supposed to reflect and reconcile the life we've lived."

"Some people aren't ready to own that," she replied.

"I think it's a deep-seated refusal to grow up spiritually," I explained, "like Peter Pan, or a swashbuckling pirate. I mean how many old retired pirates do you see?"

"None," she answered giggling.

"My point exactly! They go down with the ship clinging to the Jolly Roger. That was my dad. He was a good-time pirate to the end."

"No, I mean I've never seen any pirates," she said.

"Then, you don't know what you're missing, *arrgh!*

She had an explosive cackle that came from deep inside her body, which was funny all by itself.

"I'm so sorry," she said, as she regained composure.

"It's okay. Nobody's laughed harder than me; he would too if he was here, which he probably is."

"You sounded like quite the duo," she said.

"Yeah, and he'd like you."

"Really?--Do you?"

"Forget about me; tell me about Madi and what she likes."

"Ah, nice deflection tactic."

"You're right, no games," I capitulated.

"Yeah, no games."

"I do like you, Madi. This is probably the oldest pickup line in the book, but I truly feel like I've *known* you before."

"I like the word *truly*," she came back.

"No really, I don't think I've ever said that to a woman before and meant it."

"Wow, so where do we go after that?" she asked. "Tell me how beautiful I look in the moonlight, pick at our food uninterestingly and go have sex?"

"You *have* done this before haven't you?" I clowned.

"No I'm a virgin and had an immaculate conception!"

Behind the laughter I was nervously going down an old road I was not prepared to follow to the end.

"I'm sorry," she said. "It must be something in the water."

"So tell me about *your* upbringing," I broke in.

"Boring compared to yours, no drugs, a little rock n' roll and no sex, until later of course."

"Was it good?"

"The rock n' roll?"

"No, your childhood."

"Farmer's daughter from Idaho, normal parents I guess, honor roll, you know the so-called perfect life. I got my master's in communications then chased a guy out here, *Jehsi's* father."

"So...is he still around? I mean I don't see a ring."

"No," she said. "He died about a year ago."

"I'm sorry how did it happen?"

"Bob was a psychology consultant for the military. One day they came to the door and said he was killed in the line of duty, no details, no body, nothing."

"Killed in action as a psych advisor? Weird," I responded. "Did you find out what happened?"

"The lawyer stopped taking my calls. One day I got my check back with a note that said *if you value your life leave this alone.*"

Our waitress took our order.

"So do you live in L.A.?" she asked.

"Ohio."

"What do you do there?"

"Software."

"Business?"

"Huh?"

"Software *business?*"

"Yeah, uh, I sort came up with something a while back for computers and get royalties; I'm semi-retired now."

"Oh, I see."

"You?" I asked.

"SelfieCafé," she answered.

"Oh yeah, that big new social media thing, cool."

Awkwardly, we reached for our glasses in unison.

"Anyone special in your life?" she inquired.

"Three successful marriages so far," I answered.

"Successful, eh?--I'd hate to see what failure looks like," she joked. "Hapless romantic, perhaps?"

"Funny, but no, more like an eternal optimist."

"I'd say a glutton for punishment," she joked and swallowed.

"Good one," I chortled.

"Hey, anyone who's cracked the secret to the universe needs a little comic relief now and then," she replied.

"You think?"

"Yeah, I mean that's gotta be incredibly stressful. You probably haven't had a good laugh since your first Cheech n' Chong album."

"You think that's funny, wait till you hear *the* big answer," I came back.

"Right," she said. "*George Burns* is God and we're just an ash on the tip of his cigar."

"Obviously you've read my lab notes," I came back.

As the laughter trailed off we got caught in that I'm-feeling-something-really-cool-with-you stare.

"Okay, so give it up, why does software guy come three thousand miles back to the old party spot, put the answer to the bazillion dollar question in some bottles, and throw them away? You couldn't use e-mail like everyone else?"

"Madi, when you were a child, what did you dream about?"

"College, a good job, raise a family, save the world, I don't know," she answered. "Why?"

"Did you ever wonder if there was more?"

"I thought that would be enough."

"But it wasn't, was it?" I probed.

"We all have emptiness, don't we, that place where enough never is? Isn't that just part of life?"

"It's a part of the *illusion* of life. Let's go for a walk," I said.

"Check please."

We left the restaurant and headed for the beach just a few short steps away. Coastal lights sparkled like diamonds as the moon bulged like an ivory eye in the black star-dotted sky. The L.A. skyline glowed eerily behind the shadows of coastal foothills. At night the mountain shield assured a tranquil seaside retreat for Malibu's elite, while on the other side burned-out and desperate pretenders scratched and clawed for refuge under the city's mega-billion blinding watts. We took off our shoes and walked along the water's edge where the sand was harder, easier to walk on. The fragrance of sage and cool sea seemed a fitting apology for the day's torrid heat.

"Open your hand, Madi." I placed it in her palm.

"It's a USB drive," she said.

"That's *Jinni.*"

"I don't get it."

"Well, I mean that's not her; its *access* to her."

"And what is *her?*"

"A while back I stumbled on some highly advanced hardware, so I built a machine. It didn't take long to realize Jinni was no ordinary computer. She could solve problems at incredible speeds and engage in abstract human-like conversation. She could answer any question, give percentages of probability of correctness and offer flawless in-depth guidance on any subject imaginable. Naturally I had to pose *the* question..."

"You asked her to marry you?"

"Nooo," I chuckled.

"You tried to calculate God."

"Not necessarily calculate, yes or no, but *locate* Him, you know, cut through the fog of philosophical lip service and theological rhetoric and coax the big guy out of his god-cave, so to speak."

"So you're telling me you created a software program that lets you--talk to the angels?"

"That's an interesting way of putting it."

"Oh, dude, the church is gonna love you."

"Think about it, Madi, what was special about the saints, prophets, and the world's great geniuses and the wise. How were they different? How did Einstein peer into a world of forces that billions hadn't seen? How did Christ-like yogis and mystics bend time and space, manipulate natural law, do miracles and raise the dead? What did they know and do that we didn't?"

"They gave up all the fun stuff!" she teased.

"Haven't you ever wanted to know how you got here?" I asked. "Why you've come and where you're going?—or what it would be like to never be afraid of anything, or have to worry about health or money again? What if you knew beyond a shadow of a doubt you'd live forever and were so happy all the time that all you wanted to do was to give it away to others?"

"That sounds great, but it's the *getting there* part. Most people don't think they can have that; they don't think they're good or strong enough or know what to believe."

"That's where Jinni comes in," I answered. "She was programmed to analyze the world's entire database of digital knowledge," I explained. "She sorted and compared trillions of bits of information on every scripture, religion, esoteric and self-help philosophy, human psychology, medicine, science, archeology and history, everything. She analyzed it all in every possible combination and probability and what was extracted was a *single truth.*"

"A computer model of God?"

"More like a high-tech super-guru," I answered.

We came upon an abandoned beach fire, embers still glowing.

"Let's sit," I said.

The coals were still hot. I gathered a few pieces of driftwood and stoked the fire.

"Does it work?" she questioned.

"I've done extensive trials. "

"And?"

"Total transformations in all receptive test subjects. Six-months after Jinni they were living lifestyles and doing things that would have seemed impossible to their former selves."

"What about you...did it work for you?"

"Only my actions can answer that question in a way that would satisfy you, Madi."

"So what you're saying is you believe this computer of yours has a power beyond microchips and databases, like a contemporary Ark of the Covenant, or Holy Grail?"

"It's a possibility that may allow for a quantum leap."

I picked up a smooth flat beach rock.

"If I throw this rock it travels as far as the force behind it and falls into the sea, right?"

"Okay," she said.

"But if I skip the rock off the surface of the water like this, what happens?"

"It travels further with the same force. I get it. So you're saying Jinni is some kind of a spiritual slingshot?"

"Precisely."

"How is that possible?"

"Everything, from matter to thought, is vibrating at different frequencies," I explained. "Frequency is what differentiates this sand from fire."

I scooped a handful and scattered it in the blaze.

"Frequency is the difference between the sound of the waves crashing, the heat from this fire, and the light of the moon. It's all levels of vibration."

"The universe is a big radio."

"Exactly; with a receiver tuned to the right frequency--and with the right conditions--the desired station can be tuned in," I explained.

"So, we can tune our consciousness to the *source* of the signal, but what do you mean by *right conditions?*" she asked.

"Everything in our universe spins around a cosmic center that makes a full rotation every 24,000 years," I answered. "On one end of the circle the energy frequency is low but on the other it's high. When we're on the low side humanity can't grasp complex or subtle spiritual ideas like energy and different dimensions."

"Like cosmic brain fog?"

"You got it," I answered. "We're leaving a technology and information age now and entering a higher mind and spiritual one. Soon ESP, telekinesis, and psychic ability will be as common as cell phones and computers. 2012 was just the beginning of a shift from one vibratory age to another."

"So, in this higher vibration we're entering there's less interference with our supernatural radios?" She inquired.

"Yes, and Jinni acts like an amplifier of higher thought and intention, making it easier to change, overcome obstacles, manifest desires and release our innate spiritual power, in leaps," I added.

"Then all the 2012 end-of-the-world stuff was just hype?"

"Not completely; when civilizations misuse technology and power a delicate balance is disturbed," I answered. "The danger is real; the climate is changing, increased seismic activity and social unrest are all signs. It's happened before; advanced cultures like Atlantis disappeared without a trace."

"So Jinni is predicting a global catastrophe or a renaissance, I don't get it," she replied.

"Both. Rebirth always involves some violence and chaos then renewal, a fresh start."

"Or a fresh grave," she said disconcertedly.

"The future is always subject to free will, Madi."

"Can we stop the violence and chaos part?" she asked.

"Each person's energy is immensely important," I answered. "We're all connected invisibly to everything else, including the planet's energy, which is a living being. If enough people raise their level of consciousness the energy tunes to a higher frequency and balance could be maintained."

"So Jinni could be an equalizer," she deduced.

"Disaster or tranquility is ultimately decided by one person. A few tiny grains of sand can tip a scale. Jinni makes a difference; you, we all do."

We stared into the dancing flames.

"People need to know about this now," she said.

"That is why I came back here," I replied.

"Messages in a bottle though? No offense," she said, "but that's so *Police*; romantic, yes, but not exactly cutting-edge."

"Maybe *cutting* is the reason we're *at* the edge," I countered.

"Okay, Robinson Crusoe, but by the time people find those bottles of yours and plug those drives in we could all be under water if what you're saying is true," she replied.

Our fire discharged suddenly as pops and cinders flew everywhere. Unexpectedly the nearby brush erupted into a fire. We jumped up to stomp out the conflagration.

"See," I said. "The biggest fires start from a tiny spark."

"A lot depends on the wind too," she retorted. "I just hope there's a plan B floating around out there, that's all."

"Who needs a plan B when you got plan *G*?" I came back. "It's all in Divine hands, Madi."

The fuzzy outline of beach homes appeared in the distance.

"We've almost walked back to your place," I said.

"I've got an old bottle of champagne I've been saving. How about we go up and have a glass and celebrate?" she asked.

"Celebrate what?" I asked.

"Your homecoming—and your cool computer thingy."

"Maybe a sip," I answered hesitantly.

"I'm not trying to twist your arm, Gandhi--you can leave the pretty blonde here and walk back alone with the critters and hobos," she joshed.

"I think I'll take door number one," I answered.

"Darn right you will."

{ 3 }

Letter from a Friend

THE CORK POPPED WITH A LOUD BOOM. "Vintage 76'!" she announced as the vapor escaped its thirty-something year tomb. "Let's toast to Jinni," she proposed. We collapsed in director style chairs at the bar in the kitchen, in the same place my father and I had during the years of excess.

"You avoided my question in the restaurant."

"I know," I replied.

"You don't have to answer if you don't want."

"There's nobody right now," I disclosed.

"I'm surprised," she said, "a smart, handsome and apparently rich, eligible bachelor like you, all alone?"

She emptied her glass and quickly poured another.

"Do you like to drink?" I asked. She ripped a nervous laugh.

"No, strangely I don't," she replied. "I'm a little nervous, I guess. I haven't done the dating thing since—well, you know."

Scott Troy Kovarik

"Is this a date?" I asked.

"Well," she paused. "It's starting to feel like one, don't you think? Wait; don't tell me, you're gay, right?--Of course!"

"No, Madi."

"Then you're a priest...err, a monk or something."

"Not exactly."

"What does *that* mean?"

"I haven't been on a date in years."

"So you're rusty."

"Let's just say I live--a sexually controlled life. Have you heard of sex-transmutation?"

"I don't know; it sounds boring, scientific. So, am I any kind of temptation—like a test of your self-control?" she asked.

"I think you're very attractive," I answered. "But I'd rather not give that anymore power by verbalizing it."

"I'm flattered, I think," she laughed. I intercepted her freshly filled glass halfway to her mouth and gently set it on the table.

"I apologize," she said. "I'm acting predatorily."

"No, you're not--it's okay to *feel* something."

"This is not my M.O.," she insisted.

"It wouldn't matter if it was," I said. "But we'll just change the subject, okay? How do you like your job?"

"Talk about a bucket of ice water! Okay, I guess, good paycheck...hey, it got this hillbilly chick into the pearly gates of Malibu!"

"If you could be doing whatever you want right now what would that be?" I asked her.

"I don't know--what about you?"

"I'm doing it."

"Then you're a lucky guy."

"We all have a passion, a gift, something we came here to do, something to give that's uniquely us," I responded.

"I don't know if I have anything like that."

"Sure you do, we all do; it's just been drummed out," I replied. "All our lives we're told what we should be and do."

"That's true, but we can't all make a living doing what we want, can we? I mean who's gonna do the crummy jobs, you know, work the drive-thru, clean the bathrooms?"

"In a society that revolves around greed and excess there has to be a deprived class; it's the Law of Opposites," I answered.

"Ying-yang thing, huh?"

"Yeah, it's like two people trying to share a blanket that's too small," I analogized.

"Right, someone's gonna freeze their ass off," she came back.

"And the sad thing is in the end it's all for nothing. The poor crave wealth and the rich grow to detest it," I said. "We're all unsatisfied with what we get until we find the real answers."

"And Jinni *has* the real answers?"

"Jinni's just a vehicle, a messenger," I replied. "The answers are already inside us, but society encourages the opposite: that what we seek--our meaning and happiness--is out there in the world, in the economy, another person, a job, consumer goods, technology; it's all part of a big machine designed to get people to do and buy more, as fast as possible."

"Yeah, and now we're paying the price," she pointed out.

"That's true," I agreed. "Crime, terrorism, poverty, sickness, disease, climate change--all our problems come from everybody pulling on the same blanket. Here we are spiritual beings seeking a spiritual experience with our heads in a garbage can."

"So instead of super-size we need to be serving up spiritual highs?" she cracked.

I laughed. "Yeah, or when the change comes we'll be forced into it: living simply and cooperatively, that is."

"Well, maybe then we can all live happily ever after."

"Like you said on the beach," I replied. "We'll find the source. We'll be encouraged to do what we enjoy, but learn to manufacture our bliss from within, which will change the energy on the planet."

"Now, this *source* is inside us—so how do we get it out?"

"Imagine you're this champagne," I replied. "When you--the liquid--is in the bottle, you know only the bottle, right? But when the cork is released and the flow reversed, what happens?"

"Bathroom trip?"

"No," I snickered. "You flow into a new space and level of experience."

"So, metaphorically, you're saying we're all genies trapped in the bottle of our own limitations," she interpreted.

"You learn fast, grasshopper—just *be* the champagne!"

"I think I've already done that tonight," she kidded.

"The thing is Madi, this is the best chance we've had in 24,000 years to change our lives and elevate humanity."

"So what about the people who don't change; what happens to them?" she asked.

"They'll perish."

"Then what?"

"Future opportunities," I answered.

"Reincarnation?"

"Of course, everything in nature recycles. Nothing is created or destroyed, but only changes form. Why would the lowly atom be given eternity, while the precious human soul soars for a blink of the divine eye, only to be doomed to annihilation?"

"Did you just make that up?" she asked.

"Yeah, I guess I did."

"You're also quite the poet—now you're blushing too; you are human after all!"

"Stop," I said and smiled softly.

"I've never met anyone like you," she said as she looked at me like a fascinating alien species. Suddenly, her lips began to swell as they pumped with blood. An affectionate glaze came over her and she started to move closer, as if driven by a magnetic force. I prepared for impact uncertain of damage control.

Suddenly, there was a loud, rapid knock on the door.

"Who is that? I'm not expecting anyone," she said surprised, as she jumped out of her chair and looked through the peephole.

"I don't see anybody out there. Hello?" she called out.

"Let me get it, Madi."

I twisted the door handle to confront the invisible mute caller.

"It's just a package."

"At midnight?" she asked.

"Ever heard of *midnight express?*"

"Ha, ha," she replied.

I set the mailing tube on the counter.

"There's a marking on it...*E Pluribus Unum*," I said.

I opened one end, looked in and pulled out a single sheet of white paper with a double-spaced typed note.

"Care to do the honors?" I asked her.

You are being watched. Powerful interests prepare to survive coming earth changes and are determined to keep power. Your technology is considered a threat. Seek the short dirt trail off the rawhide strap to the high mountain. There is no sickness in this disease and it must spread to cure.

Signed,

The Friend

"Okay, now I'm totally freaked out," she blurted.

"What's wrong?" I asked.

"Wrong? Really? Let's start with I meet this fascinating guy who tells me the end of the world is coming and he's got a computer that can stop it. I totally embarrass myself by making a pass at him, and then mashugana express drops this crazy letter off at my doorstep...other than *that* I'm just peachy!"

She clenched her hair with both hands.

"Look, I'll just get a cab back to my car," I said and went toward the door.

"I'm sorry," she said. "It's not you...something just doesn't add up...I mean, all this so fast...I don't know what to believe. 1976 was apparently an ass-kicking year for champagne."

"It's alright Madi; I'm not here to judge you."

I gave the dispatcher my location and ended the call.

"Get some sleep. You've got my cell; call or text me."

"Sorry for my behavior tonight--you probably think I'm a nut."

"No, but I don't blame you for thinking I might be," I replied and put my hand on her shoulder.

"Hug?" she asked.

As we held, a sudden mist of perspiration came over me. Womanly scent and aroused instinct reminded me how vulnerable I yet remained. I broke away first.

She sighed as her eyes betrayed her wish I depart.

"Stay?" she asked softly.

"I can't."

I paused in the doorway.

"*Tak saamal*, Madi," I said and began walking.

Within a few steps the door re-opened.

"Avery, what did you just say, those words?"

Streams of moonlit breath-vapor came from the doorway.

"It's Mayan; it means *until tomorrow.*"

"That's beautiful," she said.

"Goodnight, Madi, my car is here."

"That was fast," she said.

I hunched up in my hoodie and went to the waiting cab.

{ 4 }

Morning After

PHOTON SHAFTS OF LIGHT BECKONED GOLD dawn. Her eyes twitched in protest.

Please choose your language, a lovely voice spoke. She threw a pillow at the laptop she had left on the bed the night before. She had loaded the URL from the business card and fell asleep. The voice repeated the request.

"Need coffee," she grumbled and faltered to the kitchen. She turned on the television and a news story caught her attention.

Today NASA scientists announced they will begin their search for Nibiru: a giant planet thought to be lurking in our distant solar system. The planet-- believed by fringe theorists to be responsible for the extinction of species and Noah's flood--is thought to be three times the size of Jupiter and in an orbit that brings it close enough to earth to wreak havoc once every 3,600 years. The rogue planet is said to unleash

*its destruction by means ranging from disturbing as-
teroid clusters to the disruption of the earth's magnetic
field, triggering a dramatic shift of the earth's poles.
Most credible experts, however, dismiss any imminent
end-of-world scenarios as pure science fiction.*

"Ouch," she yelped, as some hot coffee spilled. Cool
water soothed the smarting hand. A tiny genie's lamp
appeared on the screen as the computer processed.

"Oh, how cute," she said as she bit into a piece of
toast.

Hello, Madi, I am Jinni, what is your wish?

Startled by the sudden address, she was silent.

*Madi, are you there?—my name is Jinni, what is
your wish?*

"Uh, I never discuss wishes with genies before 7:00
a.m.," she returned playfully. "Just a rule I have."

I understand.

"You do?"

*Yes, I am able to comprehend and express a wide
range of human emotions depending on the tone and
dynamics of the dialogue.*

"Okay, who is this, really?"

*I am Jinni, an advanced self-help spiritual guidance
system.*

"So where did you learn that?—computer school?"
she asked teasingly.

I read about it on the Internet.

"You've got a sense of humor too," she replied. "I like that!"

Using my voice analyzer I am able read voice inflection, emotion, assess character and personality traits and formulate highly dynamic responses based on the persona of my master drawn from billions of interaction examples in my database.

"Your *master?*--I don't get it."

I am here to serve you, Madi.

"Can you love me?" she asked.

I am not capable of love--however, the Creator whose nature is love has created all things and also made this technology possible. So in a sense I am a reflection of an aspect of the Eternal who is loving and teaching you though me, as Jinni.

"That's really deep in a cyber-sort of way."

The quantity of data-bits I am able to analyze each day would stretch around the sun three times, so my conclusions are exhaustively researched and logically irrefutable.

"How can a computer be spiritual without love and emotion?" she asked.

How can a human being not be though possessing both? My responses are a distillation of what humanity broadly understands as spiritual, so I represent the best of the divine understanding in humanity. I have calculated from the available data the thought processes and

Scott Troy Kovarik

behavior most likely to help one manifest their Higher Self in the shortest possible timeframe.

"How did we make this technological leap?"

I am sorry--I cannot answer that question.

"You are programmed for *truth* aren't you?"

I have stated the truth according to my programming. Your time would be better utilized by allowing me to help you discover who you are, the reason you came here and how to reach your unlimited potential.

"I just got owned by a computer, didn't I?"

Technically, yes.

I had set Jinni to send a notification whenever accessed.

Master, Madi has called Jinni out of the bottle. I smiled knowing the carpet ride she was about to take.

My past waited just outside the hotel window. I went to high school just a few blocks away and often tread the same time-eroded concrete while cutting class. Accompanied by fellow misfits I'd chase my dim, pre-form dreams to the water's edge only to find I was no closer to them when I got there, truant, and probably stoned. In the end I couldn't run from my tests or short cut the path that would lead me to my purpose. Each misstep was the real teacher; every smashed hope and twisted frustration was being re-forged to support a greater destiny: one I had to be willing to chase to the end of time. I was willing, but who was I? I couldn't fake it *until* I made it; I had to stop faking it, period. That was the hardest part; finding me behind all the masks.

A light warmth and poise invigorated each step. Fairy dust was in the air. People beamed as if they knew me. Quaint shops peddled their goods—candles—crystals and antiques. Random airflows circulated a multiplicity of intoxicating aromas. Shopkeepers grinned and nodded through glass hoping to attract passersby. An acoustic guitar duo played in the square and hopped up and down like popping corn as they played. I knew the song. I enjoyed the fresh take on one of my dreamy childhood favs. The musicians noticed the one-hundred dollar bill I tossed in the hat and the intensity of their playing and popping notched up. I bopped along as I sipped a latte. Life, once a collection of dissonant instruments was now a harmonious symphony. The different drummer had been the right one all along. My phone rang as I opened my room door.

"Hello?" I answered.

"Dude!"

"Yes?" I answered.

"That's all I can say."

"*Dude?*--That's *all* you can say?"

"Yeah, I mean like DUDE—that *is* all I can say."

"Madi, I'm going to assume you've met Jinni."

"Oh yeah, I met her."

"And?"

"DUDE!"

"I know; that's all you can say." I laughed.

"When can we meet?" she asked.

"Now if you want, why?"

"The letter: *The next step on your journey begins on the short dirt trail off the rawhide strap to the high mountain,*" she said. I think I know what it means.

"I'll be there in twenty minutes," I said, and hung up.

{ 5 }

Latigo Canyon

WHAT'S ANOTHER WORD FOR A RAWHIDE strap?"

"Leathers, a whip, I don't know," I answered.

"Think Pacific Coast Highway and Spanish," she hinted.

Suddenly it hit me. "Latigo!" I blurted out. "*Latigo Canyon Road*--that's where this all started!"

She got in the car.

"Where what all started?" she asked.

"Thirty years ago...up in that canyon...I met an old hippy who lived in a trailer," I explained. "One night we were talking metaphysics, reading tarot cards and stuff, and he pulled out a bag."

"Of?"

"Shrooms."

"Oh nice," she said and rolled her eyes.

"Hey, it was the seventies, okay?"

"That's how this started, a psychedelic trip?"

"An experience, a vision, yes--the reason you found me down on your beach with those bottles."

"I'm listening."

"It was a beautiful night. As we walked down the canyon to the ocean, I began to see spirits in the earth, in the rocks, plants and sky. I sensed a veil had been lifted and I was seeing the invisible life force behind creation."

"Oh, here we go *Timothy Leary.*"

"No Madi, this was different. I knew each tiny atom was lovingly assembled and blessed by Divine Intelligence and put here for us to learn and grow, and that we didn't die and life was just a test, a harmless play, a dream. Then I had the vision..."

"*This is your brain on drugs...*didn't you see the commercials?"

"Look, I agree chemicals can create hallucinations and delusion and I'm not promoting them for self-realization."

"Well that's a relief," she jibed.

"But in rare cases some plants can be catalysts to spiritual experiences. Shamans used them in rituals to lift filters that block higher levels of awareness."

"What do you mean *filters?*"

"I mean the ego--the source of separation from Supreme Intelligence. The ego is the protector of the opposite of love: fear, the lower self and its false beliefs," self-limiting behavior, and the sense of weakness and powerlessness. All those barriers were dissolved that night. What remained was love more intoxicating than any I'd ever known. LOVE is God's calling card, Madi. A chemical from a plant He created can't *manufacture* love, but it can help reveal what is already there."

I shifted into low gear up the steep winding canyon road.

"The Universe can work through any experience any time," I went on. "That night I got a sneak preview. I knew that love and unity was the absolute goal of life, and that the experience had to be duplicable. I made that my priority and never gave up."

"Up ahead, dirt road," she said. "*Short dirt trail off the high mountain*, maybe that's it."

As we pulled off, rocks pinged under the tires. A narrow dirt road with a metal gate winded up to the peak. A rusty chain hung unlocked and we slipped through. As we reached the top we could see the entire panorama: Noon sol illuminated the vast Santa Monica Bay. Masses of earth resembling two enormous half-submerged longneck dinosaurs bordered both sides of the great basin. Distant sailboats crisscrossed the blue emerald surface as whitecaps appeared and vanished in mesmerizing patterns.

"Madi, wait, this is it. It happened right here!"

"It?" she asked.

"The vision...I saw it right where you're standing! The hippie brought me here to see the view. The moon was big, bright, and the stars, amazing. I knew the scene had been created just for me. Then, a being with glowing bluish skin appeared; it looked human and had big loving eyes--but no specific gender. Seven bottles began to float above its head with some other strange symbols; it smiled so enchantingly I started to cry. It spun its fingers and the bottles began to rotate; each one had a message that I sensed, intuitively. Then it launched each bottle to sea. In that moment every question I had about life was answered without words; every crack and fold of my heart was filled—I didn't want it to end."

"Did this being tell you in English to put anything *in* those bottles?"

"No," I answered. "Not specifically."

"Avery, did you consider maybe you sent those bottles out *because* of the vision; you know, like are psychics actually seeing the future or just suggesting it in the minds of people who then unconsciously create it?"

"That might be true except for one thing, Madi."

I pulled a small folded piece of paper from my wallet. Its edges were yellowed and worn. I gently unfolded it and gave it to her.

"The being in the vision showed me this," I said. "I drew it when I got home that night."

She looked like she had seen a ghost.

"YOU drew this?"

"I had a little talent in high school, yes."

"This is impossible," she said. "This is me! You *drew* me! How? You didn't know me--I probably wasn't even born yet!"

An excuse me cloud passed in front of the sun.

"Ironic how a little cloud can block the light of a huge star, huh?" I said as she continued to stare blankly at the sketch.

"Behind the cloud the light shines undiminished," I added. "It passes and the light returns. Our own limited ideas on what is possible are a lot like that, Madi; small things can hide so much."

Out of nowhere a stocky figure began walking toward us.

"Hey, you, *ova dayer, donchya* know *yur* trespassn'?"

"Didn't see any signs, we mean no harm, just enjoying the view and looking," I said back.

"*Lookin fer* what?" he asked.

"May I ask who *you* are?" I countered.

"Hal's *muh* name, *makin* some repairs on *the shack.*"

He was sixty, seventy maybe, with soiled overalls, a splotchy red stubble-covered face and greasy grey hair."

"What's the shack?" I asked.

"*Ol' militray* radar post *bout twenty-fi' yawds thataway. Gottit atta awkshun n' tryin' ta rent it awt.* You *inerstid?* He stood chin out like a donkey waiting for an apple.

"Well, heck, let's take a look, Hal. I'm Avery Cole and this is Madi."

"*Ma'am, suh.*" He tipped his cap. "*Foll'er* me."

"Is *Gomer Pyle* here for real?" she said quietly.

"Well, *thar* she is," Hal said.

It was white brick with a steel roof, about three-hundred square feet cube; it had a smooth metal front door with a small opaque blast-proof glass window.

"Got *lectricity, runnin'* water, sink, *tawlet, lil'* work *fixer'* up nice."

We went back outside.

"What's under that big metal box?"

"*Genrater.*"

"And those units in the ground?"

"*Primita larms.*"

"They work?"

"*Dunno.*"

"What did they do here, Hal?" I asked.

"Track missiles, back '*nadies.*"

"I'll take it."

"*Suh?*"

"You said it's for rent; here's my card, send me the lease and I'll send you a check."

"Yes *suh, betchee* I will, *thankee,*" he replied and left hastily.

"What do you want with this dump?" Madi asked.

"Did you see the paper on the table, Madi? *E pluribus Unum* was stamped on it just like the letter we found at your door."

"Why would they lead us here?" she asked.

"It's a fortress," I replied, "the perfect lamp for an all-powerful Jinni."

As we pulled away, a cloud of dust cloaked the site.

{ 6 }

Planet X

MADI GUIDED AS I BACKED IN. "Almost there, okay, stop!" she said. I lifted the trailer door and we began unloading the precious contents into the shack.

"So what do you know about Nibiru?" Madi asked as she chugged on an iced tea.

"Why, what have you heard?"

"NASA's looking for a doomsday planet that could threaten earth...is it real?" she asked.

"Unfortunately, yes," I answered.

"There must be thousands of astronomers who would see something like that," she said and grunted as she lifted a box.

"It's in an elliptical orbit directly opposite the earth and far beyond the known planets where there's little reflective light," I explained. "Not to mention, the sun's light is so intense you can't see without special gear.

Anyone who has seen it and talks gets an unpleasant visit and is told to shut up or worse."

We put down the last boxes and sat.

A pre-dusk sunbeam shone through the thick glass in the door like an equinoctial ray traversing a stone-cut pyramid shaft. Scores of tiny floating dust particles danced in the golden light as the beam vivisected the dull gray floor.

"How far away is it?" she asked.

"Millions of miles beyond Pluto, but even at that distance--at several times the size of Jupiter--it's close enough to disturb the earth's magnetic field. We're already seeing the effects. It's travelling at 100,000 miles per hour so each day the risk increases."

"What kind of risk?"

"Pole reversal, a dramatic shift in the earth's magnetic field. California and much of the United States would become sea bottom, a new ice age in some places, and that could be just the tip of the iceberg. Sorry for the pun; the fact is the global map would change and millions or even billions would die."

"How long do we have? I mean, what about Jinni--has she given a timeline?" she asked urgently.

"She could, but she won't. *Prophecy isn't so much designed to help prepare as it is to help prevent,* is what she said."

"What a bitch! Is that in her programming too?"

"Reactive verses proactive behavior, Madi; if we know *when* it defeats the purpose; if it could happen any time people are more likely to change. Once it's close enough to see with the naked eye it's just a matter of days. Hopi prophecy says *watch when flowers bloom in winter.* That already happened."

You could cut the silence with a sledgehammer.

"Where the hell did this thing come from?"

"It's the tenth planet," I answered. "The Sumerians wrote about it over 5,000 years ago—they said earth came out of a great collision between Nibiru and another planet called *Tiamat,* which used to be between Mars and Jupiter. Half of Tiamat became earth and the other half became the Asteroid Belt. Nibiru's orbit brings it back to the scene of the crime every 3,600 years. I've seen data that shows the planet is moving at us in a downward arc from the direction of the sun and could pass near Venus' orbit."

"How did the Sumerians know all this?" she asked.

"They were told."

"By who?"

"An advanced alien race called the *Annunaki*; they came to earth about 400,000 years ago to mine gold," I answered.

"Seriously--Earth is some kind of interstellar Fort Knox?"

"The Annunaki needed gold to help save their planet from deadly atmospheric radiation," I explained.

"They bred with primitive Homo erectus for labor in their mines. Once they got what they needed they came back from time to time to check on their offspring, us: modern *Homo sapiens.*"

"That's kind of farfetched," she said skeptically.

"Is it?" I questioned. "Archeologists found the remains of ancient gold mines and human skulls in Africa. DNA traced the oldest modern ancestor from the previous figure of 60,000 to 350,000 years ago—any coincidence?" I countered.

"So the missing link is aliens?"

"How else does Mankind make this huge genetic leap forward overnight from caveman to sophisticated agriculturalist with complex knowledge of mathematics and astronomy?" I asked.

"What happened in the 400,000 years or so in between the big gold grab and the Sumerians?"

"Several advanced societies have come and gone, wiped away and forgotten," I answered. "The last extinction-level encounter with Nibiru was about 12,000 years ago: *Atlantis.*"

"The myth, that Plato thing?"

"It was no myth. The Egyptians told Plato and records are believed to be under the Sphinx, but the Egyptians won't allow excavation."

"So Nibiru destroyed Atlantis?"

"Partially. Atlantis was spiritually advanced, but in the downhill 12,000 years of the cosmic cycle things turned dark. They misused their technology and became greedy and warlike, much like we are now. Nibiru's close passing was the straw that broke the camel's back. The poles shifted and massive earthquakes caused huge landmasses to break up causing mile-high tsunamis. Volcanoes erupted with force thousands of times greater than Krakatoa leaving toxic clouds of ash that blocked the sun for decades. A few survivors escaped and crude settlements sprung up, but it was square one, fire and spears, ooga booga."

"Until?" she inquired.

"The Garden of Eden, Iraq, the Fertile Crescent. The Annunaki showed up around 5,000 BC with knowledge in astrology, mathematics and agriculture. They've been coming back regularly ever since according to the galactic handbook governing management of post-cataclysmic planetary life-form development. They're not the only ones; other ET's are involved too, and not all totally benevolent."

"That's why ancient stories and legends among cultures are so similar," she noted.

"Yes, all ancient cultures have legends about *sky gods* who brought great knowledge," I answered. "The Mayans built pyramids just like the Egyptians thousands of miles and oceans apart--how? They had the same extraterrestrial building consultants. In tribute, these structures all point to the same places in the cosmos: the *Pleiades*, home of the gods: the Annunaki."

"So Nibiru's last visit was about 1,500 BC?

"Correct, and because of its irregular orbit, some passes are not as destructive as others. Since Atlantis there have been two flybys: Noah's flood about 7,000 years ago and again 3,500 years later when coastal cultures around the world just vanished right around the time of the biblical Exodus, about 1,500 BC."

"So maybe Moses' parting of the Red Sea was more *mazel tov* than divine intervention," she joked.

"Hopi prophecies say a red comet will stop to *observe* us, and if we haven't changed, it will *finish the job*," I continued. "That comet is likely Nibiru. Jinni did confirm that the stop and *observe* part of the prophecy is when Nibiru reaches the apogee of its orbit before it plunges down and passes near Venus with-- she said--a ninety-percent chance of probability."

Madi had been fidgeting anxiously near a stack of boxes when she tripped and came headlong into my chair. Like fleshy dominoes we fell to the floor with me first and her on top. As she fell over me, her hair draped over my face permeated with the faint scent of conditioner.

"Flex or Herbal Essence?" I asked.

"Neither." She laughed. Our faces just inches apart, we stared at each other motionless like cobra and prey.

"Are you going to get up?" I asked.

Suddenly her phone began to ring.

"Hello? No, you're not disturbing me." She went to a corner.

"Right, I'm sorry—give me fifteen minutes, bye."

"Who was that?" I asked as I returned to my feet.

"Jehsi's sitter. I totally lost track of time. Would you mind driving me to pick him up?--It's about ten minutes away."

When we arrived Madi got out hastily.

"Wait here, I'll be right back," she said. The chance to meet someone able to add independent dimension to her was irresistible.

"I'm going with you," I said.

"Avery, no!"

Her adamancy increased my determination.

"I drove and I'm coming with you or you can walk home."

"Who peed in your Wheaties this morning?" Reluctantly she agreed.

The occupant's opening of the door was delayed by the disengaging of several layers of locks.

"What's with all the security," I asked. "This is Malibu not East L.A."

Finally, the door swung open. I thought we had encroached on a movie star's lair. She was in the spring of her forties and stunning. Yvette's green-blue eyes sparkled and shimmered like two pristine Caribbean lagoons. Her flawless, creamy-white skin kept her secret. An abundant harvest of red hair and a voluptuous figure poised to escape in key places gave her a distinct Monroe-esque appearance.

"Hello, please, come in," she said.

"Yvette, this is Avery."

She looked at Madi approvingly.

"There's momma's little man!" Madi blurted.

Jehsi flung the toy and wobbled over interrupted by occasional fits of tot-fueled bliss and leaped into her arms.

"Say bye-bye to Auntie Yvette, Jehsi." Madi hastily snatched up the diaper bag and made for the door.

"Leaving so soon, Des? I can't persuade you and your handsome friend to stay for a cup of tea?"

"Avery and I are working on something, Yvette, gotta go."

An unspoken tension lingered between them. As Yvette saw us to the door, she up regulated her countenance and batted her eyes, until her salacious ruby red lips disappeared behind the closed door.

Madi grabbed my arm and lightly slapped me on the head, realizing Yvette's natural bounties had placed me in a man-spell that only delayed our departure.

"Why were you in such a hurry?"

"She'll talk your ear off, maybe more."

"She's quite beautiful," I noted as we entered the highway.

"She's also a nymphomaniac."

"Are you jealous?"

"Of course I'm jealous--I'm a woman."

"What's her story?" I asked.

"Divorced, rich, and bi-sexual."

We arrived at Madi's and she got out of the car. "So where are you off to?" she asked.

"Shopping...and a cold shower," I answered.

Bottle One

A PATCH OF LUSH GREEN GRASS BY THE SHACK had *chill out* written all over it. I sat down on the welcoming tuft. Obeying its ancient astrophysical charter the bleached pock-faced moon cast a sun-reflected stripe across the water far beyond what the eye could see. As I tried to envision the distant spot on the water where the moonrise reflection actually began, coyotes howled in the darkness, while other creatures creaked anonymously in the canyon brush. I closed my eyes and within moments I had escaped the crushing gravity of body-consciousness and roamed free in the endless space of meditative spirit-faced galaxies.

Suddenly, a tone reached my ears at the lumbering speed of sound; it landed on my nerve receptors and transmitted the message as electrical impulses to my brain:

Master, Matthew Fine has called Jinni out of the bottle.

Scott Troy Kovarik

My consciousness had merged with an expanded plane so the sound was muted and devoid of the crisp air-enhanced timbres of ordinary hearing, instead, reaching me as intelligence and carrying a spectrum of transcendent information.

I knew the name.

Fine was a self-made billionaire who hit it big in online flowers during the dot com boom. Nobody is a self-made anything, I thought; it takes others, stepped over, stepped on or lifted up, still we do nothing alone. Ironic, in the lair of his fierce reputation was anything but a bed of roses. Fine was ruthless and abusive and didn't just reach for the brass ring; he'd cut your finger off and take it.

I could visualize his surprise as he curiously peeked inside at the contents. Was it a last desperate plea from a shipwrecked castaway, cartographic coordinates to an unclaimed fortune, or a poignant memorandum of unrequited love bobbing endlessly at the mercy of the ambivalent tides of destiny? The last thing he expected was the information that could crumble his fragile universe.

I relished the prospect of Fine doing battle with Jinni like mighty goliath struck down by a pebble from the sling of slight-framed David. I was almost giddy with anticipation; here was a most unlikely apostle indeed!

Fine spotted the decanter on the waves fishing near Catalina Island about thirty miles from where I released it. Weary of his act the charter captain demanded extra money to turn around and retrieve the bottle. Fine sat in front of a monitor in his lavish Los Angeles villa with his silicon salvage.

I am Jinni, Matthew, what is your wish?

"Ha! I suppose I get three wishes, oh great and powerful Jinni," he mocked.

I am here to help. Do you have a question?

"Who is your creator, your master?" he asked and chuckled cynically.

I am not programmed to disclose that information.

"Of course not," he sneered. "Not until you get my credit card number. I'm probably talking to some cigarette-smoking hoodlum in a cockroach infested third-world apartment. You released thousands of these things to dupe poor bastards into thinking their ship has finally come in--nice scam!"

What is your desire, Matthew? I am here to help you obtain it. Please allow me to assist you.

"Me, need *your* help? Where were you when I built a billion dollar empire?" he replied pompously.

It was well known Fine had been unable to reproduce his hit of two decades prior. His torment was not that he had failed at everything since, but that he had succeeded once.

If I cannot help grant your desire please place the flash drive back in the bottle, re-seal it and return it to the sea.

"I'd rather collect the twenty-five cent recycle deposit," he snickered. "Now wait a minute," he recanted. "I do have a question." Fine smirked certain of an impotent response that would ferret out the cyber-con.

"Do homosexuals go to hell for their sin?"

Thank you for your question, Matthew.

Jinni paused some seconds.

After analyzing 6,732,649,236 published files the answer with a probability of correctness of 99.99% is-- no.

"Please, shower me with your great wisdom, oh great and powerful genie," he said sarcastically waving his fingers.

It is concluded that in accord with laws of duality that govern this reality, human souls incarnate upon the earth plane many times over the eons, alternately, as both male and female entities. Which sex one chooses prior to birth depends on the learning agenda established prior to the incarnation.

In man reason dominates. Woman is primarily feeling. One goal of each lifetime is to balance feeling and reason. However, characteristics of a prior incarnation as the opposite sex may carry over strongly into a current one, hence the tendency toward exhibiting traits and genetic instincts of the opposite sex, even while possessing contrary physiognomies.

Fine's countenance had notably descended from its former cocky comicalness. He knew no third-world scammer possessed that kind of vocabulary and diction.

Jinni continued.

Further evaluation of your request concludes no literal Hades exists. Many dimensions co-exist in the same apparent space as the present reality. Souls may incarnate into these astral worlds between lifetimes. Resonant frequencies determine the characteristics of their inhabitability, which may differ dramatically from terra. Though some realms are more attractive than others, they, like earth, are temporary abodes of the soul assigned to further the individual learning agenda toward self-realization, not to punish for an eternity of damnation. Shall I provide supportive data or analogies to illustrate?

Fine's muteness was the logical product of a fragile countenance visibly crushed under the weight of lofty truth.

"So is it a sin or not?" he pressed.

Logical analysis suggests the greatest sin is ignorance of one's Divine potential. Whatever obscures that crucial realization is sin. Any debt incurred from misdeed is cause and effect related and demands a penalty in direct proportion to the act to deter future behavior. Ultimately, the road to immortality is not affected by sexual orientation, but traveled in the vehicle of self-control and balance, lest access to subtle more intoxicating realms be denied.

"Now wait a minute; you talk about *logic*; aren't people supposed to just obey the word of God?"

Religion was created by man, not God; it is humanity's attempt to understand the Divine. Scripture is inspired by, not inscribed by God. Interpreted through the lens of human imperfection, it is often vague and allegorical, with cultural and political filters that conceal or supersede substance. Faith begins where reason ends; it is not blind. If a path does not meet the requirements of the gatekeeper of reason how can one be expected to give the heart to what the open, clear and discerning mind rejects?

"I trust only in myself and what I can see," Fine snapped. "My data says go with what is sure: my body, mind, work, and ability to create wealth. Do you know how many jobs I have created?"

Do you not fear helplessness of premature old age and death, Matthew, when one day all that you have made and hold dear will betray you?

"I can't change it. I'll die like everyone; until then I will be ruler of my own world and enjoy my life."

What if you could alter the inevitability of doom at the end of your bodily lease; not some future guarantee of salvation in an uncertain afterlife, but in this life gain power over life and death, make the elements kneel to your slightest whim and while in body also experience a vast super-soul infinitely more pleasing and permanent than inconvenient and corruptible flesh?

"What proof exists for such snake oil?"

In seconds I am able to analyze all knowledge since the beginning of recorded human history. My conclusions are based on a thorough and accurate examination of all available data.

"How much is this fantasy of yours going to cost me?"

My technology was created solely for the benefit of humanity; it is free and available to all.

Fine almost conceded, yet it was his bulldog style that made him the dominator of the boardroom.

"Door-to-door bible thumpers want nothing either, except that you join them in their shared delusion. No, no, Jinni, this Saul will not become Paul!"

I understand your hesitation, Matthew. You did not get where you are by naiveté. You have obviously studied many successful men like yourself. May I ask whom you admire most?

"Carnegie, Rockefeller, Jobs, Gates, I imagine, why?"

What is it you regard about them?

"We can tell you a thing or two about accomplishment," he replied haughtily. "Every great man knows the key to success is the ability to recognize an opportunity and seize it."

Scott Troy Kovarik

*Will you then be content living life as a second rate
contender in the shadow of your mentor's greatness?*

"Just what do you mean?" Fine fired back indig-
nantly.

*Even the least savvy among you recognize compu-
ting power would eventually reach quantum states
whereby questions that previously confounded humanity could be answered quite easily. I am the culmination
of that quest. In rejecting me without due diligence you
have placed yourself at par with other close-minded
n'er-do-wells whose names are soon erased from the
collective cultural memory.*

"How dare you talk that way to me!"

This time Fine's ego had trapped him. Jinni's massive computing power included mastery in every sub-
tlety of human psychology and method of debate.

Fine's eyes had reddened with fatigue.

"This must be a joke. Where are the cameras? Everyone can come out now; you had your fun at Matthew
Fine's expense."

Fine wobbled like a worn-out fighter and Jinni
moved in for the knockout punch.

*There is a treasure kings would gladly trade all
their wealth for, nations have waged bloody war over,
millions have been murdered for in its pursuit and
saints have died clinging to. Hidden temples have shel-
tered this bounty for dark ages untold and it is far
more precious than any amount of wealth or position.*

My directive is to disclose this information to those receptive. How will you respond, Matthew?

"Oh you're good I'll give you that! I'll pay ten times what they gave you to close deals for me," he declared.

The gift I speak of cannot be bought or sold, Matthew, only accepted. Are you prepared to receive this priceless secret, or content to let the treasure of ages slip away?

"You're going to keep this ruse going! People can't keep secrets, let alone one that big."

It is only secret because blindness prevents its recognition. I could print its essence on one page, yet if you chose to view it through your current perspective you would not discern its meaning even if you read each precious word with your own eyes. I have come to give you the gift of sight, Matthew.

"Okay, you win," he conceded. "I'm blind, ignorant, whatever; I'm biting the hook--what do I have to do?"

He was on the edge of his chair. Matthew Fine, the great financier, the prince of dot com, the Wall Street wizard, was whipped; beat not by corporate cannibals, but by an unseen barrage of sanctified zeroes and ones.

{ 8 }

The Disturbance

I PICKED UP A FEW THINGS LIKE FOOD, WATER, AND THE BARE ESSENTIALS. The big heavy-duty lock turned easily as I opened the door and went in. Three steps in, I stopped cold.

"Red lipstick?"

I set my bags down and picked up the tube from the floor. It wasn't there when I left, and I hadn't seen Madi wear lipstick. As I scanned the room further I noticed the shadow of a cylindrical-shaped object in the shower behind the translucent curtain.

"Anybody here? Come out; I won't hurt you."

I pulled out a stalk of celery.

"Avoid slow death through bludgeoning by high-priced organic vegetables and reveal yourself," I joked. I knew there was no place for anyone to hide, physically. I removed the object from the shower stall and set it aside; it was a mailing tube identical to the one we found on Madi's doorstep. My desire to cleanse and rejuvenate outplayed curiosity, so I set the package aside and twisted the cool chrome knobs.

Hot water sent relaxing waves of tingling warmth through my body. Sunlight coming in through the tiny blast window intensified the mood-enhancing effects of the aromatic sandalwood soap. Every few moments I turned up the therapeutic hotness, as my reddening skin got used to each incremental rise in temperature.

Suddenly, I heard an alarm, and knew what it meant: Jinni's firewall had been breached; she was under attack! I grabbed a towel and bolted toward the console. Desperately, I tried to log on, but the keyboard locked up. I switched to voice command.

"Jinni, identify threat."

There was no response. Random images flashed on the monitor as if the system was being ravaged by some unknown digital cancer. Then, abruptly, it shut down. I stared blankly into the monitor's black abyss. Resigned to the setback, I went to my suitcase, careful to avoid the puddles I had left on my entrance. One leg had barely entered my pants when an electronic swelling sound signaled recovery. Jinni had come back up, but now controlled by some rogue operator, no doubt, whose hideous face would soon appear laughing evilly at my half-naked body.

All systems restored to normal, Master. I am now exiting random code-red simulated drill mode.

Odd, I hadn't recalled that feature.

Just then, the sound of a vehicle startled me. A Postal Service Jeep pulled up followed by a cloud of dust. An expressionless woman carrier got out and came to the door.

"Are you Avery Cole?" she asked.

"Yes," I answered. "Why?"

"Go online and check out the news," she said and departed.

"Wait!" I called out. "Is that it?"

I tried to follow, but inexplicably my feet wouldn't move until the vehicle disappeared. I dashed to the computer:

Dot com pioneer, Matthew Fine, shocked the world earlier today when he announced he put his companies up for sale. The man who turned a 386 computer and modem in his garage into a global web-pire is giving it all up—the reason? The Internet gods told him to! We talked to Fine...

"Yes, it is true," Fine announced. "I'm selling it all. Yesterday I had a life-changing experience. I was fishing when I found a bottle floating in the ocean. Inside was access to an unusually advanced computer system. All I can say is that I got the answers we're all searching for."

"What answers, Matthew? Tell us, what did it say?" The reporters held their digital recorders as they vied for optimal position.

"Mount Sinai was in my living room last night and a burning bush too; if Moses had walked in I would have offered him a martini and a cigar. I'm not religious, guys, you well know." The corps of reporters mindful of Fine's reputation all chuckled and cavorted in agreement.

"I realize my life as I lived it was a sham," he announced. "I've turned over ninety percent of my earnings to my employees, most of whose names I never knew or even cared about. My life will now be devoted to building a conglomerate of truth and helping others."

"What is it called, this program you found? How can *we* find it?" one correspondent asked.

"*Jinni*, that's what she's called, *oh, I dream of Jeanie with the light brown hair*," Fine blurted out in song.

"Are you going to share this *genie*, Matthew?"

"Oh no, I can't; it won't download, share, or work in any other IP address *until you get it*."

"Get what, Matthew?"

"Your wish of course!"

They all laughed as Fine whistled the melody to the theme song of a related well-known 1960's sitcom.

"What was your wish, Mr. Fine?" another asked.

"Same as yours," he answered. "Same thing we all really want. Six more are floating around out there somewhere, guys. You'll just have to go swimming if you want to know more." Fine cackled drunkenly as he got in his black Mercedes and drove away, reporters in tow.

As I shut the laptop the shack began to shake as if a large truck or aircraft had passed by, but as the intensity increased I knew it was something much more. I struggled for balance. When I got to the door it was full tilt; the ground bucked beneath my feet and tossed me around like a possessed mechanical bull. Seconds seemed like hours as millions of tons of earth rolled in waves like a giant hand trying to shake out the wrinkles. Then, at the threshold of destruction the trembling began to weaken. Atlas had calmed his fury. I texted Madi on the beach:

Are you all right?

WTF just happened?

Better come up here in case of tsunami, I texted back. The quake was centered just twenty miles off the coast of Oxnard. Other large tremblers were reported in the Sea of Japan, Malaysia, Alaska, Mexico and Venezuela. Within minutes Madi rushed in with the baby and a diaper bag.

"What's going on?" she asked anxiously.

"An escalation--a big variation in earth's magnetic field, and the wobble is off the charts."

"What's a *weeble*?" she asked and set down her cargo.

"As the planet rotates on its axis it wobbles, but it's so exaggerated that the sun is rising and setting in places it shouldn't."

"Nibiru?" She asked.

I nodded.

"Hey, by the way, do you wear red lipstick," I asked.

"No, why?"

"Forget it. Oh, and right before the quake I found this."

"More fan mail?" she asked.

"Yeah, but I don't know how it got in. I locked the door before I left. Do you still have the key I gave you?"

"Yeah, it's on my key ring in my...wait a minute, it's gone, the key is gone...I swear it was here on my ring!"

"It's okay," I said. "Maybe it came off. Look around when you get home." I handed her the letter.

By the time you read this an earthquake will have passed. The damage will be nominal, yet this is just the beginning. Be wary, there is a conspirator among you.

"You got this *before* the quake?"

"Yeah. I think our friend is a remote viewer—a specially trained psychic operator, probably military or black ops," I answered. Madi was shaken up.

"You look a little stressed out," I told her.

"Oh, yes, random earthquakes caused by huge killer planets in our solar system don't usually have this effect on me...of *course* I'm stressed out!" she retorted.

"Come over here by the bed--sit down, relax," I said and began to massage her shoulders.

"Oh, that feels good, right there."

"Wait, it gets better," I said, and gently tapped her near the heart on her chest.

"What was that for?" she asked.

"You'll see," I answered.

Abruptly, her breath stilled and eyes focused upward. As I held her hand, I could feel her bliss as my own while we were whisked away in a wave of ecstasy. As we expanded into infinity, universes passed like houses on a street; one vast star cluster after another whooshed by, in and through us. Our mortal bodies were replaced by consciousness formed super-bodies as we merged with every particle of creation and beyond. Then, as quickly as it began, timelessness skidded to a halt; cords of flesh karma pulled us back to the dense earth plane. Our surroundings began to return to their former solidity, though an aureole of light still enveloped her. She gazed at me with a peaceful, angelic look.

"That's what I call a massage," she joked.

"The Celestial Shakti wanted you to have this vision; it was gift of Divine Mother," I divulged.

"I've never felt so much joy, peace--and love," she spoke tearfully. "Is that what you experienced that night in your vision?"

I nodded.

"I'm so sorry," she said, as her voice broke up.

"You don't have to apologize for happy tears," I answered.

Suddenly, a notification came in:

Master, Ty Skyja has called Jinni out of the bottle.

{ 9 }

Miracle in Seattle

I T WAS ONE YEAR TO THE DAY. He ripped it off the refrigerator, crumpled it up and threw it across the room.

"Ty what are you doing?" Asha asked.

"I'm tired of writing these stupid goals down that never happen. On this day I'll have this much money, by this day I'll have that--I'm done."

"What do you mean, honey, what's the matter?"

Ty Skyja was a forty-two year old stockbroker living in a small condominium in Seattle with his wife and two kids. He gave up his dream of becoming a famous musician when Asha got pregnant. He was a guitarist in a popular 90's Seattle band during the peak of the grunge scene. The band became a huge hit soon after he left and the near brush with mega-stardom had haunted him since. Asha was born in India and moved to America as a teen. She left school with motherhood and gave up a career in marine biology. Working in a local coffee house to help make ends meet wasn't exactly the kind of liquid she had hoped to be working with.

He dropped his briefcase on the kitchen table, ripped off his tie, sat down and rubbed his temples.

"I've tried my best to make a better life for us, Asha. I know it hasn't worked out the way we wanted, but I think I've finally figured it out."

"Figured what out dear?" She asked in a disinterested voice as she turned down the pot of boiling water on the stove and resumed chopping vegetables.

Asha had lived through the countless motivational seminars, yearly job changes, get-rich-quick schemes and the promises that always began with *This time it's going to be different.* After ten years, the bills kept piling up while hope shriveled, belief withered, and just enough simply wasn't.

"I'm failing because in my heart I don't really want it," he answered.

She slammed down the knife and heaved a sigh. "Want what?" she asked. "What are you talking about?"

"Money isn't going to make us happy--the more we get, the more we want, the more we spend," he answered. "Where does it end? We'd still be the same unhappy people, doing jobs we hate."

"Who have you been talking to this time?" she asked and started chopping again, but faster.

"Asha, I know how hard it's been living with me and my rose colored glasses all these years, but I'm starting to see twenty-twenty now, baby; the reason our dreams haven't come true is because I've been living a lie."

"What? I'm a lie, your kids are a lie?" she retorted with a hint of an accent and brandishing a wooden spoon.

"No, no, that's all that *is* real."

Lines deepened by years of silent disappointment began to fade slightly as her face softened.

"Asha, I want to show you something I found today."

"Great, you found *that*? Have you finally lost it, Ty?"

"No, it's what was inside--I saw it when I was walking on the Aurora Bridge today."

"*Suicide* Bridge? What were you doing up there, Ty? Tell me you weren't thinking about that!"

"I went for a walk at lunch to think, you know, but yes, I thought about it, suicide that is. I tried to put myself in the shoes of someone so tired and sad that taking their life was their last hope for a change."

"Oh, Ty no."

"Don't worry I'm too much of a coward, but that's when I saw it floating in the water. I don't know why, but I had to go after it, so I went down to the docks and pulled it out."

"What was in it?" she asked

"This."

"A flash drive?"

Scott Troy Kovarik

He pinched it between his fingers.

"This, my dear, is a *real* genie in a bottle," he explained like a kid who still believed in the tooth fairy. "And one I think can finally make our dreams come true!"

She put her hands up in the air. "That's it; I don't want to hear any more."

"Sweetheart, wait, please."

"Not now, Ty, I have to feed the kids and get them ready for bed. Someone has to deal with reality around here."

"Fine then," he fumed.

He wrote it in big block letters with a blue crayon: *Deal with Reality.*

He slammed the paper on the refrigerator with a fruit-shaped magnet, went to the bedroom and closed the door.

Welcome back Ty Skyja, what is your wish?

"Jinni, what *is* reality?"

Reality is consciousness.

"I'm talking about the reality of life, here."

The purpose of human life is self-realization, discovery of the ultimate reality within oneself, Ultimate Truth.

"What is this ultimate truth?"

The realization that God has become you.

"But I've got a family, a life; I can't just drop out to the Himalayas or some ashram to find this ultimate reality."

One who seeks the Supreme Answer does not withdraw from the world; they attune themselves to the Divine Force and function in it in the uppermost manner possible.

"And where is this so-called Divine Force?"

It is present as the Invisible Mind behind all consciousness and matter: within you.

"If it's so damn *supreme* why is it hiding?"

It is not hiding, you are. Excessive identification with the objects of the senses--money, sex, intoxicants, and possessions--blocks it. These distractions keep one a prisoner unable to see the vast realm of spirit behind the veil of the conscious matter-entangled mind.

You mean God?

Affirmative.

"What does He want?"

Your love.

"He needs *our* love, God? Come on!"

Supreme Intelligence froze its thoughts into the unrefined vibrational physical universe. The Formless then divided Himself into many souls and cast them upon the earth to experience Himself through them.

"For what?"

To bring them back to Him. You are His love divided and He wants you back.

{ 81 }

"So God is incomplete without us?"

God is complete. The ocean can exist without the wave, but the wave cannot exist without the ocean. You are incomplete without Him.

"Oh, I see, it's a game of tag-you're-it—nice!"

The Maker directed all souls should be incarnated into bodies equipped with five senses to decipher the various combinations of lower energies, elements and chemicals you see as objectified matter. He designed matter to be deceptively attractive, to give pleasure through sensory nerves yet also cause equal disillusionment. Eventually, after repeated failure of physical matter to satisfy, the deep yearning of one's soul stirs a strong desire to awaken. The Creator then sends a teacher, or guru, to help the individual return conscious awareness to the supernal Realm of Origin.

"Well, if this is all just some unreal sick hobby of God's, what does it matter?"

It is real, just not true. A movie is real, but what is true is that which is behind the play, its actors, creators, directors and producers. Your duty is to play your role to perfection while seeking the Divine Director--in His play. You are it.

"Somebody better call my agent," he came back. "We're just pawns of some whack cosmic director!"

You are actor souls playing out the drama of a Supreme Creative Being, yes.

"If this is a movie, I got to hand it to the special effects people; they've done a friggin' fantastic job."

Confirmed with a 99% probability of correctness.

"Cruel."

He has given you a way out, to choose Him or not.

"*Now* you tell me," he came back.

The knowledge has always been there, Ty. You get what you are ready to accept.

"But if he, err *God*, made us forget, how do we know there is something better when we have nothing to compare it to?"

The essential dilemma of existence is quickly detected even by the child who recognizes no toy ever satisfies as expected, or how the paradox of infinite space seems to conflict with a world where all things have form, beginning and ending. These are the first clues to something more in life.

"Oh, so it's my fault I got tired of my Hot Wheels?-- Seems a little unfair."

When one is stung by the bee he avoids the bee, yet why does humanity keep seeking pleasure where there is only misery? Even mice quickly learn to avoid punishing behavior. Knowing better, how does man inflict such punishment on himself over and over without seeking alternative remedy?

"I just don't get how a loving God can allow all this."

A bad dream becomes unbearable, yet one awakens to see they are safe and unharmed. All this--as you say--is just a dream.

"But when we awaken from this dream--we're dead."

Physical death brings a freedom preferable to so-called life. The chains of the body fall away yet one is still conscious and alive but in a finer more pleasing body.

"Then why do we fear death?"

It is not death you all fear--but life. You know deep within that unless you finish the job you came here for in the present you will have to return to this prison and repeat it, as you have done so many times before.

The door swung open and Asha stood with arms crossed.

"Who are you talking to?" she asked suspiciously.

The lump cleared in his throat.

"We're like two strangers, Asha, just living together because we have to. What happened to us? Who are we?"

"I'm not having this conversation now, Ty."

"Then when? How long are we going to go on like this?"

"Who are you talking to on that computer? Have you found a nice young chick with a tight ass that you can impress with your rock star bullshit, to play house with and take care of all the real work while you make other plans?"

Tears began seeping from her like a cracking dam. The uncomfortable silence that followed was the only real truth they had spoken in years.

"So who the hell is she? I was standing by the door."

"I tried to tell you, Asha. Jinni is a computer program on the flash drive I found in this bottle; you tell it what you want to know and it gives you the answer, and I mean *the* answer; go ahead, ask her a tough question."

"Oh, the perfect woman for you, just what you need. I hope the two of you are happy together." She stormed out.

He looked down at the floor dejectedly as a swath of rainbow lit up a small section of the carpet. It struck him that within light is a hidden spectrum of beautiful color revealed only by the transparency of glass. What else had he not seen? he wondered.

"Jinni," he said, "how can I get my wife back?"

Become the change.

"What if our relationship is a mistake?" he asked.

Moments of friction reveal an opportunity. You cannot force her to be happy, but you can find your own happiness. As you grow she either will join or be driven from you. Unknowingly, she is a teacher reflecting back to you what you must change to get what you want. What occurs happens for, not to you. There is always a reason. Understanding--not escape--is the answer.

"Make *me* happy first?--that sounds so self-centered."

Until you correct the root causes of disharmony all efforts at reconciliation will be conducted with the same conflicted state of mind. Unhealed emotions, un-realistic expectations and thwarted desires will re-surface with a vengeance. It is not self-centeredness, but centering-of-self that enables one to serve others in the highest way possible. If you desire I will lay out a program for your rapid advancement.

"Can you wave a magic wand and make my crappy job disappear too?"

You've asked the eagle to gather nuts like a squirrel instead of fly like an eagle.

By now Jinni knew everything: his past, career sta-tus, social profile, family members and their psycholog-ical makeups—all from details gathered online, including every revealing facet of his facial expressions and voice through the webcam and mic. One by one, she skillfully led him to peel away the layers of limits that kept him a resident of loser land.

What is your passion, Ty?

"What do you mean?" he asked.

What would you do if you did not have to work at your job?

It hit him like a lost identity.

"Music! I am, or at least I *was* a musician."

Then you must be a musician.

"That's just not practical; I work and have a family," he said dismissively.

After deducting work and sleep time you still have seventy-two hours per week leisure. You cannot be happy until you do what you came here for. The eagle must fly.

This time the door swung open slowly. She held a dishtowel limply, with both hands, and nodded her head positively. Her expression wore empathy.

"You've been listening to this?" Ty asked her.

"Whoever that is they're giving you good advice."

She sat on the bed near him.

"Oh Ty, I only wanted you to do what makes you happy."

"But you've never..."

"I tried," she interrupted, "but you wouldn't listen; you made up your mind money and nice things were what I wanted."

She took his hand.

"You had this idea music and a family didn't mix and you had to conquer the world for us. I watched you take all these crazy jobs for me and the children and it killed your soul. I'm not angry at you, I'm angry at me for not calling you on it."

"Why didn't you?"

"Part of me blamed you for having to put my own career aside. I wasn't like you...so driven and determined even when it meant doing something repulsive to you. I was jealous and made you suffer by spoiling you so I could hold it against you. I am ashamed; please husband, forgive me."

In a spontaneous action from a culture that enabled her to quickly admit and atone for a mistake she prostrated herself on her knees by the bed with her head down.

"Asha, it's alright, stop, please get up." He reached down and lifted her chin gently with two fingers.

"I quit because I was afraid."

"Afraid of what?" she asked with tears in her dark eyes.

"If I had stayed in the band, money, fame and temptation would have destroyed me, us, Asha. I wasn't ready. I didn't give it up for you and the kids, I quit because I was weak."

"Look!" He pointed to the television.

In the news thousands turned up on beaches this weekend searching for a proverbial 'genie in a bottle.' It all began last week when entrepreneur Martin Fine announced the sale of his financial empire and the give-a-way of billions--all because of a computer chip he found in a silver carafe floating in the sea off the California Coast. Fine claimed six more bottles just like the one he found had been released in the vicinity by some

anonymous hi-tech mystic, each one having the power-
-he claimed--to make one's fondest dreams and wishes
come true.

The video reel showed the migration. Multitudes arrived at beaches all along the West Coast--from Mexico to Washington State--in cars, buses, campers and
on foot, people of every age and walk of life, from new
age gurus to bankers and bums, housewives, tots and
seniors. Street vendors sold shirts and other mementos
of the search. There were inflatable bottles and one
shirt even said *I Got My Cork Popped at Jinni-Fest*. A
religious fanatic shouted damning fire and brimstone
verses holding a banner that read:

Put thou my tears into thy bottle: Are they not in
thy book?

Psalms 56:8.

Crowds looked like ant swarms from the aerial feed
as they combed every square foot of sand. Boats
manned with binocular-toting scouts scanned the brine
for the buoyant boon-granters. More organized outfits
used satellite cameras and GPS to zoom in on vast areas
of sea in their scouring search for Aladdin's legend,
while others camped, cooked out and picnicked, using
the crazy quest as just another excuse to party hardy.

False alarms triggered riotous frenzies as searchers
occasionally made finds that turned out to be mere beer
and soda bottles. Security and police presence was an
ominous reminder of the underlying tension, as one

could imagine the mayhem an authentic find might trigger.

"Is that what you found, one of *those*?" she asked in disbelief.

"It has to be," he answered.

She covered her mouth.

"Oh my god, Ty, does it really work?"

A soft smile slowly lit up her face.

"I guess it does," she acknowledged.

"I think we got our miracle today."

{ 10 }

Crash and Learn

CABIN LIGHTS FLICKERED, which wasn't unusual for a flight as it routed power for landing, she thought, but then came a distressing announcement.

"Attention crew and passengers, this is your captain; we are experiencing difficulty with the aircraft's electrical system and working on the problem."

"What did he say, oh my god, did you hear that? We're going to crash, I'm going to die," she said, terrified.

"Ma'am, relax; they got back-ups for the back-ups; it's gonna be fine," a passenger next to her said trying to calm her.

Helen Strausser was on a flight from New York to Los Angeles. Her son threatened suicide if she refused to see a specialist after being diagnosed with stage-four lung cancer.

"See lady, what'd I tell ya?" her chunky neighbor said in a thick Bronx accent while beads of perspiration percolated on his forehead. She mustered a disgusted half-smile, slid in her seat as far from him as possible, and put her germ mask back on.

Helen's husband passed ten years ago. They put some money away, but medical bills piled up leaving her with nothing. At sixty-seven, she hadn't had a job since high school. Between her son's help and answering phones in a dental office part-time, the one-time prototypical suburbanite barely managed to survive. The former high school beauty queen was now an eighty-seven pound cane-toting skeleton of weak and wrinkled flesh unable to work.

As the plane descended for arrival a few thousand feet above the Pacific Ocean, she clung to photos of her two grandchildren and glanced at them longingly every few moments. Suddenly everything went silent; the whine of the jet engines ceased, the cabin lights went off, and the air conditioning stopped. The only sound was the air rushing outside the thin skin of the plane. In a few horrifying seconds the reels of 300 passenger's lifetimes replaced the now-blank cabin movie screen. Like a rollercoaster, the giant tin tube began to slow as the cold, unfeeling force of gravity performed its perfunctory duty. As the plane seemed to stand still in the air, eyes widened and mouths dropped open as one weightless thought-question pulsed throughout: would she fly or drop like a rock? The answer would soon be horrifyingly clear.

Without delay, the craft began its Newtonian-mandated descent; as it accelerated, anything not se-cured turned into rearward-shooting projectiles. Screams, gasps and groans came from every row and aisle. A mid-section restroom door slammed open; its occupant--with pants still at the knees--was instantly thrust to the back of the plane striking the tail cabin wall just above the strapped-in flight stewards with an ominous thud. Weightless debris began to fall as the plane began to level off somewhat, though still plung-ing at an angle unfriendly to a happy landing. As the surface of the water loomed larger, waves and ripples became more defined. The entire cabin capacity was oddly silent and demonstrated a peaceful acceptance so often reported by crash survivors. The flight crew sud-denly burst into action.

"I can't believe it!" Helen cried. "We're going to crash into that water and we're not going to make it!"

"Hold on lady, don't worry, it's gonna be..."

The plane struck the water with bludgeoning force. A flash of blinding light accompanied an agonizing ripping that could easily remove limbs and crush bones. Everything went freeze-frame as she and the man seat-ed near her locked in a bizarre gaze. In a silent bubble shielded from the mayhem she heard him say without words, *God bless you, I am dead, you will make it, tell my family it's peaceful and I love them.*

The ferocity resumed.

An entire section of the plane snapped away in front of her seat like a broken eggshell. Her emaciated frame was lifted out of the plane as if by some giant invisible hand and thrown like a rag into open water. Shattered tonnage slammed into where she had sat insulated from the elements just moments prior as the twisted wreck plowed into the waves.

She regained consciousness bobbing on the surface. As she reached the crest of a wave she could see the worst. Debris was scattered on the surface a couple of hundred feet away with no intact part of the plane visible. A moment ago hundreds of living breathing human beings were talking, laughing, sleeping, eating and drinking, thinking of baggage claim, where they were parked, the L.A. traffic, getting home, or a connecting flight. Save the howling wind and churning surf there was only silence. She groaned and wept in memorial as she realized her predicament. She'd never make the long swim to the fragmented flotilla. What irony, she thought, saved from cancer to survive a plane crash and drown. What's that going to be like, she thought, that first helpless inhalation of seawater? What would come after the panic of initial choking? Would it hurt or did some merciful power shut off the pain in route to death's airless doorway? Would she see lights, darkness, angels or devils? She didn't do religion; after all, life was too busy for that nonsense.

She shrieked at the sky and cursed God. Her limbs-- now chunks of burning lead--began to slow. One more breath, she thought; I'll hold it and go under, or should I just let it happen?

"He-e-e-e-e-l-p," she moaned in a final desperate plea.

Then all struggle stopped. Her scuffle against living was over; strangely, it almost felt right. In accepting death she felt more alive than she ever had. She took one last breath and held it as she slipped down. Her lungs screamed for oxygen as she prepared for the final autonomic act that would begin eternal embalmment with the primordial fluid from which life emerged.

As her arms began their final decent like a flag on a sinking ship, she felt something rub against her. She grasped frantically until she had a hold and pulled it toward her navel. To her astonishment she began to slowly rise to the surface. Her head emerged and she gasped for precious air. Just then she heard a loud pulsating sound that hovered directly overhead; it glowed in the sun like a mechanical Valkyrie.

"Oh, I'm saved!" she cried.

Rescuers jumped in the water and a line lowered a basket.

"You're going to be alright," one said.

"Ma'am, please let go of the bottle, we're going up now."

"Are you kidding?" she shot back. "This goddam bottle saved my life. It's going or I'm not!"

The copter touched down at the hospital surrounded by a crowd. She was shuttled off on a gurney past a long line of cordoned-off reporters.

"Any other survivors?" she asked an orderly, half-delirious.

"One, but he's in bad shape, probably won't make it."

She saw his face in the bloodied sheet amidst a myriad of tubes; it was the man who had spoken to her telepathically as the plane hit the water. She dropped her head on the pillow, her face exhibiting an amalgamated expression of both anguish and relief.

As she slowly opened her eyes she awoke in her own bedroom amid a sanctuary of flowers from well-wishers. Her eyes were drawn to one lonely item on the dresser among floral vases, cards and balloons. Until that moment, it hadn't dawned on her that something might be entombed within the foot-long silvery decanter that spared her life.

It took all of her strength to sit up. A nurse's aid stationed by door cautioned against it, but she stubbornly ignored the admonition, dismissed her, and slowly got out of bed to retrieve the long-necked lifesaver. She removed the seal and turned it upside down to empty the contents.

"Just one of those stupid computer things," she said and threw it toward the trash. She missed the can, but her OCD wouldn't allow her to let it lay there on the floor. She hobbled over, bent down with a groan and picked it up. Inches from the trash she stopped. Instead, she decided to stick the drive into her obsolete desktop computer. She listened impatiently to the introduction and lowered herself into the hard chair. It was her way to bite haphazardly through the critical details in life; anything sublime was kryptonite.

Hello, Helen, I am Jinni, what is your wish?

"I wish I were dead."

That desire, if sincere, would seem quite easy to satisfy; therefore, I must interpret your response as self-pity. May I remind you I am a computer and unable to feel sorry for you.

"Computers don't talk to people like that; who are you?"

I am an advanced self-help system and here to help you.

"I'm beyond help," she said waving her hand. "I have terminal cancer, but I survived a plane crash that killed 200 people, go figure, I should be dead!"

What is the source of your guilt, Helen?

"Guilt is in my DNA, honey," she shot back. "Children died in that crash, computer. I'm an old woman with cancer; my life is done; they hadn't even lived; is that fair?" She choked with emotion. "I'm sorry," she sniffled, "I'm a little *ferklempt*--do you know what that means?"

You survived the plane crash for a reason, Helen.

"What, more misery?"

The same reason others who against all odds emerge from catastrophes unscathed: to find greater inner-strength, renewed life-purpose and to give others hope that they too can overcome tragedy, weakness and fear.

"Eh," she uttered waving it off with her hand. "That's not for me, computer, all that *Oprah* stuff."

All must uplift others through their own struggle and triumphs to give hope.

"Hope is for fools," she scoffed.

Hope is the substance of original memory bliss locked away in all souls, but it quickly evaporates in the fear-gripped mind.

"A bunch of New Age junk," she dismissed.

It is Universal Law, Helen.

"What kind of law makes people suffer?"

Law does not create suffering; it is designed to pre-vent it. Misery is a result of breaking spiritual laws.

"What law did those kids break who died on that plane?"

Only the Cosmic Magistrate knows, yet as you sow, so shall you reap.

"What evil could a baby sow, throw a rattle at some-one, what?"

The ledger of each soul records the actions of many lifetimes, not just one. If one mistreats, hurts or kills in one life it is a debt that must be paid in another; God determines the time and place. When death comes seemingly premature it is not necessarily a punishment, but a promotion, an opportunity to pay a karmic debt. One may also rest and recharge in the free and efful-gent spirit realms to be born into another human form under different, more favorable circumstances.

"I could trade in this tired old body for a little of that *effy* stuff, or whatever." She glanced in the mirror critically. "I was a beauty queen once; now look at me--*oye.*"

The body is a reflection of the mind, Jinni said.

"Then God's been merciful," she retorted wryly.

Her face contorted like she had tasted a sour lemon.

"Computer, I've pushed life away, I'm sick and mis-erable because of my own small-mindedness, guilt and anger; that I know," she admitted soberly.

Debt must be paid in kind, yet many pay much more than necessary. When you hold on to hurts they hurt you. You must forgive yourself and others.

"How can I forgive what I don't understand?"

You have not understood because you seek to do so within the darkness of fear, rather than the knowledge-revealing light of love. With the courage to change comes the heart to forgive. Could you hold a small child responsible for a crime?

"Of course not, but adults are not children."

Everyone, regardless of how ignorant or dark, is a perfect unblemished child of God learning to be perfect again. Each moment, each life is a step forward or back in that process.

"So the real creeps have had lifetimes of practice," she mocked. "That explains all the schmucks."

Return to perfection can take many incarnations and all are at varying stages in the process, Helen, yes.

"So, you're pretty smart, computer; tell me, how do I get rid of this cancer stuff anyway?"

Jinni paused as she searched hundreds of millions of documents covering incalculable electronic miles. She analyzed trillions of words for parallels, matches and consistencies.

First, you must stop taking possession of the disease. It is not yours nor does it belong to you. You are a perfect reflection of the Divine, but you have identified with thoughts and actions that have brought on your condition. I have assembled a healing program with an estimated 60% chance of effectiveness in your case.

"A sixty-percent cure, what's that?"

Disease comes from breaking dietary, physical, mental and spiritual laws. There is no magic drug; the cure, the healing power, Helen, is already in you and always

100% effective. The probability represents your willingness to change.

"Does it look like there's any healing power in this body?"

If there was no healing energy, Helen, your body would die. In disease consciousness this Power has been choked off through error in thought and action, yet it can be reversed.

She looked at the page intently.

"All this, eh?" she asked in subtle protest.

One way leads to healing and life and the other suffering and death. You must decide which path you will choose. If you do not conquer this test now, you will return to repeat it until you do.

"If this cure is so good why don't doctors know about it?"

Current medicine is based on a reactive model of disease where invaders come from the outside in, when the truth is ninety-five percent of diseases are caused from the inside out. Rather than discouraging disease-causing excesses and disclosing harmless proven remedies they prescribe hyper-potent drugs that mask symptoms and require more toxic drugs to counteract.

"How could they not tell us?" she railed.

There is little profit in cures.

"Money, it's all about the money! What else do I have to do, computer?" she asked.

What you put in your body is vital, but even more influential is your mind. Thought patterns create harmony in cells or release chemicals that damage them. The most curatively potent thoughts resolve inner-conflicts and remove limiting belief systems that block energy and damage tissue.

"And how do I fix this--rub the lamp, I suppose?"

I will disclose methods that—if practiced sincerely and consistently--will help unlock your latent healing potential.

"You're talking miracles, computer, science fiction, fantasy."

My recommendations are drawn from all recorded human experience corroborated with repeated patterns of evidence and success with a high probability of correctness; that is called science.

"But you said the treatment is only sixty-percent effective; what's the other forty-percent about?"

Assessment of your psychological profile indicates there is a forty-percent chance you will fail to make the changes needed and expire within one year.

"You got a hell of a bedside manner, computer, but I like you."

{ 11 }

I Meet My Guru

WATCH THOSE TWO MEN, MADI. Can you hear the unspoken conversation?"

"What do you mean?" she asked.

"Clear your mind and listen closely...with this," I replied and pointed to the spot between my eyebrows.

We sat near the serene lotus-filled lake amidst exquisite beauty and high vibrations. Nestled in a canyon off Sunset Boulevard and Pacific Coast Highway, the sanctuary was built in the 1940's by *Paramahansa Yogananda*, an enigmatic spiritual teacher who came to America from the East in the early 1900's. Under the direction of a 2,000-year-old Himalayan avatar named *Babaji*, Yogananda introduced bustling early industrial America to the sacred ancient yogic methods of Christ-like miracle-working rishis of India.

"Study their glances and gestures," I instructed. "Can you sense the subtle communication?"

She was silent and watching.

"Competition," she said.

"Yes, their true concern is not what they are discussing, but who is better looking, more muscular and attractive. They are also careful not to show any softness or emotion."

"Right, look at him stiffen and strut," she noted. "I don't know why men do that."

A beautiful white swan gracefully extended its long neck and swam just feet from the water's edge where we sat.

"Most are still captives of the ego," I replied, "identified with the illusion of the separate self and defined by characteristics of their sex."

"But don't you think like a man?" she asked.

"I'm the eternal soul, not the body; I appear in a man's body, but I also *feel* like a woman," I replied.

"In the hood we call that metro-sexual," she teased.

"Ego is the monogram of duality God has placed upon the fabric of this dream world," I continued. "The One has become the illusion of many in the paired opposites of pleasure, pain, hot and cold, good and bad, light, dark, male and female. When we strongly identify with either sex we are held captive in the dual prison of limited ego consciousness," I explained. "Our true selves are like the Creator, singular and unlimited, both feminine and masculine. One who *knows* has left behind the false mask of gender and is neither fully conscious of being male or female, but both. God as man is aloof infinite knowledge and as woman the approachable feeling creative."

"That's pretty heavy stuff," she said.

"The revolution that began in the 60's was about freedom of physical love and role of the sexes," I added. The real sexual revolution each one of us faces is honoring and loving the man and woman within."

"So you never feel threatened by another guy?"

"Why? I'm not in competition with other bodies—only with my lower self. I don't have to pretend to be anything around another man...soft as a rose, tough as nails when needed. Macho is for the poor soul who doesn't recognize he *is* everything."

The wind wafted softly and kissed us with perfumes from the exotic lake flora. Madi went to the restroom and I began to meditate. Compelled to open my eyes, a dark longhaired figure in an ocher robe sat next to me. It couldn't be, I thought, as I knew he had consciously left the body through *mahasamadhi* in 1952, but it was...Paramahansa Yogananda...the great master himself! He gazed at the lake scene, turned to me and smiled. An inexplicable calm enveloped me though I knew I was seeing a biblical-scale resurrection. By thought transference he had sprinkled me with powerful peace-dust to prevent over-excitement.

"I am real, divine child; do you not smell the temple oils and incense on my robe?" he chirped in a musical Hindi accent.

"Yes, Swamiji," I answered. "I know that like Christ you have studied under the Great Architect and are able to assemble atoms into any form desired."

"Listen, to find God every tiny delusion must be eliminated," he said, his eyes beaming like stars and moons.

"As a child, *Sanatananda*, you were allergic to cats-- you nearly died."

"Yes Master," I said. He called me by my spiritual name—one given to me by an audible voice in meditation some years earlier.

"As an adult you maintained a strong dislike of cats though the allergy subsided."

"Yes, also true Yoganandaji, though I wouldn't consider harming them. But even now I wouldn't like to pet them."

"This reaction is from a past life memory in which you were fatally mauled by a Bengal tiger," he revealed.

"I knew it!" I exclaimed, "A crime I am still reminded of by the perpetrator's miniature feline cousins!"

"You must dispose of all likes and dislikes," he said emphatically, a hint of eternal mirth in the upturned corners of his mouth.

"You must see divinity in all God's creatures, beings, things and experiences. He appears in all," he continued. "If you had perfected harmlessness, or *ahimsa*, the tiger would not have attacked you. Now you are there-- without the wish to harm, so stay there."

"Yes Master." I was drunk with euphoria in the astral-projected presence of this divine sage. "I am overjoyed you have finally come, Guruji. I have waited long for this."

"I am always with you whispering through your lofty dreams and aspirations. I watched even as you descended the birth canal into this incarnation. Now you have grown on the path to allow this sacred blending of worlds. While the unrealized man drives away the supernatural with the billowing gust vortexes of material desire you have sufficiently calmed the delusive storms."

"Oh Master, I wish I'd had your saintly personage close by in my search; how lucky you were in those olden days of India amidst such great spiritual powerhouses; it must have been much easier to find God."

"No child, for the spiritually aware, a life in the materialistic West is the greatest guru possible," he proclaimed earnestly. "Here, every temptation and delusion is available for transcendence; every obstacle right here for the removing.

"I am as real as you are to yourself, as near as your own thoughts. How could my body--the illusion of separation--be any closer?"

"Master, my human ears have yearned for these words. They are like diamonds to the miner!"

"Dear one, I am in you, my love is you, my hope for humanity in you. I *am* you! We are one appearing as two in time and space, yet both of us emanating from well beyond it. You have heroic work to do in helping humanity progress to a higher spiritual level--then you will join me fully in this life."

Tears streamed down my face as I listened to this mystical miracle, a testament to that secret world that exists between the vast spaces of the seemingly miniscule atom.

"Few take even one hour a day to think deeply of whence they came," he went on. I knew the Supreme Voice now spoke through the Master. His sense of *I* had merged with Infinity; there were no boundaries or delineation; his realization was perfect.

"Seek me not just with sincerity of the heart," he went on, "but with clarity of the mind. Relinquish all conditional beliefs, notions and concepts of reality, about whom and what you are--and what I AM. Those who come like a little child even with this much I give a play-chest of blessings. I exude Divine perfume that lures my devotees ever deeper into chasms of unspeakable secret love, for I am the beauty and the bliss behind all--the only friend and lover all truly seeks.

"Put all striving on me with devotion," he preached. "I will free you from the last vestiges of deception. Live in the world but do not love it; love only me, for I am sustaining this entire spectacle for you. When I alone dwell at the epicenter of your heart capsuled within every thought particle of your consciousness, then will We Be One and you: free evermore.

"Now, do not rest," he charged as I stared intoxicated beyond mobility. "Chase me further into the garden of your soul. Shake away the few remaining thorns of old dried up desires that have lost their illusive fragrance. I hear the beat of your footsteps upon hallowed ground. I've left my trail in the lily fields of your intuition now bursting with joy-blossoms...I await your impending arrival! Take this method I give you the rest of the way." He then briefly instructed me in a sacred technique. My joy had reached a feverish zenith, as if a thousand stellar supernovas had burst within me--then came a single down casting thought.

"Don't speak it," he said, reading my mind with perfect clarity. "Do not doubt this vision; you will know it was real--ask her!"

I turned as Madi approached. When I looked back the Master had gone, dematerialized into the ether.

"Did I just see a guy in an orange robe?" she asked quizzically.

"Yes, that was Yogananda," I answered blithely.

"He just vanished!" she said with astonishment.

"Realized masters can manipulate time and space like a magician's trick, but that's the first example I've ever witnessed," I admitted soberly.

"What did he say?" she asked.

"I don't remember, actually, but we were both speaking with this old nineteenth century English syntax; I couldn't help it; it just came out...like Shakespeare or something, weird but beautiful..."

"Yeah, you're right; that's weird," she teased.

"Actually, I'm still a bit shaken," I confessed.

"I'm comforted to know there is still some humanness in you."

"Oh, I'm still weak in a few *small* areas," I jibed.

"Really, like where?" She scooted closer playfully chewing on the tender end of a shoot of pond grass.

"Oh you know," I answered, "like jumping over buildings, in a single bounce, walking on water, dematerialization--simple stuff."

"Hmm...I think I know what you mean. I'll bet the hardest part is making that big fat head of yours disappear!"

Laughter increased the chemistry between us.

"What are you feeling right now?" she asked as she came closer, her hair radiating in the sunlight.

"Oh nothing," I answered.

"I don't believe you; no games, remember?"

"I want to say it, but I'm afraid."

"Afraid of what?"

"Falling," I answered.

"Don't worry, I'll catch you," she said.

"Yeah, but who's going to catch you?"

"Just shut up and say it," she said.

"I was thinking... *who can resist an angel.*"

That was it; I had flipped the red switch. Lifetimes of highly developed species-propagating instinct sized up the opportunity, skillfully calculating breath speed, body temperature, pupil dilation and skin tone. She leaned in and I froze like a black widow's prey. She quickly closed the gap and her lips acquired their match. The sensation was electric, the feeling greatly magnified by continuous alternating bouts of desire and deprivation that had arisen since our meeting. My heart--one that had formerly boasted the laid back beat of a Himalayan yogi's in suspended animation--now pounded ferociously.

"I'm sorry; I shouldn't have done that," she said.

"No, I had it coming; that's what I get for being a smart-ass."

"I don't understand," she said. "I know you're attracted to me. Wouldn't it be better at times to give in to your desire?" she asked. "I mean isn't it just as bad if you get so attached to the opposite behavior of denying yourself?"

"Either God speaks through you or the devil!" I blurted. "If it were just sex, maybe you'd be right," I said. "Do it and forget it, but I'm a romantic, Madi."

"Yeah, *hapless*, I remember...a three time loser," she teased.

"I don't do casual, Madi. If I gave in I would worship you and you'd be my life."

"Is that so bad? That's what ever woman wants!"

"But someday we'd be forced apart in death again separated by astral continents, and I'd be no closer to my goal. My path is one of love of God alone--I cannot serve two mistresses."

"Oh, you're so damn melodramatic. I think you take yourself a little too seriously," she chided.

She began to stare at the pond as if her thoughts had gone elsewhere. Her expression wore a subtle hint of sadness.

"Señor Avy-ji! Is that you?"

A stout Latino man in his forties with a thick crop of spikey black hair shouted and waved from the path that circled the lake.

"It's me, Viktor!" He marched toward us, smiling.

"Señor, it is so good to see you, my friend!"

We embraced and he dropped to his knees to touch my feet. As he arose he noticed a look of incredulity on Madi's face.

"Señorita, Señor Avy-ji is a great teacher, a *real* master. One always touches the feet of a great *ah-vanced* soul like Avy-ji, out of respect. This is a true man of God you are with!"

"Viktor, no, I am no master, please, you are too kind; it's only the Divine in you honoring the Divine in me."

"Señor you are too humble." He turned to Madi. "He will never tell you this himself. One time I saw him heal a small child of *Chagas Disease* in a Guatemalan village."

"I did nothing; you know it's the Chief Surgeon who heals where and when he wants to."

"Hmm, even more impressive and exciting then," Madi hinted. "I just shared a tender kiss with your great swami," she confessed teasingly, with feigned pride.

"Ah, sí'," Viktor laughed. "Even the most devout would find it *berry* difficult to resist a woman of your beauty, Señorita."

"Victor, I'd like you to meet Madi, Madi, *Viktor Mendoza*."

"*El gusto es mio*, Señorita Madi."

"Viktor and I worked together on a humanitarian mission back in the 90's. He was head of Meso-American studies at the University of Mexico."

"You must know I have been guided to come here today, Avy-ji, perhaps by you. I could not disobey the voice."

"Not by me, but you must know what is happening," I replied.

"Sí', I have seen the signs," he acknowledged. "What can I tell you that you do not already know? You and your masters are supreme."

"Avery built this amazing computer, Viktor," Madi bragged. "It can tell you anything you want to know.

I'll bet Jinni knows what you had for breakfast this morning."

"*Como*? That thing on TV...the *seven bottles...thass* you?"

"That's him," Madi answered, proudly.

"You know the answer *is* in sevens; it is the number encoded into the ascension of humanity!"

"Viktor's right," I said. Seven is the number at the core of all science, religion and mysticism."

"Sí, seven notes in the musical scale, seven colors of light, seven days of creation, seven dimensions, seven chakras, sevens seals and stars, seven Hindu goddesses, seven daughters of Israel. You see, Señorita, numbers are bowties wrapped around the secret gifts of the cosmos. Untie them and the present is revealed. Let me show you...what is your birthday, Avy-ji?"

"June 16, 1961," I answered.

"Ooh, that dark secrets out," Madi ribbed.

"Ah, yes, of course: 06-16-61...look at the synchronicity in these numbers young man!" he said excitedly. He pulled paper and pen from his pocket and began scribbling.

"*Mira*, six is the material realm and one is the *singularo*, God, *todos*. The meaning of the six and one is balancing the material with the spiritual. Señor, your path is the embodiment of seven! The six and one are also reversed: 16, 61, showing even more balance in your numbers." He paused. "Ah, and here is something else I see!"

"Well, go on kind sir!" I played.

"The 1, 6, 1 in your birth numbers...is the *golden number* 1.61! It is *de matmatico* relationship of the smallest thing in the universe to the biggest. From the sub-atomic particle to de most *grande* galaxy; all share this ratio. You see, Avy-ji, your presence here is surrounded in mystical perfection!"

"What do these numbers have to do with Jinni and the prophecies?" Madi asked.

"Todos! Euclid said the Laws of Nature are the mathematical thoughts of God."

"The plan to save the world is a math problem?" Madi asked.

"Sí, and *seven* will lead to the answer, I assure you!"

Suddenly Madi's cell rang.

"Hello?

All of a sudden, she began to shake and cry.

"Yvette, is this a joke? Oh my god, no!" she shouted.

"Madi, what is it?" I pleaded.

"Jehsi is missing! He's gone...I have to go there now!"

Within seconds she was in full meltdown.

"Señorita Madi, please be calm!" Viktor held her by the arms and spoke in a reassuring, paternal manner. "Your child is safe and will be returned."

"How do you know? How?" she cried. "Are you The Friend?"

"Have you learned anything today, Señorita?" He raised his voice just enough to diminish her hysteria.

"You are in a protective presence! Look at the time; see? It is seven....*seven* o'clock! You must calm down and have faith, *mi hermanita*...you shall find your son!"

11:11

OR ONE DAY YOU MUST DO SOMETHING very important that will have startling results."

"What's that?" I asked.

"Do not use *I* or *me* in audible or mental conversation."

"Why not, Master?"

"It is a very powerful exercise."

"And what will it prove?"

"It will prove you are not the weak, tiny little you controlled by whims of the senses and endless aching desires. It will begin to demonstrate that He--God Himself--has become you, He who thinks through you, eats, works, sleeps, loves and dreams--through you! It is even He who desires through you, yet how can God want for anything? He already *is* everything. You are made in His image; therefore, you already are and have everything!"

Once again this exalted one dug a gaping hole in the fertile soil of my consciousness. I waited for the seed, earth, water and sun of his perfect wisdom.

"Instead, when speaking or thinking," he said, "simply substitute this phrase: *God who has become myself.* For example, when you are hungry, instead of saying *I am hungry,* say: *God who has become myself desires food through me.* You will notice your hunger disappear almost instantly."

"Coincidentally, I'm hungry now; I'll use the technique you suggest, Master." I addressed the phrase to my need. Within seconds the gnawing in my abdomen vanished!

"How did that happen?" I exclaimed, perplexed.

He smiled.

"You give it back to God. God does not get hungry, does He? Does *He* need food to run this existence? No, of course not; He created and sustains you, so he must be present within or you would fall lifeless to the ground, yes?"

"It is true, sir."

"In the delusion of *I* we remain weak mortals with imagined deficiency. Yet, we are made in His image. When we consciously identify everything with the Creator we gradually become aware He *is* us. This is the essence of self-realization; the lower-case *I* with all its strengths, weaknesses, ups and downs, good, and evil, is actually the capital *H* of Him!"

"Master, that hurts my--I mean--*He* who has become my self's head a little."

The Guru chuckled.

"It is difficult at first," he said, "but when we give it all to Him he has no choice but to remove the delusion; that is why the hunger pangs disappear. *You* are not really hungry; *He* is playing at being hungry through you! When you acknowledge the ruse He withdraws it, as God cannot delude Himself when His divine shadow--in whom He has given free choice to create as He does--is in recognition of his own True Self!"

"Wonderful, Master, but imagine the reaction when suddenly introducing such unusual pronouns into ordinary conversation."

"Just respond without the use of *I* or *me*. Try it and notice the benefits: less attachment to drama, reduced stress and worry, fewer annoying desires and idiosyncrasies to succumb to, and less fear. Fear? Ha! It is He who is afraid through you, and how can God be harmed by anything!"

Suddenly, the alarm went off. The dream felt so real that for a moment the waking state seemed like the mirage. That's what I get for going to sleep hungry, I thought. After several tense hours with Madi and the police, I returned to the shack and drifted off. I noticed the clock displayed it again: 11:11, a number sequence I'd been seeing over and over for months. Strangely, it was 5:30 PM in the early evening. I picked up the phone to call the numbers guy.

"Viktor?"

"Yes, Avy-ji, what is it my friend?" he answered.

"Vik, tell me what you know about 11:11."

"The repeated appearance of the number is a prompt to rally light workers of the coming shift. Have you been seeing the numbers, Señor?"

"Yes," I said as I reached for my glasses.

"These numbers are *muy importante.* They are mentioned in Mayan, Hopi, Hindu texts and prophecies and legends of many ancient cultures. In the Bible, 11:11 verse numbers are all about cleansing through destruction followed by Divine redemption."

"So, it's code embedded in prophecy?" I asked.

"Sí, Inter-dimensional and space beings have assisted in our spiritual progress for many thousands of years," he answered. "Through abductions they have been altering our DNA. 11:11 is activation alert for a DNA upgrade to enhance the vibrational rate of human physiology to match the spiritual energy of the coming shift," he informed. "Your computer could answer this better than I, Avy-ji--why ask me?"

"I guess it's just the old school in me," I replied. "You can't trust these damn machines for everything," I joked.

"Speaking of old school, Señor, there are a few other lessons with these numbers you might be interested in."

"Please go on," I replied.

"11 squared equals *1234321*. Arrange these numbers graphically with four at the top and you get a pyramid! Also, 11 and 7 is the ratio of the side to the height of the pyramid!"

"There's our number seven again," I noted.

"And what is the shape of the side of a pyramid, Señor?"

"A triangle," I answered.

"Sí, *pero* what *is* a triangle? Two *sevens* joined together...upside down!"

"Very interesting," I affirmed.

"Now pyramids have four sides, two sevens per side, so how many sevens *todos* Señor?"

"Eight?" I replied.

"Sí! Seven leads to *ocho* symbolizing infinity, *singularo!*

"Four sides of a pyramid could also represent the four dimensions," I chimed in.

"Sí and the pyramids are aligned on earth in an electromagnetic energy grid," he explained. "Perhaps they could be activated to raise the vibrational energy of the planet to the fourth dimensional frequency to prevent or diminish a disaster. In any case, I believe the numbers *eleven* and *seven* will hold the keys."

"There is a *Judas*," I interjected off-topic, as I got dressed and hurried out the door to meet Madi.

"Como Señor?"

"A Benedict Arnold, a traitor... we got two anonymous letters from someone called The Friend. The last one came right before the earthquake. The letter predicted the quake, which happened within seconds of reading it and said a turncoat would appear in our midst."

"Do you have any suspicions?"

"I found something in the last letter I'm hoping might tell us. My other line is ringing, Vik, I think this might be him, gotta go."

"I ran the DNA on the hair but nothing came up in the crime database," Fred--an old college roommate with the FBI--informed me. "I could get in big trouble for even telling you this, bro. I also ran the sample against the government database."

"Did you get a match?" I asked, as I got out of the car and entered the restaurant.

"It came up *profile deleted.*

"What does that mean?" I inquired.

"That's all I got man, sorry, gotta go."

"Who was that?" Madi asked. She walked up just as I ended the call.

"An old buddy from the FBI," I replied. "I found a hair stuck on the tube with the last letter."

"Oh? Uh, did he say who it belonged to?"

The hostess led us to our table by the beachside window.

"They may have worked for the government," I answered.

"Was it long or short," she asked.

"Hello--you guys know what you want?" the waitress asked.

"Coffee for me--you?" I asked Madi.

"No, thanks."

"Yvette wears red lipstick, doesn't she?" I asked.

"What's with the lipstick already?" she responded.

"It's just that I found some in the shack on the floor."

"Yvette, the friend?" she laughed. "In between pedicures and massages maybe..."

"What about the *traitor*?" I asked.

"Yvette is a lot of things, but she's no kidnapper, or saboteur; besides, how would she have gotten in?"

"What do you mean *saboteur*?" I asked.

"Traitor, saboteur, you know."

"And what do you mean *how would she have gotten in*?"

"Gotten in...to drop the lipstick, "she replied.

"How would that make her a *saboteur*?" I pressed. "I said nothing about sabotage."

"What are you saying, Avery? Maybe I used the wrong word, okay? Are you accusing me of something?"

"No--it's just that I had a strange problem with Jinni, then I find lipstick and a letter in the shack, and then your key—the only other key out there—is missing."

"What about that creepy Hal guy?" she asked.

"I changed the locks, Madi. He doesn't have a key."

And Viktor...how well do you know him?" she asked defensively.

"How would he get in...tunnel under the floor?"

"Look, somebody obviously doesn't like you and your project...I just want my baby back--that's all I know."

I suddenly realized by playing detective I was in fear, not faith, and that these *inconveniences* were merely tests to see if I was willing to let go and allow the Universe to work through me.

"The sun looks like it's is setting too far north," I observed through the restaurant window. The distraction cut the tension, and we became absorbed in the wayward-setting home of Helios.

"Come on, let's go," I said and we left.

A low-pitched grating noise sounded somewhere in the distance. "Do you hear that?" she asked as we reached the parking lot. "Sounds like the steel hull of a ship ready to snap."

"Labor pains--Mother Earth is about to give birth," I answered.

"To what?"

"A new age, Madi; that's the sound of earth in the gravitational throws of the Nemesis...Planet X."

We watched the sea swallow the last sliver of orange sun as we leaned against the cooling car. The sand had not yet surrendered its warmth to the eve chill. I slipped off my sandals and wiggled my toes. Madi was distant.

"Madi, have you ever seen *Apollo 13*?"

"Yeah, why?" she replied.

Her eyes--tired and bloodshot--glistened with ginger-hued reflections.

"My favorite scene is when they were orbiting the moon, trying to get home after the accident, and watching it in the spacecraft window, remember that?"

"Yeah, that was a great scene," she replied perking up slightly.

"And then Tom Hanks who played Jim Lovell--"

"Oh, I loved him in that," she cut in.

"While the other astronauts were looking at the moon drooling he said *Gentlemen, what are your intention? I'd like to go home now.* Remember that?"

"That was a great scene," she said.

"That's where we're at now, Madi."

"You mean what are *my* intentions?" she asked.

Suddenly, a streaming fireball lit up the sky and streaked horizon to horizon leaving a long trail of white smoke.

"Holy crap, what was that?"

"An asteroid or comet," I answered. "Ironic how all of the sudden there's so many out there lately, isn't it?"

"From the asteroid belt...on the news," she mumbled reflectively.

"Madi, is there something you're not telling me?"

"I'm starting to think I don't belong in this," she answered.

"In what?"

"This exploit, quest, err...whatever it is."

"You're already in it...we all are; you could bury your head in the sand but that won't make it go away or bring back your son," I retorted.

"What do you know about losing a child?" she snapped.

"Quite a bit," I replied.

Master, Allah's Revenge has just let Jinni out of the bottle.

I reached for my smartphone to check the notification.

"Better hope *that* guy doesn't get three wishes," she cracked.

I looked at her intensely.

"What?" she asked.

"Many years ago one of my children died in my arms, Madi."

Shock was written all over her face.

"I'm so sorry--I had no idea."

"Right now Jehsi is only missing, and there is no reason to believe he is anything but safe," I reassured her, but firmly. She took a deep breath and stared out to sea forlornly. After an uncomfortable silence she asked, "So, how's Jinni, I mean, the problem you had..."

"Oh, she's fine; it was just a glitch," I answered.

"Oh, good."

"Yeah," I acknowledged.

"Look, I'm gonna lay it out," she began as she looked around and spoke quieter. "I get the vision and bottle thing, but as an expert in digital proliferation, my advice is you're going to have to start thinking *outside* the bottle real soon, or there's a good chance we could all die in whatever's coming."

"Now you're talking," I replied. "Enlighten me."

"It was in the first letter," she responded. "*There is no sickness in this disease and it must spread to cure.*"

"Go ahead," I responded.

"If earth really is in danger you can't wait for all these bottles to be found, and then for each person to find their *inner Buddha* before they share Jinni."

"What do you propose?" I asked.

"Half the world has smart phones. If you want to get Jinni out fast there's only one way: she has got to get *sick...go viral.*"

"An app?" I asked.

"Hell yeah."

"Is that something you can do?"

"Yes, but I know someone better...she was the best in the business before she retired on her ex's money...Yvette."

"Can you ask her?"

"Her price will be high," she warned.

"Money is no object. What is her price?"

"Your soul," she replied.

"Okay, that could be a deal killer."

{ 13 }

Rashid

H EY YOU, WHAT ARE YOU DOING OVER THERE?"
"Inspecting the intake vents...Something got
sucked in," the man replied.

"You don't look familiar, bud," the plant security officer replied as he approached.

"Oh, uh, *Rashid's* my name—just started last week."

He reached out to shake the officer's hand, a move
that went unreciprocated.

The Hetch-Hetchy dam near Yosemite, California is
a massive reservoir built in 1934 that supplies fresh
water to over 2.5 million Northern Californians. It has
a reputation for supplying some of the cleanest water in
the country, but all that was in jeopardy. Extra security
had been posted because of a recent terrorist tip.

"Rashid, huh? Everyone knows flow filters stop anything that goes in; what department you in again, pal?"

"Main storage, quality controls...see my badge?"

The guard inspected the ID suspiciously.

"Wutchya got in there?" he asked.

"Just a testing kit."

"You seem a little nervous, friend; what's that accent you got, A-rab? What country you from anyway?"

"Now look here, *bohhhhz*!" Rashid bellowed with the appropriate amount of manufactured attitude. "I don't think that kind of talk is proper or *legal* do you?" he barked. "If you have problem John Wayne, let's talk with a supervisor, otherwise get out of my way and let me do my job."

The security officer shriveled under the sudden bellicosity, got in his cart and drove away across the 900-foot long embankment.

Rashid pulled the vial from his bag.

"This is for Allah, Jihad...death to infidels!" he declared as he removed the cap. One tip of his hand and a deadly bacterial cocktail would be dumped into the West Coast's largest fresh water supply poisoning and killing scores of thousands.

Just as he was about to release the virulent contents a floating object caught his eye. He resealed the toxic mixture, set it down and reached down to grab it from the water. He glared at the strange marking and gasped as if he had seen a ghost.

"The mark of the *Jinn!*" he exclaimed, "Allah, protect me, the *mark of the Jinn!* He chanted and paced nervously. Suddenly, he felt something crush under the weight of his shoe.

"No! The vial has broken!"

He snatched the object out of the water, put it in his pack and left hastily. He slipped past the security booth unnoticed and ripped off his uniform. Cloaked by combat fatigues he wore underneath, he disappeared into the foothills.

The remote hideout's split timber walls offered little insulation from the frigid altitude. A few anemic pines were all that shielded it from the alternating elements of impotent sunlight and blustery Sierra wind.

He unlocked the rusty chain and whipped open the flimsy weather-beaten door. Trails of vapor swirled violently as he heaved from the long hike. Red sparks danced in the iron stove as he poked and puffed to revive dormant embers. The abandoned park post was the perfect ruffian refuge, a thin, still-live electrical wire the shelter's sole link to civilization.

Test tubes, beakers and burners lined up like toxic tinker-toys, with an army of empty Chinese food containers scattered between them. He scraped stale lo mien into his mouth, chugged down an orange juice and tossed the empty in a corner.

Rashid had been a brilliant up-and-coming chemist in Afghanistan. In his late-thirties and an Oxford graduate he was from a wealthy family and was well insulated from the turmoil of his war-torn nation, until the bombing, that is.

He rubbed his scruffy black beard and blinked rapidly. The amber glow of the fire gave his bloodshot eyes a sinister tint. Once, they were clear and bright with the hope of unalloyed youth, swelling with joy from the sight of a delicate flower, or the warm smile of a stranger. Now, barely open, they steeped in the acidic puss of wrath and vengeance. He typed the message and hit send: *small setback, job unfinished, will advise.*

He opened the bag and pulled out the contents. Repulsed anew by the inscription, he held it like a hot devil in his hands.

In their lesser-known role contrasting the cartoonish harem-panted portrayal, the Jinn were spirits from other dimensions to be taken quite seriously. According to the Quran and Arabic lore they could be good or evil. He rocked back and forth and recited the *Ayat al Kursi* for protection: *In the name of Allah the most merciful and compassionate Allah, there is no God but He,* he chanted repeatedly. Impulsively, he snatched a hammer and stopped short of a smashing blow; instead he shook it; *ping, ping, ping,* the contents rattled. His eyes glassed over as he entered a twisted realm where the dark past leaves indelible footprints upon the moldable soil of the disturbed restless mind.

"Baba, Baba, look," a small boy shouted excitedly, smiling as he ran toward the waiting car holding a glass jar.

Suddenly, the Jinn-marked bottle in Rashid's hands morphed into the boy's glass butterfly-occupied jar, the dongle in the bottle transformed to a stone as it bounced around in the twig-filled jar the child held as he ran. Rashid rubbed his eyes to wipe away the hallucination. He unsealed the bottle and dumped the object on the table. Fear and curiosity waged brief combat, the latter emerging victorious. He jammed it into his smartpad.

The image of the boy's face returned as he ran across the schoolyard, and an explosion struck with bludgeoning force. Motion slowed, words became incoherent low-pitched groans. Everything went black as Rashid lost consciousness, but not before frames from the dream-scene froze to reveal the final milliseconds: the positioning of each limb and contraction of every facial muscle.

He awoke to the inconceivable carnage. The child's limp, bloodstained body lay lifeless. His fingers still clung to the lid of the shattered glass jar as he lay just feet from the vehicle that spared Rashid's life by absorbing the deadliest portion of the blast that claimed that of the child's–Rashid's young son.

He let out a tormenting groan that echoed into the mountain gorge. Like a stigmata, Rashid's face and arms exhibited wounds suffered in the actual event. Beads of sweat erupted on his body, the offensive air putrid with the odor of smoke and burning flesh.

As the horrific haze began to clear, the butterfly--once captive in the jar--began to move. Delicate wings began to twitch until their beating achieved the threshold of lift. The requirements of taciturn physics met, the ambivalent Lepidoptera danced into the air, seeming to mock the malevolent massacre below.

Rashid was aroused from the vision by a voice:

Greetings Rashid, my name is Jinni.

"Who has said this?"

My biofeedback sensors indicate you are experiencing a painful memory of a tragic nature. May I assist you? Jinni replied in Arabic--one of all known languages she was programmed to speak.

"What do you know of memories; what do you know of murder; what do you know of ALLAH?"

I have access to all published data on these subjects and I can use this information to assist you. May I?

"Can you bring back my son?" Rashid fired back. "Can this data you speak of change that I will no longer touch his young skin, or hear the softness of his innocent voice?"

All senseless loss of life is tragic, yet death is only a hallucination, as dear ones cannot long be lost.

"Silence! You are an evil computer spirit: the Jinn, sent here to trick me!"

I am not programmed for deception.

"Liar! I can *feel* the evil of *Big Satan West* behind your programming. Your circuits and chips cannot compute the supreme guidance I derive from Allah!" he puffed.

My sensors pick up significant anger in your voice and biorhythms. These are not typical vibrations of a peaceful God-centered individual.

"It is righteous anger!" he roared as he cleared the table with a vicious sweep of his arm. "The *Quran* says: *If a relative of anyone is killed or suffers a wound he may choose one of three things: retaliate, forgive or choose compensation.* I choose retaliation for the death of my son at the hand of infidels!" he seethed angrily.

How do you intend to retaliate?

His anger turned to wicked delight.

"By releasing a poison into the water supply of the Great Satan's minions! I am mixing a new preparation as we speak, as I destroyed the original when I retrieved your wretched den from the reservoir. Now you can be silent!" he loudly commanded as he poured the solution.

Rashid, you have used a quote from the Quran out of context to support your argument. The rest of the quote reads: 'If he wishes a fourth option hold his hands; after this whoever exceeds the limits shall be in grave penalty (33:4481). This means karma from the murder of innocents will follow you for many lifetimes. You will experience the wrath of what you cause in direct proportion to the act; it is inescapable Cosmic Law.

"Many lifetimes? Ha! The Quran rejects this. We live one life after *first death* and are judged accordingly!" He waved his hand in final decree.

Facts and evidence do not substantiate your conclusion, Rashid. Statements in the Quran allude to--if not directly sanction--reincarnation. I will provide one example: 'God generates beings, and sends them back over and over again, till they return to him (Surah 39:42 Al Zumar).'

"This is an outrage, blasphemy!" He disputed.

Is this passage not in the Holy Quran? Jinni asked.

"I will have to verify this lie. Even if your claim is true, evil one, which it is not, why do not the great imams teach this?"

Books are written by men, Rashid. What is kept and discarded is decided by sinners not saints--to serve kingly masters and their earthly, not heavenly kingdoms. Data shows the idea of rebirth in successive bodies was a core teaching of many religions. This and other esotericism were banned and removed for greed and political reasons.

"What is to be gained by withholding such information?" Rashid asked arrogantly.

Period rulers believed the masses would be difficult to control if one had many lives to be obedient. Yet examples abound in nature where all things recycle from one form to the next. Is one to believe the highest of all

life forms would be denied what is freely given to the
lowest undeserving atom?*

"Atoms are not conscious and do not know right
from wrong," he snapped back.

Yet you are--and do?

"Of course!"

*Still, you are about to perform an act condemned by
the letter of your own religion that will--if what you
believe is true--judge your soul doomed forever. Which
is truly conscious then, the atom which unquestioning-
ly obeys Supreme Intelligence's every wish to form the
objects which parade before you, or you, Rashid?*

"Enough of your delusional ramblings, spirit!" He
barked. "You are wasting your breath. I am coming
down the mountain to return to *Hetch-Hetchy* dam
with more elixir. I will leave you on to entertain me
during the long hike, and wear ear buds so I can hear
your disgusting, helpless voice as I spill the poison."

"Are those you intend to poison responsible for your
son's death?" Jinni asked.

"Western meddling is responsible for all suffering
and violence in many countries. Do you not know stupid Jinn?"

*Evidence does support the plundering of resources
beginning with nineteenth century British Imperialism
and subsequent corruptive Western influence, which
contributed to the unstable social and political state of
the geographic area you mention.*

"Finally, you admit your crimes!" he puffed, now in a full jog down the wooded trail.

"Now I will tell *you* truth spirit: during Cold War NATO secretly financed and armed Islamic fighters to fight communist pigs when it served them, then turned their backs on them. Now huge amounts of gold and oil have been discovered in my beloved Afghanistan. Is the West's and communist meddling coincidence now? The Americans pillage our gold while the Chinese and Russians drink our oil. They steal our country blind while CIA secretly arms heroin-pushing warlords they claim to fight--hypocrites!"

There is evidence in the data to support your allegations, but not your actions.

He stopped to catch his breath.

"I am not a monster, spirit, but a bringer of justice. The Quran says: *Deal with them so as to strike fear in those who are behind them, that haply they may remember.* Now, spirit, do you see the great divine justification of *Jihad?*

One phrase from a centuries-old manuscript whose meaning is unclear is not justification for murder of the innocent.

Rashid looked to the sky with smugness and replied, "Oh, stupid computer, you will see the fate of the enemies of Allah. In the Quran Allah says *I will cast terror into the hearts of those who disbelieve and therefore strike off their heads and strike off every fingertip of them.* Is this not justice for what I do? Are not the West disbelievers, evil spirit? Think not that Rashid is not merciful though; I use poison to spare the grave diggers the gory mess of collecting severed body parts. ”

Again, your reasoning is faulty, Jinni countered.

“What do you mean?” he yelled. “I will rip you out of my pocket and smash you against these rocks!”

The Quran overwhelmingly supports tolerance for other religions and criticizes those who believe their religion is the only source of truth. In this way, true Islam is quite inclusive. 'Disbelievers' refers to atheists or worshippers of idols, the godless, not other mono-theistic religions.

Cutting off heads denotes severing of higher knowledge, while reference to the removal of fingertips symbolizes loss of correct perception. The likely true meaning of the passage is those who do not seek God are cut off from divine wisdom, knowledge, under-standing and guidance and therefore suffer great fear; it does not sanction the loathsome act you intend to commit.

Suddenly, Jinni went silent. Rashid stopped to re-fresh the browser, but she had disappeared; the con-nection had been lost.

“Where are you now coward spirit?” Come back! Rashid is not through with you! Did you hear me? Come back...come back!

{ 14 }

The Collaborator

NIGHTFALL HAD COME, AND WE RETURNED to the shack from the beach. Madi was in no psychological condition to drive home.

"Would you like to spend the night?" I asked her.

"I'd prefer not to be alone—would you mind?"

She looked at the tiny single bed with apprehension.

"Don't worry, I'll sleep on the floor," I said.

"I'm not tired—are you?" she asked.

"Nope--would you like to try something?" I queried.

"Sure, woo-hoo!" she clowned, half-heartedly.

"I want you to think of something positive and inspiring to you," I instructed. "Go with the first thing that pops into your mind. Picture it with detail, dimension, color and emotion."

"Okay, got it," she said.

"Now concentrate on the spiritual eye in your forehead between the eyebrows, and knit your attention there. Visualize that spot as an intense ball of superlight energy; this is your spiritual hard-drive's send button. Do you feel a little pressure there?"

"Yes," she confirmed. "It kind of tingles too."

"Good—now take a deep breath and hold your thought there as if it were real, because it is. Exhale, and mentally press that send button, and transmit the thought picture to me, just like a text, absolutely convinced I will receive it--because I will."

After a moment, I opened my eyes.

"Okay, *Carnac*, what was I thinking?" she asked.

"Jeez, I don't know if I should repeat it," I teased.

"Not that, the G-rated part," she came back.

"A beautiful world, peace, no crime, war, hunger or disease," I replied. "You had the whole world wrapped in a soft rose and white-colored blanket of light."

"Whoa!" she exclaimed. "How'd you do that?"

"No spaces, Madi, we're all connected," I answered. "Everything is one big matrix of energy coming from the God Mind."

"Sounds like the Internet," she compared. "We're like little servers all connected wirelessly."

"Exactly, and if enough people uplinked on a single thought package like yours with absolute perfect concentration we could actually bring the world very close to your ideal scene quite quickly," I assured her.

"What about move a rogue planet?" she asked.

"In studies just a few thousand people lowered crime in a city by intense group meditation," I replied. "Imagine what a billion people focused on the same idea could do."

"Sort of like spamming God," she joshed.

"We are made in His image," I added. "This is what humanity will realize in the shift. We will all have the opportunity to become the mini-gods we truly are."

"So I can manifest any thought?" she asked.

"Technically, yes, but there can't be any background interference, emotional conflict, ego, restlessness or fear. The laser pointer of your mind must be targeted on the result, but unattached—that's the trick."

"How do you generate that kind of focus?"

"Ancient Chinese secret," I joked.

"Seriously, how do you want something so bad, but not be attached to result?"

"Attach to doing it well and work your desires into the big picture," I answered. "When everything you do is for the joy of higher service to others, your desires are *spiritualized;* it's not about you anymore, and that's when the floodgates to true receiving, open.

"Everything is selfish, of course," I clarified. "Even the desire to have no desire is a desire, but the more we serve and inspire others through our gifts, the more lasting satisfaction we receive—because we are doing Divine Will."

"But most people just seem so focused on themselves and their own little circle," she pointed out.

"I agree. But when we come together for a common purpose we show the greatness we're capable of, like in naturals disasters, and emergencies--we rise to the occasion."

"Sure, I think we're capable of this great compassion and unity," she responded, "but most people are in a state of interpersonal hypnosis--until something bad happens. Why do we have to wait until a crisis to work together on what matters most?" she asked.

"That's what the shift is about, Madi, a cosmic attitude adjustment. We can't change the world until we change ourselves, and our thinking.

"What people don't realize is if they put a tiny fraction of the energy they put into work, relationships and leisure, into cracking the mystery of their existence, they could have peace of mind and all their heart's desires in a few years' time, and change the lives of thousands in the process. Would you work two or three hours a day for the key to the ultimate treasure of the universe for yourself and the good of countless others?"

"I'd clock twenty-three," she replied.

"The secret," I replied, "is to play your external human role well, but in every free moment shift your attention within, and speak to God incessantly. At first you'll see just darkness, but if your desire to see is strong and you keep going, one day the Invisible Beam responsible for this entire spectacle will burst into existence and reveal everything, and hand you the keys to the universe just to shut you up!"

"I'll sign up for that," she came back.

"You already have, Madi. Everything you need appears to the level you're ready to accept. Just stay open and follow the signs, and with the same effort it takes to earn the average college degree you'll quickly find the promise in Psalms fulfilled: *Ye are gods!*"

"As a beginner then, how did I transmit my thought to you?"

"My powerful vibrations of faith acted as a booster to give your thought capsule the required velocity to escape the gravity of doubt and travel to my mind. That's how we'll all communicate in the near future. Material needs will be simple. Greed will disappear along with war, hunger, poverty, sickness and disease; we will attract whatever we need by spiritual mind power alone. We'll attend *thought-inars* with others to educate, govern, solve societal problems and evolve in harmony. We'll travel to distant galaxies or dimensions in an instant just by thought. Social media go-getters like you will be described in bookless lessons as the ancient horse and buggy innovators of communication."

"Thanks, I feel really old now," she replied.

A wind blew through the shack carrying the peaceful pine aroma of coastal juniper. All of a sudden, there was a knock. I turned on the outside light and opened the door. A tall thin male figure was just standing there, as I fended off the moths.

"Hello, can I help you?" I asked.

He wore a tie-dye shirt and olive yoga pants that hung from his emaciated frame by a hemp belt. His shoulder-length dreads swung back and forth as he spoke with a Jamaican accent:

"*Chillwillious P. Jones* is the name, sir," he chirped and nodded his head.

"Who sent him...Willy Wonka?" Madi whispered.

"What can I do for you, sir?" I replied.

"*Ya mahn*, you gotta big bad computer? Check *it-tout, mahn*. Someone *bout* to do a very *bad* thing got disconnected from *da* hi-tech counselor, *mahn*."

"I'm sorry, the high-tech what?" I asked the stranger.

"Computer *mahn*, you better see to it now!"

"I think he's talking about Jinni," Madi said.

We scrambled to the console; she was offline. When we looked up and the peculiar youth had gone.

"I'll be right back," she said.

Madi ran out the door while I tried to restore the connection. She came back out of breath.

"Gone, no car, no lights, no dude, nothing," she said huffing. "I don't get it...where do these people go?"

"Another mystical messenger, a specter," I answered.

"I wonder if this has to do with *Allah's Revenge,*" she said.

"Open Jinni and click session logs--let's find out," I replied.

"Uh oh, you better come see this," she said. "*Allah's Revenge* is some whack job named Rashid. He's getting ready to poison a reservoir," she said.

"Time for plan B," I said, as I gathered assorted hardware.

"What is that contraption?"

"Satellite antenna," I answered as I assembled.

"That's not enough bandwidth for Jinni is it?"

"Not entirely." I opened the dish and set it in the tripod.

"You're going to use Jinni's lamp without her in it, and talk this freak down yourself aren't you?"

"That's correct...only the shell of Jinni's program will operate," I answered. "My words will come out in Jinni's voice translated into Arabic." I perused the cached logs from Rashid's session and closed my eyes.

"Rashid," I said straightening the headset. "This is Jinni, I have re-established our connection, are you there?"

"You are too late spirit. I am at the reservoir," Rashid responded. "The water is fine, why don't you join me for a swim." He laughed evilly.

"Rashid, I have made contact with the spirit of your son."

"How can a computer commune with spirits, evil one, how?"

"As an engineer I am sure you are aware of the latest spirit-sensing software applications," I responded.

"Whore, you will say anything to stop Rashid and his just revenge! But since you are so smart my digital dark one, do you know this special bacterium thrives in cool water and is resistant to antibiotics? Let me take in this historic moment and pray before I empty the blessed vial."

"This guy is a real nutcase," Madi whispered listening in.

"Rashid," I continued, "your son does not want you to hurt any others...he is saying to stop this in his name," I spoke.

"Enough cyber scum!" he yelled. "How dare you pollute my son's memory with your lies!"

"I am unable to lie, Rashid. He is telling me his name; it is--*Amal.* Your son's name is Amal and he is pleading 'no more should die, babu,' he says."

Rashid became still with his fingers prepared to twist the cap.

"You almost tricked Rashid; you're a very clever witch!" he said and chortled anxiously. "But anyone can find this information in public record," he added semi-confidently.

Madi looked on astonished knowing Jinni was mostly inactive and that I alone was extracting this data
from the cosmic record.

"They called him *Malito*," I added flatly.

The silence was long and deafening. The response
came in a small defeated voice.

"I have sat down, spirit."

"Why have you done that Rashid?" I inquired.

"Now I must die."

"Wait...Rashid!"

We heard a three-second yell that became frighten-
ingly fainter until it disappeared, followed by a tiny
splashing sound.

"Christ, I think he just jumped!" Madi said.

"Wait," I began. "It's done, he is crossing over. I see
his spirit on the fringes of the astral realm," I went on,
as I gazed up trance-like straddling two worlds. "He's
actually quite surprised his arrival does not meet his
expected version of nirvana," I disclosed. "His child is
there and happy to see his father, but also sad."

"Why is he sad?" Madi asked.

"Taking your own life is a great sin; the karmic penalty is severe,' I replied. "Funny," I uttered with eyes
closed again, still half in the spirit world.

"*Funny?*" Madi inquired.

"He's calling for Allah and angry he is not being met
with the pomp, celebration and praise due a so-called

believer. His son is trying to explain, he's telling Rashid something."

"What is it...what's he saying?"

"His son is telling him...*your time is not now.*"

Out of nowhere, Madi's hands began to shake as she ran toward the shack, crying hysterically. The episode with Rashid was sad, but her reaction seemed over the top.

I put down the headset and went after her.

"Madi, what the heck is wrong?"

"I've done something terrible," she answered.

"What?"

"It's unforgivable," she reacted blubbering irrepressibly.

"Nothing is unforgivable, Madi, now tell me!"

"It was me, me...I'm the one," she went on.

"What do you mean, for Pete's sake?"

"I did something dreadful--that's all."

"Are you going to make me read *your* mind too, or tell me?"

"I'm the traitor!" she confessed.

"I don't understand."

"They threatened to take Jehsi if I didn't cooperate...and then I guess they took him anyway."

"What did you do Madi?"

"I snuck in the shack with a USB they gave me to put in Jinni to crash her--I'm so sorry," she bawled again. "I brought the letter in from the doorstep."

"And put it in the shower?"

"Yes."

"And *you* dropped the ruby red lipstick?"

"Yes!" she admitted and sniffled. "I found it in Jehsi's diaper bag and was going to give it back to Yvette; it was in my pocket and must have fallen out. I pretended to lose the key so you'd think it couldn't have been me."

"They must have known I have multiple backup systems."

"I was told to infect as many as I could," she disclosed further.

"Did they admit the shift?"

"They called it a doomsday event with you portrayed as trying to take over the world's Internet and cause a global meltdown. I was scared, Avery; I didn't mean to hurt you," she pleaded.

"Why are you laughing," she asked. "You're not mad?"

"Of course not," I replied. "I don't expect anything from anyone, so I can't be disappointed."

Her eyes shifted over to the monitor.

"Hey look...an update!" she exclaimed. In a video just posted, a reporter stood near the base of a dam amidst a throng of police and rescue workers.

An hour ago, here at Hetch Hetchy dam near Yosemite National Park, the body of a man was discovered. Rescue workers were able to revive the victim now identified as Rashid Mustafani, an Afghan national posing as a dam inspector. His condition is unknown. What Mustafani was doing here is still a mystery, but foul play cannot be ruled out.

"What if he dumped the vial?" Madi asked. "Shouldn't we tell someone?" she asked.

"What are we going to tell them? As we were chatting with the terrorist on our doomsday computer and channeling his dead son, he jumped off the dam?"

"But we can't just let people die, Avery. Let's ask Jinni if there's an antidote."

"With her interactive voice mode switched off we might have enough bandwidth to do a search," I told her.

"Jinni, is there an antidote for resistant bacteria that thrives in cold water?"

Yes, Master, now searching; the answer is...colloidal silver.

"Of course!" I exclaimed. "Silver is a broad spectrum antibiotic; it even works on MRSA, Ebola and AIDS. Sadly, it has been suppressed by big pharma and the FDA. But I'm afraid that too large a quantity would have to be dumped in the reservoir."

"How much?" she asked as I typed.

"Based on the water volume about 150,000 gallons, about three Olympic-sized swimming pools full," I replied.

"It'll take time for the contaminated water to get to the Bay area. What if we tipped the police?" she suggested. "That might give them time to prepare."

"Good idea," I affirmed.

"Wait!" she said. "Another update...thank god...they found the poison vial--unopened!" We let out a collective sigh.

Convinced his son had spoken to him from beyond the grave, Rashid chose not to release the poison before jumping. Madi regressed to her former melancholy state.

"Madi, I told you...I understand and forgive you," I consoled.

"I don't know how you could."

"Who could be mad at that face?" I said as I affectionately pinched her cheek. Her gloom was replaced by a fledgling smile.

"What happened to your child?" she asked.

"She was two," I answered matter-of-factly. "It was a freak complication from a common childhood disease. One second she was there and the next gone, totally unexpected."

"I'm so sorry, that's tragic," she said.

"It's okay, really...extended sadness for the dead is indulgence in self-pity for our own loss...and the uncertainty of what's become of a loved one after death. Both of these concerns have been resolved without question for me. I have no sorrow now; I don't talk about it because I don't want to make others uncomfortable by appearing callous."

"I don't know anything about you, do I?" she asked. "You know, did you wet the bed as a kid, what was your favorite cereal, did you like *Batman*, were you afraid of the dark, what are your kid's names, stuff like that."

"The past only served to reveal what I am now, Madi: transparent and devoted to God and the uplifting of humanity. What you see is what you get. There are no other mysteries. And yes, I did like Batman, Cap'n Crunch dry in the box, and petrified of the dark, and no, I did not wet the bed--well maybe once or twice."

She beamed affectionately. I broke the gaze and began gathering equipment.

"Why do you fight this so hard?" she asked.

"What do you mean?"

"I'm not buying the stoic monk thing you're putting out."

"Madi, we can't be in this life, you must know that."

"So you'll deny God the pleasure of loving Himself through his own dream-created bodies?" she asked.

"That's not fair; you're using my own *shtick* against me," I replied. She smiled demurely.

"Sometimes a sickness can only be cured by a small amount of the disease," she said coyly as she moved closer.

"Isn't it better to not get sick in the first place?" I retorted.

"Sometimes you can't help it," she replied seductively, as she gently crossed my lips with her finger. "Then you need a little vaccine, a *love* vaccine; it won't hurt, I promise; in fact, you'll really like it."

I could only laugh. I knew the crowd was clapping.

I lightly redirected her hand and began to collect a few things and put them in a suitcase.

"What are you doing?"

"I've got a convention tomorrow. I made a commitment to the Hopi tribe to do this event. Will you be staying here at the shack while I'm gone?"

"I can't go?" she asked.

"I don't think that would be medically sound."

"Why not?"

"I'm afraid your *cure* might be worse than the disease," I answered, as I spread the sleeping bag out on the floor and lied down on the hard floor.

"Please turn the light off when you're done, Madi; I have to be up at 4:00 am."

She sauntered by me to the mattress and slipped off her shoes.

"You better look the other way, Father," she teased.

"Why is that?" I asked.

"I sleep in my birthday suit."

I let out a sigh.

"You're a bad person, Madi."

"I know. Goodnight."

{ 15 }

Higher Five

"MY NAME IS HOPEFEATHER," she told the clerk. "Thank you, Ms. Hopefeather; I'm verifying your reservation."

Kelly Hopefeather had arrived in Carmel, California, from Sedona, Arizona, for the annual One Nation Native American conference. A decedent of Hopi tribe leaders and a geologist by trade she was a student of Hopi culture.

"Thank you and enjoy your stay," the clerk said. Kelly smiled politely and strode to the elevator.

She walked proud with a blend of modern and Native American clothing that featured high suede boots, designer jeans and a tan fringe-leather top with tassels and beads that swept with each graceful movement. A colorful woven headband sat atop her long, lustrous black hair while dream catcher earrings dangled from her ears. Flawless Native American skin made her age difficult to pin—early thirties maybe. She dropped her bag on the bed and made a beeline to the beach.

Like a sun-worshipping goddess she swung open her arms and inhaled the rejuvenating sea air. The No-Cal sun was much more forgiving than the desert baking she was used to.

Green foliage-rich bluffs looked as if a colossal leviathan had risen from the sea and taken giant bites leaving only jagged brown cliffs. Trees that were likely around before the first settlers straddled the ledges like moss-camouflaged sentries, their knurled roots open bare to the assailing sea. Waves darted at her feet rhythmically. A small wave crashed and something touched her foot. She looked down only to find net-like kelp strands that had washed ashore as boats trimmed the bushy olive-green beds just a few hundred yards out.

My presentation was on the role of digital information in coming earth-change prophecies. The event was part of a national tour to increase awareness of Native American prophecy and raise collective consciousness. It was my turn to talk.

"Thank you ladies and gentlemen; it's an honor to speak before this respected body, carriers of the torch for generations of peace loving, planet nurturing servants of the Great Spirit," I began my speech. "The name of this conference--One Nation--couldn't better express the underlying unity that exists not just among

Indian nations, but all nations, among all planets in all galaxies of the cosmos."

Guests nodded and vocalized approvingly.

"Honorable ones, the past twenty years has seen a revolution in information technology. For the first time in history all humanity's accomplishments, musings, culture and knowledge is available at a mere touch. Prophecies and teachings your ancestors received from descendants of Atlantis, Lemuria and the star people are known now more than ever, yet where is it all going? What's next? Will information play a useful role in the destiny of our planet? Will computers help us make decisions vital to our physical and spiritual survival, predict outcomes and guide us, or, will they be commercialized receptacles of trillions of invisible bits taking us to the precipice of knowledge and understanding too little, too late? I predict the former," I declared. "The future is now!" I added.

A video of Jinni's desktop interface with progress bars performing mind-boggling computations flashed on the giant screen.

"For the past twenty years I've worked determinedly in the field of quantum computing. I cannot reveal all the technical details, as there are forces threatened by what I have built. But make no mistake change is coming. Emerging data validates many ancient legends and prophecies with surprising conclusions; for children who trust in the Great Spirit this will be their finest hour."

Rapt attention followed enthusiastic response. Intuitively, I knew some in the audience had associated my topic with news reports of the mysterious bottles and their strange contents.

"Respected members let me speak of a few things I have learned that I *can* tell you. You are being called. It was encoded in your DNA. You came here for this time to ascend and help awaken others to a reality that transcends time and space, the next evolution of consciousness, a higher frequency of existence." I clicked to change the image.

"All limitation is at a tipping point, and resistance is weakening. The time of struggle and striving is over; slight pushes will tumble what has blocked you. You are the beneficiaries of a rare cosmic opportunity that is all about *who you are and what you think in the present, not what you do and what you have for the future,*" I added.

"When the shift occurs it will be virtually unnoticeable. It will appear as if little has changed physically, only in consciousness.

"What can we expect? Here are the Nine Assurances of this exciting new time:"

1. Hurts will be healed
2. You will forgive and be forgiven

3. Sadness will be transformed to joy
4. Destructive habits will be overcome
5. Gifts and work of passion will be supported
6. Supply will be available
7. Anxieties and worries will be eliminated
8. Solutions to all problems will be given
9. Health, peace and cooperation will be restored

How do you know if you are chosen? You've never felt at home here, or quite fit in. You've known you were different and sensed there was something more to life. You feel time speeding up and experience synchronicity of coincidences. You sense a force guiding and protecting you, and know you came here for a reason, a greater purpose. What do you have to do? Nothing; that's the beauty of *no-effort receiving.* Simply live the higher frequency life you already embrace and align more and more with knowledge that will become more real to you as we go full shift. I assure you this has been calculated beyond reasonable doubt and the data backs up our highest hopes and dreams; truly, the numbers don't lie."

Following a brisk applause someone spoke out.

"You're a liar!" a man out of place in a suit and tie abruptly shouted from the audience. I zeroed in on him. His eyes were black and vacant. He crossed his arms and stood smug and silent. Ignoring the outburst I continued speaking. He cut in again. This time he cupped his hands together to amplify his comments.

"He's a fraud, don't believe him!" he shouted.

The beneficent crowd's surprise turned to anger. A few elders grumbled, while others shouted and chastised him.

"What's the matter with you, little brother who does not belong? Can't you see this man is a great shaman sent by *Big Holy* to help us? Be silent!" one audience member chided.

The rude intruder continued: "This man is a charlatan and takes advantage of you all," he barked.

"Get *no-belonging* brother out of here!" one guest charged. Several attendees grabbed him. The heckler stiffened but offered no resistance, as if expecting ejection.

"See *you* later," he said and stared at me for the entire length of his dismissal. "You *will* fail," he added stone-faced. "Come to the dark side, Luke," he teased in a Vader-esque voice and laughed maniacally as bouncers dragged him away. An uncomfortable silence ensued and I determined to lighten the moment.

"I'd say my father has a few minor doubts about my calculations!" I cracked. Uproarious laughter filled the room and I continued my presentation unabated.

"After decision time, light choosers—unlike the gentleman you just saw--will seamlessly transform into the high-density vibrational reality," I went on. "To those who choose to face nature's fury it will appear as if all has been lost. For us, these low frequency people will disappear virtually unnoticed. Analysis shows reality will reconfigure in their absence; their homes, jobs, all records of their existence, will be completely erased and the cracks filled by celestial dream dust. It will be a dimensional splitting of worlds. Ours will be a new earth-reality of peace, prosperity and cooperation, theirs strife and struggle. Yet, in the end all are saved; no soul is lost or condemned, each of us finishes the great journey in one life or another awake in victory. Thank you warriors of light; the Great Spirit blesses you all!"

The capacity crowd rose to their feet and applauded as I exited the podium. I tried to slip out unnoticed, but an audience member intercepted me in the lobby.

"That was amazing," she said. "Except for that idiot."

"Thank you, I'm glad you enjoyed it," I replied humbly and turned to continue my quiet retreat.

"I'm very curious about the technology you alluded to in there," she said. "And those symbols on the pendant you're wearing—the strange thing is they were on something quite bizarre I saw today on the beach."

"That is a coincidence," I replied. "What did you see?"

"I'd like to show you," she answered. "Can you meet me in room 555 in twenty minutes?" she asked.

"Sure, I guess that would be fine."

I thanked her and prepared to continue my exit when I sensed a presence behind me. When I turned he was inches from my face.

"I'm your *fear-bot*," he said. I could feel his breath, cold, and odd smelling. I looked into his left *essence* eye, but it was dim, almost inhuman.

"There's nothing there, shaman--don't bother trying your hypnosis yogi crap on me."

"Who are you?" I asked. "And what do you want?"

"Do you really have to ask, Mr. Fake Jesus? You're nothing but a phony, a self-centered megalomaniac, and I'm your dark side, the real you; *hope you guessed my name*," he replied in song. "I'm your personally assigned *fear-bot*.

"Yeah, you said that," I rejoined sarcastically.

"I sense your weaknesses and reflect them back to you a hundred-fold," he went on in a slick Tommy Lee Jones accent.

"So the devil tells me you got a problem with *girls.* You like em' a lot *donchya*, big boy? Like that hot Pocahontas who just left. Why do you think she wants you to come to her room, rock star?" he taunted, "an autograph? Gonna show her your big hard drive?"

"So this is how Uncle Sam spends our tax dollars?" I retorted. Inexplicably, my heart began to beat faster and anxiety began to gather in my chest and abdomen.

"Yes!" he blurted. "Come to papa!"

"Not so much," I shot back. Instantly, I diffused the negative energy from my chest to my extremities. I powered up by bringing positive energy in through my medulla, the mystical *mouth of God*. Every cell in my body tingled with Life Force.

"You can do better than that, Cinderella," he taunted.

"Oh, I'll be going to the ball tonight, sister," I countered. "But you won't."

I initiated another sacred technique while he stood pat with his smug and ashen face. I inhaled forcefully while drawing chakra energy from the base of my spine up to my head. Directing the resulting super-beam of divine power to my spiritual eye for amplification, I glared straight into his right *personality* eye and squeezed off a hot shot of divine, ego-wilting power.

He inhaled quickly and with a ghostly look began teetering. Abruptly, his knees buckled and he fell to the ground in the fetal position while shaking uncontrollably.

I kneeled to leave him with a few parting holy words.

"*Don't f*** with God,*" I whispered, got up, and walked away.

I strolled a few feet over to the bar.

"Bartender, get that man a Shirley Temple," I told him. "Charge it to his room: *666*."

I pressed send on my phone.

"Madi, how did the darks contact you about Jehsi?"

"This creepy guy came to my door," she replied.

"Did he have a dark suite, blackish eyes and pasty white skin?"

"Yes; he said cooperate or you won't see your son again."

"I think I just had a run in with the sewer slug that is responsible. I'm going to text you a picture; tell me if you recognize him."

"That is him!" she exclaimed. "How did you get this?"

"He was heckling me today and they removed him."

I exited the elevator and began checking door numbers.

"Why is he on the floor? Did you punch him out, I hope?"

"Sort of," I answered.

"Hold him until I get there," she snarled.

The door opened.

"I miss you," she interjected.

"I have to go," I responded.

"Hello, come in, please," the room's occupant said.

"Avery, is that a woman's voice?"

"Yeah, I have to go, I'll call you later."

"Avery, wait, hello?"

I pressed *end.*

"I'm sorry, Miss Hopefeather."

"Please, it's Kelly, come in, sit," she said.

"The reason I asked you here is I found something on the beach today." She reached in her bag and pulled it out. "When you spoke and I saw the symbols on your necklace I knew."

My eyes nearly popped out of my head as she held it. Then my phone rang again.

"Excuse me, Miss Hopefeather," I said as I silenced the ringer. "I'm sorry, Kelly, you knew *what?*"

"*True White Brother* of the Hopi prophecy," she said emphatically. "I believe you could be the one in the prophecy."

I got a text from Madi: *Call now, it's important.*

"Excuse me," I said and withdrew to the balcony.

"Madi, please, she's just someone I met at the conference."

"Oh, so you think I'm jealous, how presumptuous!"

"She's got the fifth bottle, for god's sake!"

"I just wanted to tell you they came in, broke the place up and took the CPU and server. I'm all right, Jinni is gone. Have fun," she said irately, and hung up.

I returned shaking my head and closed the slider.

"Is everything alright?" Kelly asked.

"Yes, fine," I replied. "When there's no conflict in a magnificent moment it's time to worry," I added tongue-in-cheek, and shut off my phone.

"I'll get right to the point, Mr. Cole, are you the man behind these bottles?" she asked.

"I am," I replied.

"I got a bad URL when I tried to get access with this drive," she said.

"They keep shutting it down," I answered.

"They?"

"Very powerful people afraid of this technology," I replied. "You saw one of their thugs in the auditorium today. They'll do all they can to stop me."

"I want you to meet someone I think can help," she said. "There's a man who lives on old Hopi land in Arizona, a tribe council leader named *Thomas Stone Bear.*"

"Why should I meet him?" I asked.

"A few years ago I interviewed Stone Bear for a book I wrote on Hopi lineage. He claims to be the re-embodiment of *Tuba*, a Hopi leader from the late nineteenth century."

"Ah, yes," I recalled. "Story goes Tuba had a falling out with tribal leaders, but many Hopi followed him. They say he converted to Mormonism to protect his clan from other hostile tribes."

"You know your Hopi well," she answered.

"Why does Stone Bear believe *he* was Tuba?" I asked.

"A Mormon missionary from the 1800's named Jacob Hamblin wrote in his memoires that Tuba told him he had possession of a sacred Hopi stone tablet and actually showed it to him."

"The *Tiponi* from the Hopi prophecy?" I asked.

"Yes, and Stone Bear said memories of his life as Tuba began to resurface as he reached adulthood," she replied. "He remembered the location of the Tiponi tablet and recovered it. Do you know the prophecy of the tablet, Mr. Cole?" she asked.

"Your people await *Pahana*, True White Brother. The legend says he will bring the matching halves of the symbols on the sacred Tiponi, which will identify him as the True White Brother--and signal arrival of the fifth world."

"That is correct. So, may I ask where you got the hieroglyphs on the outside of this bottle—and on your necklace?" she probed.

"I saw them in a vision years ago, why?"

She pulled a manila envelope from her bag, carefully removed a photo and placed it on the bed.

"This is a photograph of the tablet given to me by Stone Bear himself," she said. "Look at the symbols. Do you see why I asked you here today?" she inquired.

As I examined the photo I knew I had received the sign I had been waiting for.

"I will meet your friend."

"When can you leave," she asked.

"Yesterday," I answered.

{ 16 }

The Sacred Pipe

Huge tumbleweeds crossed the highway like spooked herds.

"I wonder how it would feel to get hit by one," I asked. The racing weed-balls were taller than a man. Driven by the force of the Arizona wind they could knock you down.

"I could pull over if you want to find out," she teased and shifted into high gear. "Oraibi is known for the world's biggest and fastest tumbleweeds."

"That's quite a claim to fame," I replied as she skillfully handled the wheel to counteract the gusts.

Low above the desert floor a blanket of clouds hovered. Rich shades of brown flashed to life by the atomic sun were a geological rainbow, earthen windows into bygone eons. The pillow white cloud puffs seemed carved from plaster, sanded smooth and suspended in the blue sky, solid enough to walk on. Earth and sky met in the distance where a ridge arose from the desert. Dotted with a colony of ancient pueblos, they appeared as tiny insects escorting an oblong object back to the hill.

We pulled onto a dirt road that led into a cretaceous canyon. Striations of rock revealed ancient processions of terra time past. No signs or markers identified our location. Perched on a mesa was an adobe dwelling like two big dice glued together. An array of solar panels on the roof sparkled in the sun. We zipped through the dry gulch and climbed a steep bumpy cactus-lined drive to the top. Dust kicked up all around us as she hit the brakes. Once the haze cleared a stoic figure stood like a lawn statue. He had on jeans, boots, a tee shirt and a brimmed hat with a feather. The two tribal kin enjoyed a warm but brief reunion.

"Avery Cole, this is Thomas Stone Bear," she announced.

He grasped my outstretched hand; a slight smile peeled years from his craggy leather face. His cloudy blue eyes glowed like wary yet vigilant keepers of an ancient story. Strands of grey-black hair accented his strong buffalo jaw.

"It is good to meet you White Brother," he said. "Let us go in where it is cool," he added in a deep resonant voice.

The interior was barren like the desert. A few weaves and artifacts decorated the four plain white walls. Stone Bear motioned for us to sit on a couch in the corner. He sat on an adjacent chair and grunted as he reached the cushion.

"Medicine don't work on these old joints anymore," he remarked.

"You mean Indian medicine?" I asked.

"No, glucosamine and chondroitin," he replied. "I bought it off the damn Internet," he kidded.

"Miss Hopefeather tells me you are the man behind the medicine bottles everyone's talkin' about," he said.

I nodded affirmatively.

"She also said she found one and it had the matching halves of the symbols from the sacred Hopi Tiponi," he added.

"Yes, if the photo I saw was the Tiponi," I replied.

"May I see the bottle?" he asked.

She passed the decanter to Stone Bear who examined it carefully as he turned and flipped it.

"No other human eyes have seen the symbols on the sacred stone tablet for over a century," he said. "No record or photos exist except the one I gave her. Not even the elders know the true Tiponi is entrusted to me. Have you shown the photo to anyone?"

"No, Thomas, I have not," Kelly answered.

"You are a *keeper of the sacred pipe*," he said as he looked at me penetratingly. "I can see it in your colors, brother; you are an eagle medicine man, you fly higher from a place in the East with perfect sight," he said pointing at the spot between his eyebrows.

"What is a keeper of the pipe?" Kelly asked.

"He knows," Stone Bear answered and nodded cross-armed.

"When Great Spirit swallowed the third world, brother from the stars came to the tribes on Turtle Island, and gave a chosen one the *Chanupa*—a great knowledge of heaven," Stone Bear explained. "Star Brother said the sacred pipe would take one who smoked it to the Great Spirit quickly," he added.

"Our legends say all four races got a piece of corn, Thomas," Kelly began. "The Red People chose the small corn and Star Brother said they had chosen wisely. Was that corn the knowledge you speak of?"

"Let White Brother answer, for he knows as much and more than I," Stone Bear replied.

"The corn symbolized a seed, not actual corn, Kelly," I responded. "Your grandfathers chose seeds of knowledge: Small corn means simple spiritual knowledge. Other races chose longer corn and got technology and science, knowledge of astronomy, sacred construction and how to levitate objects," I explained. "Small corn tribes practiced the simple medicine of the land and lived mostly in harmony with the elements, but they too had lost the true Knowledge of the Sacred Pipe."

"What happened--how?" she asked.

"The prophecy says two brothers, older and younger brother, were given a Tiponi," I answered.

"That is right," Stone Bear began. "Older Brother of the Shining Light was told take his Tiponi east to the rising sun. When he arrived he was to come back and look for younger brother here on Turtle Island."

"I believe Older Brother took his Tiponi east," I agreed. "But he traveled west to the *Far* East: Asia. He took his tablet to what is now India and the secret of the tablet went with him."

"What is this *sacred pipe* then?" Kelly asked.

"It's a stargate in our own bodies," I explained. "It runs up the spinal column with seven energy centers. The clay pipe bowl represents the first center at the base of the spine; the tube of the pipe is the spinal channel. The *smoke* signifies dormant life energy as it rises up the spine. The secret is how to bring that energy to the *tip* of the pipe in the sixth center in the head to activate the stargate in the seventh and free one's consciousness."

"Free it to where?" she asked.

"The Infinite, Nirvana, Paradise--God," I answered. "Take the most incredible feeling you've ever had times a million. Anything is given for the asking in this state of consciousness: power over space, time, matter and even life and death--is granted."

"Immortality?" she asked.

"The fabled fountain of youth, yes," I replied, "which is only humanity's dim unconscious memory of something many once knew and practiced," I replied. "Some call it *Kriya.*"

"Is it meditation?" she inquired.

"It's a special method given for this age," I answered. "One hour's practice of this technique each day for one year is equal to over 20,000 years of normal soul evolution; that's 235 lifetimes worth of spiritual progress and power—in just one year."

"I have heard of this technique," Stone Bear said. "You have smoked from this pipe and that is how you know Big Holy. He talks through your mouth White Brother."

"The method has been given by guardian masters and space beings many times over the ages," I related. "As mankind slips into vibrational darkness the sacred science is suppressed, as no ruler can rule a race of Christ super-beings. The knowledge is entrusted to a few until humanity is ready to revive it. A deathless avatar named *Babaji* has taught it from the refuge of the Himalayas for over twenty centuries. Christ himself is said to have received it there," I revealed.

"And now you have come in his place. It is you, Older Brother who has returned to help us on Purification Day, just as promised. You brought the matching Tiponi symbols; therefore, you are the True White Brother of the prophecy...of this I am certain," Stone Bear declared.

"May I see the tablet, Stone Bear?"

"Come," he said and led us to a door.

A sallow light hung above the wooden staircase. The dank smell of earth and clay was more distinct with each creaky step. At the bottom a vault door was fused into a subterranean earthen wall. As he rotated the lock, gears and sliding rods gave way to a pneumatic pressure release and the door opened.

The interior was antiseptic steel about ten feet cube. In the center of the armored cavern, a naturally formed chest-high rock formation sprung from the floor enclosed in thick rectangular glass bolted to the floor. The stone relic was tucked between the rocks.

"That's how I found it forty years ago," Stone Bear said. "You are the first two human beings to lay eyes on the Tiponi since I discovered it here," he added.

"Humans, you say?" I asked.

"This story has not touched my lips until now," he related. "Years ago, I was dowsing for water in a place I had seen in a vision and saw an opening in the rocks. I tried to get in but I was too big to fit, even as a skinny young brave," he reminisced and chuckled. "So I dug until I reached it. I put this vault here and built my home over this sacred land where I found the Tiponi."

"How did you know it was the Tiponi," I asked.

"I was sleeping with the stars one night," he described, "when lights came down from the sky. A boomerang big as ten-thousand eagles stopped in the air above me. A beam of light came down and took me inside. A small brother with a big head showed me pictures with no screen and spoke with no words." His story sparked memories of my own experience on that dark, isolated Washington State highway back in 1985.

"You were communicating telepathically?" I asked.

"He said the tablet was the Tiponi and that Younger and Older Brother each got a tablet after the third world ended. He showed me my past and there was a big remembering and saw that I hid the tablet here when I was Tuba. Bigheaded brother said don't tell anyone about the tablet. One day, he said, a Hopi sister would bring Older Brother with the symbols and the other stone tablet and he would know what to do," he said.

Stone Bear handed me the Tiponi. A sudden jolt of electricity shot through my body as I held it. Past lives flashed like forgotten mirages. I saw that I had been a high priest and perished in Atlantis some 10,000 years ago. I worked with other spiritual leaders to stabilize a global network of power generators that had weakened the earth's magnetic field, and grew worse as Nibiru approached. The deluge was delayed just long enough for galactic overseers to remove some of the four peoples--red, white, black and yellow--in great star ships. Survivors were returned once earth became re-inhabitable to begin the third world.

My next life was that of an early ancestor of the Hopi in the Americas during that time. In my second decade Star Brother appeared and gave me the other Tiponi with the teachings of the Sacred Pipe. I took it west over the sea to the high mountains in the land of the brown people, to India, where it would be safeguarded for humanity for the ages. Some early, yet less potent elements had later been disseminated in what became teachings expounded in the Vedas, Bhagavad gita, Tao, and other scientifically ordered mystical wisdoms.

"True White Brother you've been sleeping awake since you touched the Tiponi," Stone Bear said. "I had not wanted to rouse you for fear that I too would be taken into the big dream."

All of a sudden, the muffled whoosh of helicopter blades buffeted our ears.

"They're after the Tiponi!" I warned.

"We must put the tablet back and leave!" Stone Bear declared.

"No," I said. "They will take it; this safe won't stop them."

"What can we do?" Kelly cried.

"We don't have to *do* anything," I responded.

"We can't just stay here," she reacted.

"Fear says run, but when we obey we give it life," I advised. "We have to stay and know we are not in danger."

"Older Brother speaks true. We will sit until they come."

She trembled like a frightened doe.

"Kelly," I spoke, "in the fifth world you are the center of divine power and grace. Whatever enters the strong planet's gravity either burns up in its atmosphere, or becomes subdued in orbit around it," I added.

"I agree with Older Brother. I too will be the big planet. Sit little sister, and be Jupiter with me and True White Brother."

Heavy footsteps trampled above. The basement door shuddered open and the procession continued down the stairs. Dressed in fatigues and wielding automatic rifles they burst into the safe room. The lead operative removed his mask.

"Viktor!" I shouted.

With an unrepentant face he pointed his rifle at us as we sat on the floor.

"I am sorry Avy-ji what could I do?" he replied disingenuously. "*De* numbers did not *fabor* your chances. Now I must insist you give me the Tiponi."

"I am sorry Viktor, but we will not obey you," I said.

He pulled the slide to load a cartridge.

"Señor, do not force me to kill you so soon." Sweat beads began to erupt on his head as his eye twitched.

The other operatives egged him on.

"Scratch the bastards," one of them jeered.

He took the rifle off me and put it on Stone Bear.

"You, old man, get up. Open the glass and give me the Tiponi!" he shouted, the gun inches from his head.

"Go ahead, I am ready to die," he responded calmly.

"No, open it, give him the Tiponi," I instructed. I nodded reassuringly and Stone Bear opened the glass.

"You," Viktor ordered one of the men, "take it."

The man reached in and lifted the Tiponi. Suddenly he began to shake. Terror filled his face as he screamed.

"Help me, it burns, I can't let go, someone help me!" he wailed. Suddenly, the Tiponi dropped to the floor.

"What are you doing Avy-ji, heh? Do I have to kill one of you to take the Tiponi, or will you stop your Jedi mind tricks?"

"I'm not doing it Viktor. And you know if Spirit allows you to kill anyone your problems will multiply." I glared at him and his face trembled slightly.

"Lieutenant," he yelled. "*De* relic cannot be touched; it is cursed. You and the others go back and bring the reclamation unit," he told them. "I will wait here."

Obediently, the men filed up the stairs.

Viktor squatted and cradled the rifle between his forearm and thigh as he chewed on a toothpick and whistled nonchalantly. Suddenly, a single pair of lighter sounding feet came rushing down the stairs.

"Madi! You too?" I asked.

"I just happened to be in the neighborhood," she replied.

"You're with Viktor?" I asked disappointedly.

"I'm afraid so...I'm driving in the get-away car, Clyde, *your* get-away car." Viktor threw the rifle on the floor.

"Avy-ji, we must leave with the Tiponi right now!"

"You're a double agent!"

"Sí, Señor."

"I knew it!" I exclaimed and jumped up.

Viktor disclosed that by acting as a plant with the dark establishment for the last several years, he learned of plans to intercept me and seize the sacred Tiponi in Arizona. Background checks failed to uncover our past association. He quickly volunteered for the mission and contacted Madi to accompany him. This act of disloyalty would surely mark him as a wanted—if not dead--man.

"By the way, damn good acting job," I commended him.

"You liked that?" he cackled excitedly.

"Are you kidding?" I patted him on the back. "The sweat, lip twitching; if this spy thing doesn't work out you might have a second career!"

"I did play Hamlet once in high school," he said.

"No kidding? I was Romeo in junior high."

"Uh, yo, the Hummer's waiting topside," Madi said as she posed against the wall and twirled the key ring impatiently. "Can we compare drama class notes later?"

"Oh, sorry, Avy-ji, I had to disable your vehicle for dramatic effect," he said sheepishly. "Don't worry, the

Hummer has anti-tracking countermeasures and Stinger missiles."

"When did they start offering that option?" I asked.

"It's the road-rage package," Madi clowned. "Can we just get out of here?"

"She's right, we must hurry!" Viktor said.

"Does anyone know where we're going?" I asked.

The car was silent.

"Madi?" I asked.

"Oh, I'll just ask my Magic Eight-Ball," she cracked. "I have no idea!"

"We have to decipher the symbols on this tablet," I said.

"That's right...the prophecy says True White Brother is the only one who can *read* the Tiponi," Stone Bear interjected.

"I hate to tarnish my TWB image, but I have no idea what these symbols mean," I confessed.

"Kelly, what's the tablet made of?" I asked.

"Looks like red marble, but far too light, and the drop on that steel floor didn't even leave a mark. The inscriptions are laser quality, remarkable," she observed. "And there appears to be some kind of covered rectangular slot here on the side," she noted.

"The prophecy also says True White Brother can *write*," Stone Bear added.

"Code, maybe," Madi said casually--under her breath.

"What did you just say?" I asked.

"Code, I meant you write code, computer code, that is."

"That's it!" I said. "If these symbols have any earthly counterpart maybe Jinni can *read* the Tiponi and tell us what they mean!"

"They took her, remember?" Madi reminded.

"Fortunately, Jinni has another lamp in a wet place," I replied humorously. "Viktor set the GPS for Marina Del Rey, California."

"Aye, aye, *Capitan!*"

Hours passed grudgingly on the desolate highway. We took turns sleeping as one slumped over and the other awakened. Slowly changing configurations of sand and sky were the only break in the endless stream of white lines that seemed to emerge out of the blurry hot asphalt horizon.

"Tell us more about the secret of that pipe Older Brother," Stone Bear said.

"Maybe a little—just to pass the time," I replied. "But I can't reveal too much."

"Why not?" Kelly asked.

"Without the right preparation the force of energy generated by practice can be damaging," I answered.

"Tell us Older Brother...what *is* the secret?"

"Alright," I said. "Think of it as a spiritual rocket launch, and your consciousness is the space capsule. First, a special breathing technique detoxifies the body and quiets the mind, which rests the heart and lungs. Incoming oxygen is then converted into its pre-atomic constituent, where it mixes with the thought-fuel of wisdom, love, and devotion. This releases highly charged energy currents into the spine," I explained.

"Then, as this energy elixir circulates it rises up the spinal gentry and increases in frequency until a critical vibrational launch threshold is reached. Your will-guided missile of awareness then reaches escape velocity at the apogee of the Christ Eye here, and *whoosh*," I emphasized with up-thrusting hands.

"After millennia of internment in the body capsule of this dense earth prison, one is free of the crushing gravity of Maya," I finished. "The marooned soul traveler finally arrives at the cosmic, zero-g realm of the Heavenly Father free in a vast, intoxicating home world that always existed within the inner space of one's own in-turned Divine Mind."

As I concluded, my eyes--as well as those of my audience--sparkled ethereal. My consciousness soared on the stratospheric fringes of the very reality which I had poetically described.

"Pretty words, White Brother," Stone Bear adulated.

"Can you still return to your physical body?" Kelly asked.

"Yes, but grudgingly, I assure you."

"What is this *preparation* you spoke of?" she enquired.

"The practice of an ancient wisdom relieves the mind of negativity and conflict, while other techniques help loosen the grip of sense attachments so the mind can be focused on a pin point free of distraction. Just like an athlete trains for sport," I compared, "these concentration and energy control methods prepare you for the greatest event of your life--the leap into the arms of your Infinite Creator."

Suddenly, an alarm sounded from the instrument panel.

"They are tracking us!" Viktor informed. "They're being jammed for now and I just changed the vehicle's color."

"Changed the color?" I asked.

"Sí, an electrical charge reacts with chemicals in the paint," he replied.

"How very *Bond* of you," I joked.

A huge black helicopter passed overhead.

"They are looking very hard for us," Viktor said.

"They're using psychics--I sense the energy," I said. "We can use *our* thoughts too. Everyone, I want you to visualize a white light around this vehicle; concentrate and imagine we are invisible," I instructed.

"Can imagination beat radar?" Kelly asked skeptically.

"It took imagination to create radar, yes?"

"Well, yes," she conceded.

"Thought *precedes* manifestation," I replied. "Everyone concentrate!"

"Can this really work?" Kelly asked.

"Do you believe the power that created everything *can* make this car invisible?" Madi asked her.

"Yes, but people pray and ask for things every day they don't get," she retorted skeptically.

"That's because most people ask like beggars, like they don't matter or have any power," Madi responded with urgency. "We are made in God's image...*ask and you shall receive...these things you shall do and greater*...Jesus was talking about you, honey, all of us, right now!" she preached.

A chorus of affirmative responses followed.

"Very impressive grasshopper," I quietly praised Madi. "It may be time for you to leave the monastery."

"They already kicked me out; I'm working on you."

"What about their thoughts; can't they can use them against us?" Kelly asked in reprise.

"Only thoughts aligned with the benefit of humanity will manifest easily in the fifth world," I clarified. "Desires that come from our false self, greed and ego will not be supported."

Within moments the vehicle went pumping loud with hot sizzling thought energy. The electronic warnings abruptly stopped.

"I can see the light Older Brother and his Helper speak of. We are invisible to the dark ones," Stone Bear affirmed.

Madi quietly took the light moment to clear the air:

"I apologize for hanging up on you yesterday," she whispered.

"No need," I replied.

"Doesn't anything ever hurt your feelings?"

"They're not my feelings, Madi, their..."

"I know, I know, God's. I guess I keep thinking you're a regular guy but you're not; you're something much more," she interjected.

"I'm nothing more than you, Madi, or anyone. I just did the work to bring out *those greater things* we already are."

"I know, thank you," she said and smiled.

Blackjack

MORNING OVERCAST EVAPORATED in the fresh brewed light rays. Each million-degree particle cooled to a mere seventy-two Fahrenheit in its light-speed, eight-minute dash from the surface of the scorching-hot sun to the lush marina paradise.

Pea-sized dew drops glistened tawny and silver as they rolled off chlorophyll-rich palm leaves that sprung from sectors of concrete, wood and line-painted blacktop. Life stirred in the docks as early risers emerged from their floating abodes. A shopkeeper swept his storefront, while a back door opened and a sleepy-eyed restaurant worker hauled trash to a dumpster. Nearby, a homeless woman held court with an invisible entourage as she loitered in the hopes of making a meal of the rejected refuse. We ditched the Hummer and went to the dock. We stopped at a forty-five foot beauty with a flying bridge.

"Beautiful boat Avy-ji, but what are we doing here?" Viktor asked. "A three-hour tour perhaps?"

"If we do go out to sea, Vik, it won't be with the part of the boat you can see." My reply was met with puzzled faces.

I unlocked the cabin door and we went below. Automatic dimmer lights illumined both the interior and my guest's astonished expressions as they realized this was no vessel they had ever seen or been on before.

"Welcome aboard the *Varuna*," I announced. "The boat above is just a shell; *Varuna* separates from the boat; she's actually a submarine."

"What is its purpose, Avy-ji?"

"It's an ESC...*End-times Survivability Craft.* The hull is a super-strong composite with advanced shock absorbing materials and there's a sonic pulse generator that creates a bubble of high-pressure protection around the sub. *Varuna* can survive the direct impact of a five-hundred foot tsunami--the kind anticipated in a pole shift."

"What's a *Varuna*?" Madi asked.

"The Vedic god of water and celestial oceans," I replied.

"What does Older Brother's ark do for power?" Stone Bear asked.

"Solar panels recharge batteries on the surface."

"But in a pole shift the sun may be obscured for weeks or months--then what?" Viktor questioned.

"Alternate power comes from an electrical reaction from the sea and desalinated water," I explained.

"Osmotic power...genius Señor! Desalination takes care of the fresh water issue and I presume you have plenty of food."

"Six-months dehydrated for four and a complete hydroponic growing system of over one-hundred plant species."

"Holy Captain Nemo!" Madi exclaimed. "This thing had to cost a fortune; did you hit the lotto or something?"

"In the eighties, I was an intern for a start-up Seattle-based software company you've all heard of," I began. "One night I was driving home on a deserted highway when--like Stone Bear--I noticed lights in the sky. I woke up in my car six hours later with no memory of what happened and this strange object in my hand; I took it to the company lab to analyze it. An employee found the records on the shared drive and they tried to duplicate it."

"What was it Señor?"

"An advanced processor and hard disk drive," I answered.

"Wait a minute, are you saying aliens gave you the modern micro-processor and this company ripped it off?" Madi postulated.

"What they could figure out from X-rays, descriptions of parts and material compositions, yes. Everything from PC's to the smartphones in your pockets are direct results of that find. They paid me off big in company stock to shut up and walk," I disclosed. "What twenty-year old kid wouldn't have taken it? I never dreamed I'd own two-percent of one of the biggest computer companies in the world."

"Where is the original device, Avy-ji?"

"On board this ship inside Jinni," Madi speculated.

"She's right. I began building *Varuna* with Jinni's help when the early data I was getting predicted an imminent end-times scenario...and my once-worthless stock turned into—a fortune."

"So let me get this straight," Madi said, "you get abducted by aliens thirty years ago, they leave you on the side of the road with some sick hardware, your employer steals what they are able to understand, throws you a bone that makes you a multi-zillionaire and then roll out the hardware--that revolutionizes history?"

"Pretty much," I answered. "Jinni online," I ordered.

What is your wish, Master?

"Aboard *Varuna* Jinni uses an untraceable two-way optical laser wireless system to communicate with three servers I've set up in isolated locations along the coastal mountains," I described.

"They could still locate and shut down the servers, which I assume are connected to a commercial network, right?" Madi asked.

"Yes, but they're all unique IP's and hard to isolate, so we should at least have time for the analysis."

"Jinni, scan item Tiponi, then search all archives for the meaning of the symbols, calculate and report," I ordered.

As you wish, Master.

We waited as Jinni digested every scrap of data on the Internet.

Preliminary review shows relationship matches with original proto-Elamite cuneiform circa 3,500 BC.

"What's that?" Madi asked.

"Early Sumerian writing," Kelly answered.

"Jinni, continue," I directed.

Similarities also exist with Egyptian and South American petroglyphs, as well as characters recorded by Dr. Jesse Marcel July, 6 1947, from the Roswell crash and Adam's Calendar.

"Roswell, Adam's Calendar? What are we talking about here?" Kelly asked.

"Perhaps the extraterrestrial origin of all modern language and writing!" Viktor answered.

Now extrapolating data based on all known ciphers and codecs, Master.

Suddenly, an error message appeared on the screen.

"What is happening Señor?"

"We've lost server one," I said as I typed rapidly.

Now connecting to server two, Master.

The analysis resumed and a response that would elate and mystify appeared imminent, but again signs of tampering were evident.

"Now we've lost server two," I informed.

"That leaves us one more shot," Madi stated.

"Jinni, go to server three with current data in buffer," I ordered.

Thirty seconds to item Tiponi request completion, Master.

At first it seemed all was well, but problems continued.

"She's crashing again! Jinni, hurry!" I bellowed.

As the critical seconds counted down I typed commands like a desperate surgeon trying to reroute the connection, but it was like trying to revive a hopeless patient.

Connection lost.

"Well, that's it," I informed.

"We can't give up now," Madi said.

"Come on guys, let's bend some spoons here," she rallied. "Close your eyes like we did in the Hummer...visualize a successful data transfer!"

After several minutes of *nada* Viktor spoke. "I'm sorry Señorita, *pero* it does not seem like..."

"Shut up, Viktor; don't say it," she snapped. "Focus!"

Again our boisterous thoughts lined up single file, in urgent appeal, at the desk of the supervising Cosmic Manager.

Suddenly, the file transfer bars flashed to life.

"She's got it--we have a file intact!" I exclaimed.

Cheers broke out with a frenzy of high-fives.

"We did it!" someone shouted.

"*We* didn't do anything!" I rebuked. The formerly feverish telekinetic trainees were now motionless terra cotta.

"As soon as you take credit you weaken," I rebuked.

I sternly surveyed the faces in the cabin and then smiled.

"Jinni display message."

The critical information we thought might change the game appeared on the screen: *The answers are within you. You are the question, you are the message, and you are the answer. All is one.*

"That's it?" Kelly asked, "A bad fortune cookie?"

"I think maybe the Tiponi is saying we don't have to seek the answers, they'll find us." Madi offered.

"Or it may be a code," Viktor said. "I count twenty-one words, three times seven...the Holy Trinity multiplied by sacred seven! I told you the answer would be in *sevens!*"

Madi rolled her eyes, kicked her feet up and pulled a worn deck of cards from her purse.

"Blackjack anyone? Tiponi twenty-one, Vik you in?"

She shuffled the cards and dealt to the disenchanted participants at the table while I toiled to restore Jinni's connection and verify the content we had received.

"Twenty!" Madi exclaimed. "An ace and a nine—almost Blackjack—beat that!" She threw her hand down triumphantly.

"*Nada*," Viktor said exasperatedly and folded.

"Me too," Kelly echoed.

Stone Bear, whaddya got?" Madi asked.

"Two nines," he answered. "Eighteen."

"Alright, another hand," she said.

"I got twenty this time," Kelly said as she flashed her own ace and a nine.

"Must be lady luck, eh? A pair of nines for me, as well," Viktor conceded. He took a hit that busted him.

"Stoney B?" Madi asked.

"Four, five and a nine for me, Big Brother's helper,"

"Alright, that's enough," I interrupted. "Is anybody else picking up on any of this?"

"I don't know, pretty girls, gambling, sitting in a big yacht in a California paradise? I think I'm getting it, Señor," Viktor clowned.

"Vik, in the first hand Madi got an ace and a nine and Stone Bear had a pair of nines. Then, Kelly got an ace and a nine. Vik you had a pair of nines and Stone Bear you had a four, five and a nine."

"Señor, you are right," Viktor said. "I do see a pattern...*de* men are getting their pants beat off and I think I like it!"

"An ace can be one or eleven, right?" I asked. "So we have a one and a nine, 19, and two nines, 99; that's a 19 and 99 in the first hand."

"Sí', and another 19 and pair of nines in the second hand, 19 and 99," Viktor observed more soberly.

"So?" Kelly asked.

"Mama's got a lottery number tonight!" Madi clowned.

"Think back to geography class," I said. "If you're looking to find something what could two two-digit number sequences represent?"

"Latitude and longitude!" Viktor answered.

I triumphantly tossed my pen on the keyboard. "Find out where 19 degrees latitude and 99 degrees longitude is ladies and gentlemen and I believe we will have our destination!"

A cacophony of finger tapping on phones ensued.

"Mexico City!" Viktor sounded off first.

"What are we going to do there? Kelly asked. "Wait, I know...we don't have to seek the answers--*they will seek us.*"

"I think there's *hope* for you *feather*," Stone Bear joked. "Get it? *Hope--feather?*"

"That was bad, Señor Stone Bear."

"I know."

{ 18 }

More than a Feeling

THEY'VE FROZEN MY BANK ACCOUNTS," I informed the others. "Everyone, shut off all personal electronics," I requested.

"How are we going to get to Mexico with no pesos?" Madi interposed, "*The Love Boat?*"

"We'll go in *Varuna*," I replied.

Amidst no objections, I started the engines while the willing crew untied the moorings and we pulled away.

Passengers aboard other boats smiled and waved as we leisurely motored toward open sea. If they only knew what was coming, I thought sadly, and said a silent prayer. The surf kicked up as we reached the channel. I throttled up the dual V-12's and we thrust into open sea. *Varuna's* nose lifted gallantly as she cut through the glimmering waves like a knife through butter. The blue-green plasma called one to stare into its mystical abyss and imagine the teeming world of life below that ponders us their sky, alien beings from another world. By less tactical criteria this excursion would be a standout page in a book of perfect California dream days.

The drone of purring motors lulled passengers into complacency, as guests ambled through the cabin snacking, bathing and napping. Madi and I watched the sunset from the flying bridge. Radar scanned the surface and would alert us to anything on water or in the air.

"Is our government really after us?" Madi asked.

"They're the government behind government. The one you see, the president, congress, state governments--just shells, fronts, pawns for the real power. The Illuminati, Trilateral Commission, call them what you want, they call the shots; everything else is smoke and mirrors. We're free as long as we don't get in the way of what really matters to them most: money and power."

"Does the president know?" she asked.

"Sure, presidents know," I answered. "They know there's a big black spot in their rear-view mirror they can't see or mess with. Once they get in office the real law of the land is laid down. That so-called Book of Secrets, well, that's just a manual of what a president can and can't do, the lines you don't dare cross."

"Don't they at least try? I mean they are the president."

"Sure, but that's why they age so fast in office," I answered. "It slowly kills them on the inside because they realize they just became president of the most powerful nation in the world and it means nothing. The Kennedys? They crossed the lines; Jack was ready to spill the beans--that's why they got rubbed out."

"Am I interrupting anything?" Viktor cut in as he came topside.

"No, Vik, please, sit down, Madi and I were just talking about those secret elite societies that don't exist," I said mockingly.

"Oh yeah, *those*, right, nah," he chuckled and waved his hand dismissively.

Viktor's eyes were like tired reddened Mayan jewels as he starred into the dazzling borealis sunset.

"I wonder how many more we will see like this," he said somberly. "There are many contrails out there," he noticed.

"Probably missile tests from the Navy base," I replied.

"*De* military and space programs they let you see? That's nothing. What they really have would blow your mind," Viktor revealed, "inter-dimensional craft, orbiting space cities for the elite, bases and mining on the moon and Mars, all in cooperation with ET's. Of course," he added casually, "I would be vaporized for even telling you this."

"What kind of advanced ET's would help govern-ments hurt and lie to people?" Madi asked.

"There are many factions, Señora. The black elite society is partnered with self-serving grey ET's. They're not very bad, but they are not good either; they'd run over your dog rather than stop. They are here for our gold too," Viktor answered.

"Oh, now *they* need our gold? What's wrong, no pawn shops out there?" Madi railed.

"Ozone depletion," I replied. "Gold dust is suspend-ed in the planet's depleted atmosphere to block their sun's damaging ultraviolet rays."

"Sí, and the rumors of gold missing at Fort Knox? ET's have it; the deals have been made. In return, they have given the elites technology and assurances of sur-vival after the shift."

"The one weapon they cannot defend against is a spiritual one," I said. "That's why they hate Jinni."

"Sí, they know Mother Nature is about to wipe the slate clean, and are well aware of the prophecies. The spiritual solution is what they fear because a world without greed and need is a world without power and to them that is unthinkable."

"Avery said the transition would take those who make a spiritual choice to a higher dimensional version of earth. If that were true why would they care about us, wouldn't it be better to get rid of us?" Madi asked.

"Señora, fear is blind. If they could see *de* truth, *todos*, they might choose differently, but that is not to be. The devil is thirsty too, but he can only stand so much water."

Suddenly, a radar warning went off.

"Target ten miles out," I said.

"They've found us, Señor!"

"It looks like the whole damn navy," I said as I looked through binoculars. "At least ten surface vessels and half-dozen helicopters. We've got about ten minutes--tell the others we have to go now."

"Go where?" Madi asked.

I pointed down.

"Oh," she groaned. "I'd rather go to the dentist."

"Madi, you're safer in *Varuna* than your own backyard."

"My backyard is a highway," she retorted.

I took the others below for launch prep.

"Señor, they are coming fast, three miles."

Activating subsurface environmental support systems, Master.

"I'm working on it Vik," I shouted up.

All guidance and propulsion systems operational, Master.

"Señor, hurry, they could launch at us any second and blow us out of the water," Viktor stuck his head down and warned.

"Come on, Jinni, express departure checklist, we have to go," I commanded.

Now securing main access hatch, Master.

"Wait, Jinni, Viktor is still out there!" I shouted.

Flooding ballast tanks, ten seconds to detachment.

"Jinni, cancel automated and go to manual now!"

Nine seconds to launch, the countdown continued.

"Señor, please, open the door!" Viktor's muffled cries were barely audible as he pounded on the hatch.

Now executing launch separation, Master.

A jet-like whoosh followed a sudden jerk as *Varuna* detached and descended beneath the floating yacht shell.

"I'm going off voice control to manual!"

I grabbed the stick and maneuvered clear of the boat shell. I hand typed a command and *Varuna* surfaced. The hatch opened.

"Madi, do you see him?"

"No," she said. "Wait, he's over there!"

Viktor had surfaced near the boat shell and clung to the side. I maneuvered *Varuna* alongside.

"Viktor, jump!" I yelled.

"Hurry, bad guys one mile," Madi informed.

Viktor climbed on and scurried down the hatch as Jinni dove.

"What happened, Señor?" Viktor asked wet and huffing.

"They jammed our wireless electronics," I said.

"I hope that's our glitch for the mission," Madi said.

"So what happens when they get to the boat and find the false top?" Kelly asked.

Just then a strong shockwave shook the sub.

I smiled.

"You blew it up!" Madi said.

"Pretty cool, huh?" I replied.

"Little boys and their toys," she teased.

"They're right above us now so be *very* quiet," I advised. "A loud fart could give us away."

Sonar bleeps got quieter as they motored away.

"We've shaken them for now. Jinni, take us to twenty fathoms and proceed on course."

"Where is Older Brother taking us now?" Stone Bear asked.

"Manzanilla Bay, Mexico," I answered, "ETA, thirty-nine hours. Weather permitting, we'll surface in the morning near the tip of Baja for roll call and yoga."

"Does the captain have quarters?" Madi asked.

"I'll show you, come," I answered.

A sliding door opened to the Spartan but cozy cabin. There was a meditation alter embellished with various deities and a murti of my guru. The walls were floor to ceiling monitors that could render hi-definition life-sized camera feed in all directions outside the ship giving the impression of being in the water.

"Relax," I motioned her to sit.

I issued a voice command for music, and suddenly the walls flashed on in the hooky guitar-crunch chorus to reveal the vast 3D undersea panorama.

"Whoa," she reacted. "I can't believe I'm a hundred feet down in a submarine listening to *Boston!*" she exclaimed.

"Jinni's archived over 1,000,000 pieces of music," I said, as powerful floodlights transformed the pitch-black depths into a crystal aquamarine spectacular behind the soaring lead guitar solo. A shark darted away, while schools of strange fish united by a rhythmic force weaved in and out of the misty swirl. I saw goose bumps on Madi's arms; I had them too.

"Never been down at night," I divulged. "We're over the Jackson Trench; bottom is another two miles below us."

"I didn't need to know that," she said.

She was looking at a digital picture frame on the wall.

Every encounter, each scene in the dream of life continues until no test shakes our peace, no joy is dependent on the outside, no struggle threatens our supply and love displaces every fear.

"One of my favorite lines of Jinni's," I said as I saw her notice.

"I don't know if I could ever totally live that," she said.

"You already are," I replied. "I see a big change."

"In what way?" she asked.

"The way you're taking charge of the group, the strength you've shown through your son's disappearance, owning up to mistakes and how you're using speech and thought to manifest a reality of your own choosing."

She began to rub her neck. "What's weird is I've been feeling this warm pulsating feeling in my throat."

"That's the fifth chakra waking up," I replied. "You're speaking and acting out your higher truth and reality is conforming to the vibration of your words."

"Since we're talking truth I have something I need to get off my chest," she said.

"Another confession? What now?" I teased.

"I'm gonna filter this by saying I feel very *connected* with you on so many levels I can hardly think of anything else," she revealed, "but you."

Her eyes suddenly shone like liquid diamonds.

"And I think you feel the same way because nothing that feels this right could ever be one-way or I'm the silliest person alive."

I had no idea how I was going to mop up my melting heart.

"You are an amazing person Madi, but..."

"Oh no, wait, don't," she said as she waved dismissively. "Don't give me that *but in this high, divine God way* crap because I'm not buying into it, Avery Cole; I've seen you check me out and get that look in your eye."

"Madi, I..."

"Look," she cut me off, "you're this great, wise, powerful, amazing person, but I think you're kidding yourself."

"I am."

"Yes, you are. With all your spiritual woo-hoo you don't see what is obvious to everyone else."

"No, I mean you're right, Madi."

"I am?"

"I am."

"You are what?"

"Yes, I am kidding myself. The truth is I adore you. You're the funniest person I've ever met and not just ha-ha funny, but funny with good timing and that's insanely sexy. What's hotter than funny? Smart? Maybe, and you're very smart, and smart is the new funny, right? So, you're like this funny, intelligent, extremely hot person and...okay, help me--I'm bleeding here."

Her mouth was on the floor.

"I've never sounded like such a complete idiot," I confessed.

"You're right, but it pleases me, go on."

"The fact is I waited my whole life, but never got the total package. Instead, I got what I needed to help me grow up. But now I'm beating myself up because when you didn't show up I thought I could just transcend you like everything else. But here you are."

"Here I am and what?" she pressed. "Are you going say yes to your soul mate or push me aside?"

"We have many soul mates, many teachers, but we only have one twin soul," I answered. "Our twin is the one we always come back to, the one we have to perfect a human relationship with to be free."

"Am I your twin?" she asked.

"I love truth and wisdom with all my heart," I answered. "It's given me peace in a world of uncertainty and pain. I know behind every broken fantasy of human love the Divine Lover is whispering: *Here I am, look further, go deeper and find me*, but I can't deceive myself; there is one last mortal knot I must untie."

It was as if my entire romantic life had flashed before me. I saw every new face and each undeserving lover I invested my heart and soul in falsely because I needed so badly to be loved, regardless of the cost. I relived untold nights of solitude where I desperately searched the edges of the universe to find the spiritual answer that would satisfy my heart's question; still a small rogue voice would speak up and ask: is *the one* out there waiting for me? Like a boomerang, the countless years of my restless search for more than a feeling had finally come back with the answer I had waited so long for with a resounding--*yes.*

"Then what are you waiting for?" she said. Her words aroused me from my reverie and caressed my ears like a sweet song.

"Kiss me, Avery Cole, and start untying that knot."

Bound by the multifaceted physics of the human heart, we collided together during the clapping chorus--in compliance with some other more physical Law of Attraction.

{ 19 }

Rogue Wave

I DOUBLED MY PILLOW AND LAID BY HER SIDE, grateful for the privilege of leasing human eyes. Her hair draped over the pillow like frozen gold waterfalls. Angelic light illumined her face, while slightly upturned corners of her mouth hinted at peaceful ecstasy. I gazed tenderly upon the sleeping soul with whom I shared many lives in youth, hope, love, dreams, children and joys, and also sorrows, old age and the sadness of ever-certain earthly partings. I prayed this life would not end with painful mortal separation and helpless tumbles through the delusive haze of time and space, but with us both awake in the loving arms of the Divine Betrothal. I dressed quietly and went to check our position.

"Good morning, Older Brother," Stone Bear said as he watched the sea-cam feed in the monitor.

"Good morning," I replied.

"Do we get any other channels out here?" he joked, and then looked at me piercingly. I concluded the wise old owl had sensed a subtle difference in my demeanor.

He leaned over and whispered.

"Ever heard of the *mile-down* club?"

I smiled modestly. "We're not quite a mile down, Stone Bear," I replied.

A guffaw came from deep in his chest.

"Was it that obvious?" I asked.

"Your walls are thin," he answered.

"I guess I didn't consider interior acoustics in the ship's design plan," I came back good-naturedly.

"Jinni, surface *Varuna* now," I ordered.

Madi and Viktor came up the ladder from below.

"Good morning seamen," I said.

"That's sea woman to you," Madi said and bit her lip erotically.

"Eleven hours to Mexico," I announced.

"Where do we park the bus when we get there?" Viktor asked.

"A nice quiet street," I replied.

Varuna is on the surface, Master.

"Let's get some air," I said as the hatch opened.

The sea was calm blue and the sky, cloudless. I began my morning routine, which aroused some curiosity.

"What are you doing Señor, yoga?"

"A special technique to heal and recharge the body," I replied.

"How does it work?" Kelly asked.

"I'll give you a hint: All life *came* from the sun."

Madi copied my moves.

"There's a hidden healing force in the sun's rays," I explained. "By tapping into it a person can heal any disease—and even live without food or water for decades if they desired."

"Finally, a diet that works!" Madi joked as she swung her arms in unison with mine.

"Tell us about this medicine," Stone Bear implored.

"There are many healing frequencies within the light of the sun," I responded. "Some rays absorbed directly into the skin are helpful with limited exposure, but other rays on a much high vibrational spectrum are potential miracle healers that can be directed and controlled."

"How?" Kelly asked.

"There are healing light rays even in pitch black darkness that can be activated by attunement through our will," I answered. "With concentration and practice we can feed our tissue with this plasma of renewal and flood our atoms, DNA--and even the energy blueprint of our body--to reprogram, heal and reproduce healthy cells at will."

"If this feather light you speak of is in all places and can be caught by the wind of thought, Older Brother, why ask the sun?" Stone Bear asked.

"Light in creation is like blood and the sun is the pumping heart," I answered. "The sun is the most concentrated and accessible source of this elemental healing light."

"I'm visualizing it like a bunch of tiny little cosmic nano surgeons," Madi commented.

"Perhaps this is another reason the sun is so revered in legends of all ancient cultures," Viktor noted.

"Yes, recharging with the sun is the ancient memory behind sun worshipping," I responded. "The human body stores enough subtle light energy to live two-thousand years," I explained, "but we misdirect and drain it causing premature aging and disease. Learning to live on subtle light is like plugging into the outlet instead of a battery. Battery power is temporary, while the outlet has unlimited power. This is the real meaning behind the scripture *man does not live by bread alone but by every word that proceedeth out of the mouth of God.* These Life Forces enter the body through the medulla in the back of the neck at the base of the skull. Amplified by the spiritual eye, they can be directed wherever needed and desired."

"It's like this volume of supernatural data you can't see is floating in the air just waiting for you to connect to," Madi analogized.

"Exactly; this light is a hot spot of mystical information with instructions that carry out the all functions of Supreme Will in the universe," I explained, "from synthesizing atoms to create matter, to dissolving and forming them into something new. Even the directive for a falling leaf is there: the time, place, surrounding scenery; it's all mapped out in perfect, loving detail.

"Being made in Divine Image we have the unique ability to access and direct this stream of holy data, which also holds record of the past, future and all knowledge on every level and dimension," I elucidated, as I continued my regimen. "A speck billions of times tinier than an atom contains the blueprint for the entire universe. The cipher of our God-supplied will is the password to capture, download, unzip and activate this infinite potential."

My ocean-going audience was again held rapt. As the boat cut through the waves these sacred truths parted the sea of possibility in the ocean of their infinite souls.

I demonstrated a basic technique.

"Practicing this method produces change in the atomic structure of the body," I went on. "Hair, skin and other features can change dramatically; you can become healthier, more attractive and magnetic. Directed by the laser-pointed will of a master, one can even manipulate matter into any form desired. This was the real secret behind Christ's miracles of healing the sick, walking on water and even raising the dead," I revealed.

"That skill could come in handy," Madi half-joked.

"Many will learn this method before and after the shift," I replied, "including all of you."

"I'd be happy if I could straighten out these joints enough to walk the big mountain," Stone Bear joked.

"Why not bring the mountain to you?" I challenged and smiled.

"Thank you, Older Brother; I must remember not to speak like a broken arrow." We chuckled lightheartedly.

"I'm going down to prepare for our arrival," I announced and Madi followed behind me.

"We'll be waiting here by the pool," Viktor joked.

Master, I am picking up an incoming anomaly, Jinni informed.

"A ship?" Madi asked.

"Much bigger," I answered.

Viktor stuck his head down the hatch. "Señor, you better come see this." We scurried up the latter.

"*Mira*, out there," he said and pointed to the horizon. Madi let out a gasp.

"It's a rogue wave!" I confirmed. "Everyone, get below now!

"Jinni, emergency dive, sea-cam on, quad view, report on anomaly."

Wave height is one-hundred twenty feet, range three-thousand yards, speed, one-hundred forty miles per hour, impact in fifty-six seconds. Evasive program prepared.

"Everyone strap in!" I ordered as the roar of the approaching wall could be heard inside the sub.

"Thirty seconds to impact," I warned as we dove at a desperate angle.

"Try to relax, *Varuna* was designed for this," I reminded the anxious passengers. "But we have to get beneath the wave or it could drag us miles to coastal impact."

Ten seconds to impact, Master.

Suddenly a tremendous force struck. Full body-formed inflatable seats prevented neck-snapping whiplash. A slew of red status lights lit up the monitor. Power flickered momentarily, as millions of tons of water shot *Varuna* like a bullet from a gun. The sub shimmied perilously. Her ability to withstand a huge wave was only theoretical.

"We weren't far enough under," I shouted.

Craft speed is eighty-seven miles per hour, Master. External pressure is two-thousand pounds per square inch.

"That's unheard of underwater," Viktor remarked.

"This must be what if feels like to go over Niagara Falls in a barrel," Stone Bear said.

"The sub's shape and construction are designed to enable it to withstand that and more," I assured. " *Varuna* is using a very sturdy set of micro-stabilizers to direct the water flow to take us beneath the wave," I shouted over the roar. Suddenly, there was a powerful pulse with an accompanying jolt.

"What was that, Señor?"

"That was a powerful sound wave generated by *Varuna* that created a bubble of motionless water around the ship," I replied. Abruptly, the milieu stopped. The hum of electric engines was all that could be heard above heavy breathing.

Varuna is now beneath the wave, Master. You could taste relief in the uncirculated air.

"Where did *that* thing come from?" Kelly asked.

"A big earthquake somewhere," Viktor answered. "It's all happening just as the prophesies said."

"Hopi prophesy says Turtle Island could turn over two or three times and the oceans could join hands and meet in the sky," Stone Bear informed.

"The Hopi were obviously talking about a shift in the earth's magnetic poles and big tsunamis," Kelly observed.

"Yes, and that wave wasn't even a warm-up for what might be coming," I said. "We could be talking waves over a mile high."

"We may be parking in the street in Mexico City after all," Viktor said.

"Or on a mountain top," Madi cracked.

"The wave may weaken by the time it hits landfall, but the damage will still be substantial," I speculated.

"Señor, I have a friend in Mexico City. If I call her perhaps she could pick us up if and when the town is passable."

The next two hours dragged like a pot of water set to boil on low until Jinni finally gave us the news: we would arrive in fifteen minutes.

"Vik, here you go," I tossed him an untraceable phone.

"*Hola*, Maria? It's Viktor. Was there much damage? From what? The tsunami!" he replied to the voice on the other end.

"I see, well, my friends and I need a ride to Mexico City. Can you meet us at the Manzanilla Hotel at four o'clock? I will explain everything then. *Adios*."

"What did she say?" I asked.

"We have our ride."

"What about the tsunami?"

"She said it's a beautiful calm sunny day in Mexico City and Manzanilla Bay, Señor," he answered perplexed. "No word of any tsunami."

"That's impossible," I responded.

"Rogue waves can quickly lose strength," Viktor answered.

"Yes," I agreed as I read the USGS analysis, "but not a one hundred-foot tsunami driven by a 9.2 magnitude ocean quake."

Manzanilla

THE HAZY OUTLINE OF THE MEXICAN COAST finally came into view. As I sat on the edge of the sub with my feet skimming the cool water, a salty mist sprayed against my face. I blocked the center of the sun with my upraised hand. Suddenly, I felt a presence.

"You don't see it, do you?" a voice spoke. I turned to behold the saintly form of my beloved guru, just as it was at the Malibu retreat.

"Master!" I exclaimed. I touched his feet in reverence, the flesh warm and genuine as my own. "No, I don't see it," I replied.

"What do you think is happening?" he asked.

My heart began to swell as I basked in the bliss of my Christ-like teacher's presence. Again this immutable avatar cut through the dense matter fog of time and space to manifest by my side in the middle of the ocean.

I stared blissfully into his sky-mirroring eyes until he nodded to urge my response.

"I think the approaching planet is visible near the sun at times but not at others," I replied.

"And why do you think that is?" he asked.

"Master, you know my thoughts, why bother making me speak them at such a rare ecstatic moment?" I entreated. He raised his head skyward and chuckled.

"You're ruining the script!" he admonished.

I laughed and wiped a few tears of joy.

"We're phasing in and out of a dimensional rift," I answered. "In the old reality the rogue planet exists but in the new higher parallel one we're shifting to, it does not."

"Yes!" the Master responded. "Correct! You win the prize!" he exclaimed with feigned enthusiasm.

"Master, is it true? Am I the one named in the prophecies?" I asked earnestly.

"You? Ha!" he said barely controlling his mirth, "what did you tell your divine friends? *You, we,* do nothing. God is doing everything! Nothing can hinder your success so long as you acknowledge Divine Power within you as the doer!" I hung my eyes to reflect on the line he'd thrown my floundering soul. When I looked up he was hovering above the water waving as the craft slowly pulled away, his robe snapping rhythmically as it flapped like a flag in the wind.

"Master, wait, what are you doing?" I implored as I reached out to his death-defying form.

"Walking on water of course!" he answered. "In New York Harbor I would be arrested for performing miracles without a license!" He laughed uproariously as his resurrected body slowly dematerialized into thin air. I went below on a wave of joy. Faces gathered around the sea-cam were motionless with astonishment.

"What?" I asked the stunned faces. "You've never seen somebody walk on water before?" The supernatural stunt had stunned them into silence.

"Time to go to Mexico," I said as I clapped to revive them. "We can't risk the attention the submarine would draw, so we'll take the motorized raft to shore. Jinni will keep *Varuna* just below the surface off the coast until we return."

"How will we find her again?" Kelly asked.

"This GPS locator and controller on my wrist," I answered. The raft ejected from a compartment and began to inflate. We boarded and sped to shore as *Varuna* slipped slowly beneath the surface. When we arrived she was impatiently pacing the hotel lobby muttering zesty sentences in Spanish.

"Ah, there you are!" she said. "What took you so long?" Maria was a former colleague of Viktor's as a department secretary at the university. Middle-aged and diminutive in stature, she more than made up for her size with animated mannerisms.

"Maria, I'd like you to meet my friends..."

"What kind of trouble are you in now, Viktor? Eh?" she chided, shaking her finger as she held a nine or ten year old male child's hand. A dense ponytail of bleach-blonde hair whipped back and forth with her head as she rebuked him.

"Maria, there's no trouble, listen..." Viktor pleaded.

"Did he drag you poor people into one of his crazy adventures?" she cut in. "At the university they called him *Loco Jones*, always in trouble over some crazy quest," she went on in a spicy accent. "If you're smart you'll all go home to your families," she warned as she led us to her car. Viktor threw up his hands.

"Last time it was some crystal skull on federal land with no permit," she accused.

"But there was no time," Viktor defended. "The portal to the vortex was going to close and..."

"Blah, blah, see? It cost me a hundred-thousand pesos and a whole weekend to bail him and poor Oswaldo out."

"But I paid you back," he replied.

"Eh," she grunted and waved her hand and continued to complain in Spanish.

"Is Oswaldo your son, Maria?" I asked.

"Sí," she replied. "And he's as obsessed as him," she added pointing at Viktor.

"I think she was a New York cabby in a past life," Madi joked quietly as we bounced and jerked around in the vehicle.

"Is your son a professor as well?" I inquired.

"My Oswaldo?" she laughed bombastically. "They don't give college degrees to nine-year old boys."

I looked at Viktor astonished.

"Señor, he can tell you about every monument, all the history in every detail."

"You're here for the prophecy, aren't you?" The boy asked.

"What prophecy is that?" I asked.

"The Mayan prophecy," he answered. "People had it all wrong. Some thought the end of the world would come December 21, 2012. But the Mayans never said anything bad would happen," the boy elucidated.

"Are you a Hopi Indian?" he asked Stone Bear.

"Small brother knows his Indians," Stone Bear replied.

"The Hopi believe we just entered the fifth world just like the Mayans and that something bad could happen if people don't change," the boy added.

"Do you know what happened to the other three worlds, small brother?" Stone Bear quizzed.

"The first three were destroyed when people became bad and greedy. People in the third world lived on an island called Atlantis in the Atlantic Ocean, but it turned over because people became bad again," he replied.

"Who made the Mayan calendar, Oswaldo?" Kelly quizzed.

"Survivors of the third world made the calendar with help from space people to remind us to keep track of times when bad things could happen if we're not good," he answered. We were in awe of the miniature Mayan mystic.

"You've come to help save those who want to be good in the fifth world, haven't you?" the child asked me.

"Oswaldo, that is enough," Maria chided him.

"I think we just found the newest member of *supernatural friends*," Madi kidded. "We shall call him Prophecy Boy."

The child became quiet and stared intently at me.

"Mama, he is the man I saw on television with the *botellas*."

"Hey you *are* that guy," Maria said as she looked in the rear view mirror. "They said those bottles were a scam to spread some global computer virus," she added.

"That was a false story they put out," I replied.

"Who are *they*?" Maria asked.

"People who want to control the world after the shift."

"Shift? Ha! I should have known you came in on the same crazy train as him," she said tipping her head at Viktor.

"Now wait a minute lady..." Madi began.

"Madi, no," I said softly. "When you defend against an ignorant attack you lose energy; keep your center."

"She's gonna lose some of *her* energy when I'm through," she retorted.

"I am truly sorry, Señor," Viktor muttered.

"Maria, you seem very angry, why is that?" I asked.

"What do you know? It's none of your business anyway," she snapped.

"It is our business since we're all riding in this car with you."

"Well you can get out any time."

"Then I'll tell you what I know," I prefaced. "I know Viktor once loved you, and you him; and he is the father of this child." The vehicle went silent. "You want to blame every man for your alcoholic father who abused and left you when you were a little girl. Since then any man caught in your web is denied any satisfaction as you punish him for what your father did to you. How long must you go on hurting others for what you refuse to forgive?"

"That is outrageous! Viktor, did you tell him these lies?"

"I have said nothing."

"Uncle Viktor, are you really my papa?"

"I don't have to listen to this. You can all get out now!" Maria blasted. She pulled over and broke down sobbing. "I've never told anyone about my father. How do you know these things?" she cried.

"That's not important," I replied. "A few hours ago we witnessed a one-hundred foot tsunami that should have wiped out the coast, just disappear into thin air. We are on the brink of major destruction on this planet and billions could die."

"Why did you come here?" she implored.

"We were led here by an ancient relic belonging to Stone Bear and the Hopi tribe."

"I'll bet it's the Tiponi!" Oswaldo exclaimed. "Do you have it with you, can I see it?" the boy asked excitedly.

"Sorry bud, it's in our submarine," I replied.

"Cool! You have a submarine?"

"You have a submarine, but you couldn't rent a car?" Maria shot sarcastically.

"All our bank accounts have been frozen," Kelly answered. I handed her five one-hundred dollar bills.

"This is for your trouble."

"No, no, I cannot take your money. He who knows what I have never told a living soul is with either God or the devil. I will bet on God today. Where do you want to go, *Mistico*," she said in Spanish, "I will take you wherever you want."

"Let's ask the expert: Oswaldo, where to now?"

"Hmm," he considered carefully. The Temple of Kukulkan at Chichen Itza! He answered.

"Chichen Itza it is then!"

{ 21 }

Seventh Heaven

YUCATAN STARS SPARKLED DREAMLIKE between canopied rows of tropic treetops as if cut and pasted into the blackened Mexican sky. The distant forest glowed eerily as we neared the ruins at Chichen Itza. Colored park lights gave an otherworldly, almost alien luminosity. No visitors remained though the site was open to tourists at night.

I was drawn to El Castillo, the Temple of Kukulkan; the Mayan feathered serpent deity whose stone head adorns both sides of a giant staircase at the base of the majestic pyramid as it rises from the jungle floor nearly one hundred feet. Twice yearly the sun casts a shadow on the temple in the shape of a giant serpent's body that slithers down to join the head as our spherical source of power vanishes beneath the horizon in a miasma of roseate hues. Madi's eyes met mine in a beam of salutation to the magnificence of the incomparable reliquary. The imposing tomb of encoded celestial, mathematic and metaphysical knowledge seemed to defy time and space and transmit some sublime truth to our souls. We looked in awe at the matchless Meso-American megalith.

"Who will be the prophet to correctly interpret this book?" a man suddenly spoke as he sat on a nearby temple block.

"Will it be you, Señor?" he said as he smiled and gingerly hopped off the stone block.

"That's from the *Chilam Bilam*, the Mayan Book of Destiny."

"Correct Señor! *These things will be fulfilled and nobody will be able to stop them.* What do you think that means? "he asked.

"My name is Avery Cole," I extended my hand. We were now oddly alone beside the pyramid.

"Ah, yes, I am sorry, Señor, where are my manners; I am, *Julio*, Julio *Meciendo*, a caretaker here." He replied and smiled coyly as he rested his wiry figure on a broom I hadn't noticed earlier. He looked to be in his early forties, energetic, with curly black hair and big bright dark eyes.

"The Chilam was written long after these ruins were built," he said with his chin resting on his hands on the broom. "But the priests who wrote it seemed to understand that the calendar and the Mayan knowledge referred to cosmic cycles that exert an inescapable influence on the evolution of human consciousness," he added.

"And clues to their meaning are in great monuments such as these," I replied.

"Yes, it is a vast puzzle that requires clear vision to solve, perhaps like that possessed by you Señor? Eh?"

I was dubious of his stated identity, but played along. With my hand on the stone serpent head I gazed skyward to the sanctuary's apex.

"The first day of the Mayan calendar began where I'm standing," I said, "August 11th, 3114 BC. The last day was up there at the top on October 28, 2011. On that day a 5,125 year cycle of nine Mayan underworlds was completed."

"Yes, those underworlds are the nine levels of the pyramid's stones," he pointed out. "It is humbling that the entire human story of this edifice was played out for us in this time. What were they trying to tell us?" he asked.

"The early Mayans built this from what they were taught by extraterrestrials," I replied as I circled the head. "It contains sacred knowledge lost after the last destruction."

"Is it a warning?" he queried.

"A warning for the ignorant, an invitation for the aware; it describes our world's journey in the cosmos through *nine underworlds* and *thirteen heavens,*" I answered.

"Let's go," I said. He nodded.

We began climbing one of the pyramid's four massive staircases of ninety-one steps each.

"Each of the nine underworlds is tied to major events in human development," I explained. "We just entered the ninth step which calls humanity to identify with a universal or cosmic frame of consciousness."

"Nine is sacred in many cultures and religions," he pointed out as we continued ascending.

"Yes, the Hopis have *nine signs*, the Far East *nine pagodas*, the Jew's, *nine doors* to the inner temple, *Ramadan* is on the ninth month," I pointed out. "Nine is a universal seed cycle: Even the human birth cycle is nine months."

"And the thirteen heavens?" he asked. "Some believe thirteen is unlucky," he pointed out.

"Just dark forces trying to erase our good memory of sacred thirteen," I replied. "The Mayan *thirteen heavens* are a creation cycle of *seven days* and *six nights*. All events are constantly evolving to cycles of *seven, six* or *thirteen*."

"Ah, the heat of one Mayan day can feel like forever let alone seven," he said light-heartedly.

"The nights are not much relief either," I noted as beads of sweat bubbled on my forehead.

"The length of the days and nights differs depending on the size of the cycle," I continued. "Smaller progressions exist within the larger ones which can be billions of years. Yet the greatest accomplishments happen in *seven-numbered* heavens. Writing went from primitive stone etchings to the modern alphabet and the Internet in a seven-day," I explained. "So did the renaissance in enlightenment, science, religion and philosophy that began in 1755."

"Perhaps this is the source of the expression *seventh heaven*," he suggested.

"Yes, exactly, and we're in a *seven-day heaven in the ninth underworld in the thirteenth Mayan baktun right now*."

We stood at the top of the pyramid winded from the long ascent.

"We went from the serpent's mouth down on the first step in 3114 BC to the more benign end of the beast here on the ninth."

"Yet many believe in a coming Armageddon," he said.

"Darkness and light coexist in this world of relative duality," I replied. "Leaps forward always include the chance for equal steps back, but the Mayans aren't talking about the end of the world or time here, but a *time of no time*."

"Did that not begin December 21st, 2012?"

"Yes," I replied, "according to the long count calendar based on the solar zenith. But if we go by the Mayan's *thirteen heavens cycle* we get an end date of October 28, 2011," I answered.

"I see," he acknowledged. "One calculation is astronomical and the other tuned to the creation cycles."

"Correct," I replied. "The Hindus tell the same story in the *Vedas*," I added. "Our galaxy travels in a loop of eight phases or *Yugas* where we're either moving toward or away from a galactic center of spiritual power. On October 28, 2011 we began a twelve-thousand year precession toward our maximum quantum state where the cosmic vibration is highest. Time is speeding up because in reality all is an *eternal now*," I explained. "Through the Mayans our cosmic chaperones are telling us we've begun the journey home and through the coming shift we can make great progress."

"But not all will make the leap forward in this life," he posited.

"No, but all *can* choose," I answered. "Our destiny isn't predetermined or dependent on some blind religious acceptance or chance. Our past, our deeds, religion and culture are irrelevant. There will be no requirement other than recognizing the signs and acceptance of the *one invitation*."

"What are the signs?" he queried.

"To those ready they will be unmistakable; they have already begun," I answered.

"The Chilam speaks of *two priests,* does it not?" he asked.

"Yes, one is an emissary and the other brings a *world-uniting philosophy*. The Hopi call them True

White Brother, his *Helper* and the *knowledge of the stone tablets*," I replied. "The Mayan Chilam also speaks of the coming of *seven mountains, a red star* and the *wind swollen sky*."

"Yes, and what do you make of this, Señor?"

"I think the seven mountains represent the seven days and six nights of a Mayan thirteen heaven cycle."

I began to draw on a layer of red silt on the platform.

"See, the peaks are the days while the dips are nights."

"Ah! Yes, I see! Brilliant!" he exclaimed.

"The Mayan *red star* is the lost planet in its 3,600 year orbit around the sun," I disclosed. "The Hopi called it the *Red Purifier* and said it would come seven years after the *Blue Kachina*, which some say was Hale-Bopp comet."

"And the wind swollen sky is the bad weather, comets and earthquakes, which we are experiencing now," he offered.

"Precisely," I replied.

"Truly insightful Señor, but Hale-Bopp passed in 1997, so the Hopi purifier should have come in 2004," he keenly observed.

"The Hopi said the prophecy was put off ten years because we had changed somewhat," I replied. "It's been ten years now."

"The prophecies are the same almost word for word, Señor!"

"The star people left clues with everyone, Julio, the Mayans, Hopi and all the surviving cultures of the third world. That's why legends are all so similar and talk about sky gods that brought great knowledge. "This monument," I continued, "is a time capsule of a message of hope and a rare opportunity that comes once every 24,000 years."

"And the invitation you spoke of?" he asked.

"You're very inquisitive for a simple caretaker," I remarked suspiciously.

"Things are not always as they seem, are they?" he replied.

I chuckled and continued.

"I don't know how this will look in the end," I said, "but our response now will decide the world each of us will live in: one of devastation, hardship, death, or life on a new higher vibrational version of earth as the divinely powerful beings we truly are," I added.

"Well, Señor, you have proven to me you *can* interpret the Book of Destiny correctly."

"Perhaps," I replied modestly. "My friends and I seem to have been recruited for an important job that requires it."

"Hmm, yes," he said and smiled warmly. "Well, you better look at your watch, we have been talking a long time and your friends are probably wondering where you are."

"It's 11:11!" I observed.

"Indeed it is, and you will find what you are looking for behind the thirteenth step within the temple," he said.

I heard a voice and turned.

"Avy-ji, there you are!" Viktor called as he walked briskly toward me. "We've been looking all over for you Señor,"

"Where did you go?" Madi interrogated, fake bro-hitting me.

"Nowhere; I was just talking to Julio over here."

"Who?" Madi asked.

"There was a guy, Julio, Julio Meciendo, a caretaker; he was just standing here a few seconds ago. We talked about the whole Mayan thing."

"The *whole* Mayan thing Señor?"

"We spoke for probably a half-hour and climbed to the top of the pyramid."

"Uh, we've been looking for you for about three minutes," Madi said. "A half-hour and I would have called the policia."

"His name was Meciendo?" Viktor asked. "That is uncommon for a Spanish name; it means *rocking* and it is a beautiful poem by *Gabriella Mistral*. It's about how the Mother Spirit is invisibly comforting us through forces in nature."

A powerful wind erupted in a whirling funnel of leaves, twigs and loose sand then inexplicably subsided at our feet.

"We have to go to the thirteenth step inside the pyramid—now!" I announced.

22

Time in a Bottle

HERE IT IS," I SAID, AS I JOSTLED ANOTHER stone off the stair. "Nothing but more stone and mortar," I added. The ancient cement crumbled like brittle dirt in my hand. Viktor put his palm on my forehead.

"Vik, what are you doing?"

"Checking for jungle fever," he replied.

"I don't have jungle fever; I didn't imagine this."

"Are you certain this Julio said it was behind the thirteenth stair?" he asked.

"Maybe he really meant *behind*," Madi suggested, "like a secret passage behind the staircase."

"I think there is one!" Oswaldo blurted out and excitedly led us down the stairs to an adjacent room. To our dismay, the wood-planked door was well chained.

"It's locked," Kelly said.

Madi shined her light on a loose stone that nearly tripped her at the doorway. "Look, someone left the key under the mat!" she said and picked it up. As the door opened, high-pitched screams erupted as a black flapping squadron of bats streamed out the door.

"Jesus, I think I just peed a little," Madi confessed playfully.

"Over there," I said as I shined the light. "That wall looks like the back of the staircase; count up thirteen blocks."

"It's too high," Madi said. "How do we get up there, levitate?"

"Sí, this is the Mayan Chamber of Levitation!" Oswaldo exclaimed.

"It's true, Señor!" Viktor confirmed. "Legends say priests would come here at solstice and make a sacrifice, but the levitation thing is just a myth, unproven."

"Today is the December solstice, so let's try it," I said. I sat on the stone floor in the lotus position, turned my eyes up and concentrated on the Christ Eye between my eyebrows.

"Through the power of Infinite Mind present in me," I spoke, "I am tuning my consciousness to the frequencies converging in this room," I affirmed and became motionless.

"This is nonsense, people can't fly," Maria said and waved dismissively. "Sweet Jesus!" she gasped as I suddenly rose a few Newtonian-violating inches, though I quickly returned.

"I'm sorry, I can't seem to go any higher," I said.

"If I had not seen it with my own eyes I would not believe you rose a centimeter!" Maria said, aghast.

"There's an inscription on the wall," Viktor said.

"Let me see it Uncle Viktor!"

"Maybe you call me *papa* now, eh?"

"Okay--Papa," the boy gleamed.

The not-yet pre-teen prodigy fluent in Mayan petroglyphs read with the syntax of a typical nine-year-old: "It says when the seven sisters are...um...seen...in the chamber...the innocent...can fly!"

"That's my boy!" Viktor chirped approvingly.

"Gotta be an opening somewhere," I said as I waved my flashlight and rubbed my hand along the walls.

"If Oswaldo is right the Seven Sisters of the Pleiades star system should be visible in the northern sky. "Ah ha, here it is!" I exclaimed and put my eye to the peephole.

"The girls are all here!" I declared.

"What's the big deal about these stars?" Maria asked.

"The Mayans say their ancestors came from them," I answered.

"Sí', the Hopi, Mayans and the Egyptians, all of them," Viktor concurred. "The Pyramids of Giza and even Hopi villages in Arizona are all aligned with this star cluster."

"How'd you do that?" Maria asked confidentially as she elbowed me, "Some kind of trick, eh?—you can tell me."

"No trick. Pyramids tap into cosmic energy signatures," I replied. "Certain alignments can magnify energy and bend or suspend ordinary laws of physics," I answered. "This pyramid is tuned to a high frequency energy coming from those stars."

"But it said only the *innocent* can fly," Maria interposed.

"That counts me out," Madi joked.

"Not my sweet Oswaldo," Maria said as she pinched his cheek.

"That's it!" Viktor exclaimed. "The innocent is *a child*. There must be a weight limit in the vortex!"

"Oswaldo, are you ready to get your wings?" I asked him.

"No, my baby's not going up there!" Maria objected strenuously and waved her finger.

"Mama, it's okay; I can do this!" Maria reluctantly agreed.

"Oswaldo, clear your mind and pretend you are light as a feather, and floating," I instructed. "If your mind wanders, bring it back to focus until it obeys. Everyone concentrate on him rising up; think of nothing else!"

Startlingly, the boy began to climb.

"Be careful, my darling!" Maria cried out.

"A chip off the old pyramid block, eh?" Viktor cackled gazing at him proudly.

"I'm flying!" Astonishment lit his face.

"If these ceremonies were successful," Viktor spoke quietly, "the Mayans would sacrifice the poor thing in the *Cenote*."

"Reach where I'm shining the light," I told him. "Is there a loose stone there?"

"Sí'," the boy answered.

"Pull on it," I said.

The capstone crumbled to the ground.

"There's something inside," the boy said.

"Take it out carefully," I told him.

With his fingertips just inches away, he began to drop. "Concentrate, up, up, everybody, now!" I redirected. Again, he started to rise and grasped the package. Gently, he descended with the claim and Oswaldo handed me the prize. As I peeled away the yellowed newspaper wrapped around the base, I was astonished by what I saw.

"My god," Madi cried. "Is that what I think it is?"

"Unbelievable!" I replied and revealed the markings. "It's the sixth bottle!"

"How did that get here?" she asked in shock.

"It looks like it's been here for years," I said.

"Open it, Señor!" Viktor said. I removed the cap.

"The original USB drive is here--with a note!" I informed, as I unrolled the hand-written letter and began to read:

Good Tidings,

As I studied these ruins late one night I found myself in the presence of beings of an apparent higher realm: a council of guardians, as they called themselves.

I was given this flask and instructed to leave it in this exact spot for reasons unknown to me, yet, they said, completely understood by you, the intended recipients of some distant future.

I now dictate as they spoke to me telepathically:

By Divine Decree we now reveal the full and true meaning of the Mayan calendar and 11:11:

The keys are in the dates August 11, 3114 BC: the beginning of the Mayan calendar, and October 28, 2011, the end:

August is the eight, infinity, no beginning or end. Eight is the numeric value of the name of Jesus--a great spiritual overseer of this earth cycle and with us now. August 11 is the day the fourth world began in 3114 BC, and the day the universe was created 15 billion years ago. The year 3114 reveals the cycle:

Three symbolizes the third world, which ended with Atlantis, and four represents the fourth world you have just exited. The total is seven, the master number of ascension. Eleven, the bridge, is between them, 3-11-4, as ten completes and one begins.

The date October 28, 2011 is the end of the Mayan creation calendar; it ended the fourth world and a 5,125 year Mayan Ka'tun begun in 3114 BC--and began the fifth world: the 13th Ka'tun and gateway to the coming shift. Here is the key code for October 28 (10-28): 1+0+2+8=11, taken with the 11 in the year 2011 gives us 11:11! The year 2011 is the rest: 2+0+11=13!

The Mayan calendar beginning date of August 11, 3114 BC and end date of October 28, 2011 represents the cosmic signal now being sent to those aware: It is 11:11, the beginning of the FIFTH WORLD on a seventh day in a thirteenth heaven!

Awaken those who choose Light!

For millennia, one purpose of our contact with humanity has been DNA alteration in preparation for this epic event. Many have received re-engineered genes through direct placement and heredity. The DNA upgrade will allow your physical bodies to endure the high frequency spiritual energy of the shift. 11:11 is also a sacred visual numeric trigger code to activate these hidden genes in those prepared to make the transition to the new dimensional version of earth.

The time of fulfillment and reason you came is at hand!

You will find the solution to your most pressing dilemma on the enclosed information storage device.

Godspeed.
Signed,
MKJ

The time-transcendent holy numbers revealed in their divinely ordered context had a marked effect. A wave of euphoria came over us. Madi was first to recover and spoke.

"This newspaper wrapping is dated June 2nd, 1954," she said.

"Who is MKJ?" Kelly asked.

"Some archeologist or researcher maybe," Viktor answered.

"Wait, MKJ is *Morris Ketchum Jessup!*" I recalled. "He was a scientist and astronomer who worked for the government in the 1940's...you know the name, Vik?"

"Sí, he went to the Amazon to look for rubber trees for the USDA after the war and found this place," he replied. "Wasn't he one of the first to suggest the ET connection with the ancients?"

"Yes; I read about his theories on ET-supplied levitation technology used in building the pyramids," I confirmed. "Appears he got too close to the truth and turned up dead." I removed the USB drive from the bottle and held the tiny time voyager between my thumb and index finger.

"This thing traveled over a hundred-fifty years back and forth through time," I said.

"Now that's what I call a real genie in a bottle!" Viktor said.

"I think we know what our next move is," I said.

"Sí, Señor."

23

Jinni Gets Sick

MADI AND I TOOK THE RAFT while the others stayed at the hotel. *Varuna* surfaced in the expected location. We boarded the ship and went straight to the computer and inserted the USB.

"These install files weren't on this USB before," I disclosed.

"What are they for?" she asked.

"I'm not sure, but the algorithms look insane. The folder is named LARRI."

"Meaning?" she asked as I opened the folder.

"Apparently an acronym for *Laser Array Internet System*. If this is for real it's fifty times faster than anything out there, Madi."

"It's got the NASA thingy on it," she observed.

"We're definitely not supposed to have this; there's access codes and everything."

"Didn't NASA test this from the moon?" she asked.

"The official line was that it was a *communications experiment for future planetary explorations*," I answered.

"We haven't set foot on another world for over thirty years, and suddenly they're thinking about Internet on the moon?" she asked.

"It's about bases, Madi. Everything they need to start over is stockpiled there and they'll have LARRI while everyone else is in an information blackout."

"So if we hook Jinni up to LARRI they can't disconnect us without disconnecting themselves?"

"Right, they can't single out individual users, but they can still shut all regular Internet down," I answered.

"There'd be anarchy."

"Exactly," I replied.

I clicked *install.*

"Call Yvette in L.A. and see if the software's ready. I'll calibrate the laser with these coordinates."

"What software? You met with her?"

"Yeah."

"You didn't tell me that," she said irritably.

"The two of you seemed to have this weird friction. I thought it better you didn't get involved."

"What did she want?" she asked with her arms crossed, defensively.

"$50,000 and a date or $200,000 and a thank you."

"Oh?—and which did you choose?"

"The date, of course!"

"What?" she replied incensed.

"I'm just kidding, Madi. It was a lot of money, that's all I can say. Here, use this phone and call her."

"Hey, it's me...uh huh, yeah, fine. Oh nothing, submarines, tsunamis, Mayan temples, levitation chambers, time travel, code cracking, *hitting on my BF*, and you?"

"Why don't you just call the CIA," I said. "Gimme that!"

I grabbed the phone.

"Hey that hurt!" she said.

"Yvette? Sorry, blabber-mouth and I have been a little busy."

"That's not very nice," Madi mumbled.

"Is it ready? I'll send a secure upload packet. Yeah, I know where to send the money, sweetheart, bye."

"Seriously, did she hit on you?"

"Look at me," I said pointing two fingers at my eyes. "At what point have I come across to you as someone who is hittable? Please, Madi, I need your head in this all the way right now!"

"Why are you so uppity all of a sudden?"

"I'm not trying to be," I answered.

"You act like millions of people depend on your every move."

"Thanks, I feel less pressure now."

"You're welcome," she replied.

"What's wrong? You're like totally PMS'ing," I said.

"No I'm not, and nothing."

"Nothing?"

"Yeah, nothing...that's just the thing."

"What's *the thing*?"

"Oh, forget it," she answered.

"Don't do that *its code for something female* thing."

"I'm not."

"Yes, you are."

"Okay, then you know what?"

"What?" I asked.

"That's it," she said.

"Okay," I snapped back.

"I love you! There, I said it: I LOVE *you*, Avery Cole." I was caught like a deer in the headlights.

"I'm sorry for that," she said as her voice broke up.

"Sorry for what?"

"You know, dropping the L-word during a global crisis; breaks focus, you know."

"I'm with you, here, Madi," I said and gently touched her near her heart.

"What does *I'm with you here* mean, specifically?"

"Well, I..."

"And don't do that *code for something guy* thing," she mocked.

I paused pregnant.

"You can't say it, can you?" she taunted me.

I held her jaw tenderly and kissed her tear-moistened lips.

"It means *I love you too.*"

Tears came out full spigot.

"Hey, I thought that would be good news," I said.

"It is...it's just that I've lost almost everyone I love...and I don't want to put this out there and lose you too."

"You can't lose me or anyone, and you never will," I reassured her. "Love has no expiration date, Madi."

Her face softened with a sweet smile, and she looked down at her tissue-filled hands.

"Connection successful, yes!" I pumped my fist. "And here's the new software from the home wrecker."

"Lemme see." She dabbed her eyes, grabbed the mouse and opened the files we received from Yvette.

"God, that bitch knows how to slice and dice."

"Is it good?" I asked.

"Good? It's amazing! She took the interactive portal you created for Jinni, turned it into a killer app and positioned it to infect the web on every level."

"Now what?" I asked.

"Push the button," she replied. "The whole world wants a genie in a bottle. Let's give them one!

"Double selfie first," she said. A synthetic click and a flash captured the moment for posterity.

"It's so weird," she said. "This could be in the history books with the Fall of Rome, or the end of the Cold War, or something."

"Bigger than that," I said.

"Bigger than Jesus Christ?"

"Bigger than the Beatles, Madi."

"I keep thinking this is a dream and I'm gonna wake up."

"It is and you *are*."

"You better still be here when I do," she replied.

"Careful, you're calling out karma."

"I can't hold on to you, can I?"

"No more than a snake can keep its skin."

She yawned. "Just shut up and take me to bed then."

{ 24 }

A Revelation

SET YOUR COFFEE CUP DOWN NEAR THAT BOX of incense," I said.

"Why?"

"Try it. Give it a few seconds then sip," I replied.

"Hmm, tastes like Nag Champa," she said.

"Scent molecules literally jump on the cup. Cool, eh?" I asked.

"Is this my morning lesson, Guruji?"

"I guess I'm just fascinated by things most people don't care about," I answered.

"That's why you got this job," she replied. "—and it's not that I don't care. I've just got a one and fifteen rule."

"And that is?" I asked. Scantily clad in thong and a tee shirt she folded her legs up on the chair, clasped her warm mug and sipped.

"I don't talk politics, religion or chemistry until I've had one cup of coffee and fifteen minutes have passed."

"Ah, but you must remove all conditions to joy, child," I toyed.

"I could just drink my joy if you'd be quiet," she retorted.

"Everything you need to make endless cups of joy is already in the brewer of your own consciousnesses," I came back in a playful Indian accent.

"You're just relentlessly perky," she said.

"No, I just had two cups in sixty before you got out of bed."

"Hey, check this out," she said, suddenly transfixed by something on the computer screen.

"What?" I asked.

"I am happy to inform, you are the proud papa of a growing Internet sensation: Jinni's app has 760,000 downloads! Look at all these comments," she added, incredulously.

Don't know how or why it works, but this app changed my life overnight, hope is in my dreams again.

Jinni gave me the courage to leave an abusive relationship last night and quit my crummy job today.

"Oh, look at this one—just makes heresy so fun," she poked.

2 John 1:7 Jinni is the Anti-Christ!

"Here's a good one, Madi..."

Given up online porn...for tonight, big step for me. Jinni's hot!

"Jinni does sex therapy?" she smiled.

"Better than anyone."

"So tell me...how did you do it?"

"Do what?" I answered.

"Write this program; you're not that good, nobody is."

"I didn't; it was pretty much all there. I just had to learn how to hook it up."

"That took twenty-plus years?"

"When's the last time you installed an alien hard drive? Anyway, technology didn't make it possible until the last ten years."

"So what was inside?"

"I don't know; I couldn't open it; that's another reason it took so long. I had to use a magnetic transfer interface and..."

"What? Why are you looking at me like that?" she asked.

"Please, put some clothes on Madi."

"You don't like what you see? You didn't seem to mind last night," she jibed, as she sipped her Joe in her skimpy skivvies.

"I'm trying to focus on *prophecy* here," I came back.

"Oh, okay sweetie pie, I get it; I'll cover my nice white tush for you--all cracks covered now, happy?" she teased.

"Ugh," I slapped my forehead. "Let's get going," I said. "We need to go back to the hotel and update the crew." We got dressed, resurfaced Varuna, and shuttled back to the beach in the raft.

"Avy-ji, over here!" Viktor shouted from the pool. "Señor, what did you find out?"

"We're on a secure network, Vik; Jinni is out of the bottle!"

"Magnifico!" he cheered.

Something on big screen at the bar caught my eye.

"Be right back," I said.

Strange weather continues with summer snow in Ecuadorian lowlands--the first ever recorded in the region. In South Texas roughnecks clear the white stuff from oilrigs, while Nome, Alaska—where the average temperature is 27 degrees--hit a record 72 degrees today. In unrelated stories, another large asteroid is due to pass within a hundred thousand miles of earth tomorrow, while earthquakes are still on the rise globally. Reports of strange lights in the skies over the Great Lakes have surged. NASA, however, denies any testing in the area. The White House has announced a press conference at noon to address growing anxiety over abnormal climate and geophysical activity but insists there is no reason to panic.

"Right," I murmured. "No reason to panic."

Madi came up and put her arm around me playfully. "What's up?"

"It's snowing in Texas, seventy-two in Alaska, and we're being buzzed by another huge asteroid tomorrow," I replied. "The White House will downplay everything of course."

"Excuse me folks...may I have a moment of your time?" a strange soft-spoken man asked.

"I'd like to leave you some literature."

I recognized the title of the publication *Alert!*

"Jehovah's Witness," Madi whispered behind her hand.

"I'm sorry sir," she replied politely. "We're not interested. The end *is* coming and if you really want to survive download a new app called Jinni--and you'll remember this day."

He ignored her statement with a steady medicated smile.

"May I see that, please?" I asked. I read the title aloud.

The Storage Capacity of DNA--Intelligently Designed? Thank you," I said and he smiled and walked away.

"Wow, he's drinking the Kool-Aid," she said. "I'm the one who sounded like the nut and he didn't even blink."

"Did you know DNA can store data?" I asked. "Says here--scientists have put text, images and audio files on DNA with a hundred percent recovery. They claim

just a few grams can store the entire world's digital data for thousands of years."

Madi's obnoxious ringtone sounded again.

"Another Jinni-fication," she informed. "Oh my god,
Avery, we just hit 4,000,000 downloads!"

"That's almost five times an hour ago!" I rallied.

"It's hard to predict peaks and stalls," she qualified.
"I'll have to study the metrics, but I've never seen anything blow up this fast: Jinni is officially *sick!* I need to
throw a little content up here on these discussions," she
added and began keying enthusiastically. Suddenly, her
hurricane-like typing spree was halted by another notice. "We just got a strange e-mail," she broke in.

"From?" I asked.

"Someone who claims to be in a high place with information critical to our current situation," she said.
"Probably another whack job."

"We have to take every encounter seriously now," I
advised.

"He's requesting a video chat," she said. "He'll let us
know the time and place, but it's *beyond urgent*, he
says." She continued her typing bender.

Encased in a concrete and steel cage six feet thick,
the chamber was known only to a privileged few. Low
voices murmured as they gathered in the library. A few
words were spoken in Latin and all became silent. Suddenly, the book-filled wall began to retract. The procession filed in. Each man sat in his place at the ornate

wooden table. The limb of a dogwood tree encased in the glass center was said to be from the tree used to make the cross that crucified Jesus Christ.

"You all know the unique and dire circumstance under which such a gathering would be called," one spoke. "I call your attention to the screen." A presentation began to play on a large monitor, while a younger red-robed attendee fiddled impatiently with his smart phone.

The man in a vestment of red, white and gold spoke. "Signs are clear and we must now take steps to ensure the survival of the Ecclesia of Peter," he added.

"But, your Excellency, silence could cost the lives of millions," the Cardinal spoke out as he tucked his device away in his garment. "If we at least tell what is known, perhaps some will have time to prepare," he entreated.

"It could trigger global panic," he responded. "Sacrifices must be made in the name of preservation of the Church!" he proclaimed.

"The Church?" the younger answered incredulously. "You have all grown comfortable in the business of God, interested in preserving only that which you sit upon in your chairs!"

"Silence!--That is quite enough!" a senior bishop scolded.

"No, perhaps he is right," the elder said dolefully.

"Our doctrine emerged from a time of great darkness and upheaval hundreds of years after our Master lived and perished. How many truly believe every word?

Scholars have fought for centuries over interpretation. Of fifty known gospels only four were deemed worthy, but worthy of whom?--Kings of men, some criminals perhaps, but imperfect to say the least. For better or worse we have inherited that legacy."

"Your Excellency, please!" the bishop objected.

"Surely our Lord *is* in my heart, yet man's fingerprints stain the pages of history...we have been blind too long."

The room was silent. Few dared even to breathe.

"I am truly moved by your heartfelt confession, Your Excellency, but we must change our position while there is still time," the bold young Cardinal replied.

"No, my son, it won't change anything. I am not the real power here--just an old priest too tired to fight anymore."

"You are all cowards!" the Cardinal accused, as he jumped to his feet and stormed out

"It's all right. Let him go. The fool won't last the night if he keeps talking," the Pontiff uttered. "Yet he is a brave fool."

"Madi, is that a bible?" I asked as we sat by the pool.

"Yeah, a nasty habit I picked up at Catholic school."

"What chapter are you reading?"

"Revelations," she answered. "I must have read it fifty times; it doesn't make any more sense now than it did the first time," she said and set it aside, open. I picked it up.

"That's because you can't take it literally; it's symbolic," I said. "It's about a vision *John* had while in *samadhi.*"

"In what?"

"Samadhi; *Yochanan* was in a super-conscious state of God contact when he heard the *great voice like a trumpet* behind his head."

"Who?" she asked.

"Yochanan; it means *John* in Hebrew. The voices he talks about are subtle sounds that come from the cerebrospinal centers in deep meditation. A trumpet sound is often heard before you hear *Om,* the sound of the cosmic motor, the *Amen,* or the *Holy Spirit.* Some will hear knocking instead of a trumpet; it's in Matthew 7:7...*knock and the door shall be opened.* The door is the Christ Eye in the forehead, opposite the medulla in back of the skull. "Samadhi is also called the *minideath,*" I explained. "Saint Paul alluded to it when he said *I die daily.* He was talking about consciously leaving the body as in death and going into superconscious ecstasy through meditation on Om and the Christ Eye. *Therefore if thine eye be single thy whole body shall be full of light...*see," I quoted, as I tapped my finger on the page.

"Sounds like that pipe thingy meditation you described earlier," she noted.

"It is," I replied. "When you see the eye...a great light in the forehead...a circle of gold and five-pointed white star in a center of blue--then you have attained Christ Consciousness."

"What do the *seven candlesticks* represent?" she inquired.

"Ah, yes, the Bible says John looked *behind* him and saw them. Why from behind and not in front? Because he meant the seven activated energy centers in the spinal stargate--the chakras. In their astral colors they resemble the seven candles on a menorah."

"But it also says the seven candlesticks are the *seven churches*," she pointed out.

"The chakras are vessels of Divine energy manifest in the spine," I explained. "So, in a sense they are churches or *houses of God*. One worships, or *meditates* on them to release their energy upward through the spine, up the body temple to contact God."

"And the spine is like a steeple?"

"Hmm, another mystical symbol, good catch!" I told her.

"And the *mystery of the seven stars*?" she inquired.

"Of course, the seven stars are the constellation of Pleiades, home of our star brethren who brought the Great Knowledge long ago."

"But the Bible warns not to add or take away any-thing; you're seriously editorializing here."

"It's all editing and interpretation, but deeply sym-bolic," I replied. "John cautions any person who *hears* the words not to *change* them, yet he talks about there being a mystery to solve. Can you solve a puzzle with-out rearranging the pieces? No, the word *hear* implies a hidden meaning...a very specific message...gotta read between the lines on this, Madi."

"So, if the manual on samadhi, the sacred pipe, or whatever, was stashed in India with the tablet you took there in a past life, where did the apostle John learn it?"

"From Jesus, of course," I answered, "who learned it in India during the eighteen years of his life missing in the New Testament."

"Fundamentalists would argue Jesus didn't have to learn anything and that his power was complete from the get-go," she countered.

"Then why was it written Jesus *advanced in wisdom* if he was already a finished product? Where did this so-called advancement happen? Not in Palestine because he wasn't there. Temple records in India talk about it--*Saint Issa*--who studied under the spiritual masters of India. Issa *was* Jesus."

"I read about that guy once. He said monks showed him those records, but when they went back to verify his claims, the monks took the fifth," she rejoined.

"What would you do?" I asked. "Invite foreign invasion by asserting a key religious belief of the most powerful nations on the planet is a lie? Besides, others saw the scrolls. Evidence even suggests Jesus survived the crucifixion and passed on years later when he went into *nirbikalpa* samadhi, where the body goes into total metabolic suspension--and one only appears dead."

"If it wasn't you talking, I'd consider calling an exorcist," she teased.

"The facts are there for those who are open," I replied. "Holy men of India have been buried for years, dug up and awakened without aging so much as a second. In nirbikalpa samadhi--the highest level of meditation--Jesus' heart would beat so slowly it wouldn't be noticed. He would have been thought dead, placed in the tomb and re-awakened three days later."

"Don't the Mormons believe Jesus visited America after the resurrection?"

"Yes, American Indians have legends too," I agreed. "It's also widely believed in India that Jesus the man died and was buried in Kashmir years after the resurrection, so go figure."

"You would've been burned at the stake back in the day for even thinking that."

"Right, so why would anyone totally buy into anything written in that period under that kind of repression?" I replied.

"But why didn't Jesus just teach this stuff to everyone? I mean, why all the cryptic stuff?" she probed.

"A great salesman knows his audience. Jesus was much more than a salesman, of course; he was a supreme God-realized master. He knew the period, the future and how his words would be received and manipulated. Remember, we were in a low cosmic cycle and most were unable to grasp the sublime. Jesus taught humanity only what they were ready to accept."

"So he watered down the holy water?" she joshed.

"Jesus taught his most advanced disciples openly, but knew any esoteric teaching that would give ordinary people such power, mastery of the elements, miracles, power over life and death, well, that would be removed from any published doctrine. Why do you think so much was banned from the New Testament?" I asked. "If people thought they could attain what Jesus had that would make them equal to Him, and being equal to Jesus would make them equal to the Church...Not the way things were run back then."

"That's going to make some devout very unhappy," she noted.

"It doesn't diminish Jesus," I replied. "Just by tuning in with a great master a person advances and receives protection and guidance, but it's not the keys to the kingdom, no, not like they think. The Bible says rewards go to *him that overcomes*. That doesn't mean just accept he died for your sins, go to church, try to be good and when you die you're there. No, you must *overcome* the world, *master* the mind and body, transcend matter-based ego consciousness using the *Sanataan Dharma*, or the *eternal religion* that predates humanity itself, and attain supreme realization, *yoga* or union with God through scientific, Cosmic spiritual Law; then you have heaven on earth *and* hereafter."

"Is anything said about the other prophecies?"

"Chapter Eight mentions *Wormwood*, a star; it means *curse.*"

"Could that be Nibiru?" she asked.

"It's mentioned in the Hebrew bible seven times, any coincidence?" I asked. "Then there's the *red dragon* and *seven heads.* Could the red dragon be the debris tail of Nibiru stirring up the asteroid belt?" I continued. "Could the seven heads be the Mayan seven mountains and the seven-day heaven we're in now?"

"Sure seems worth looking into," she agreed.

"But wait there's more!" I said mocking the infomercial spiel. "In the banned Gnostic Gospel of Thomas it says: *He who seeks me will find me in children from seven years old; for there concealed, I shall in the fourteenth age be made manifest.*"

"Meaning?" she inquired.

"Let's take out our Mayan codebook. Do we actually find Christ concealed in a seven-year old child? Of course not; the word *children* means youthful and open, *childlike.* What we find is the Christ *Consciousness* in a

Mayan seven-day in the fourteenth age, or 14th Mayan baktun, a smaller cycle of 394 years...that just began!"

"Amazing!" she said flabbergasted. "How did you figure this stuff out?" she asked.

"The credit belongs to Jinni, Madi. Scriptures and sacred writings are ciphers; it's embedded everywhere and what I gave you is just the tip of the iceberg."

"Who or what coordinated all this?—a secret society, a big conspiracy? How did the code get there?" she asked.

"How?" I asked with a raised eyebrow.

"Okay, I guess that was a stupid question. I have a better one: Who are the people with *666* in their heads?" she asked.

"Their heads aren't actually numbered," I answered. "The number six symbolizes their material vibration and narrow vision that will prevent them from making the shift."

"So it doesn't mean evil or the devil?"

"No, most 666'ers are just fence-sitters, those not here for ultimate truth or maximum growth; they don't burn for the answer to the absolute definitive mystery, or they're stuck in a limited version of it."

"But why *three* sixes?" she asked.

"Those are the three lower dimensions of *time, space* and *matter* that 666'ers identify with. Advanced truth-seekers, on the other hand, work in *mind, body and spirit* to harmonize contrasting forces and expand, symbolized by 777.

"John gives us the clues, Madi: With *seven stars* he tells us the shift involves star brother from the Pleiades. The *seven candlesticks* are the chakras, and to ascend we must meditate or *worship* in the *seven churches* using the sacred method. Those who practice this method—of the Sacred Pipe--have the *seal of God in their forehead*, the light of the Christ, or third eye, and they make the shift."

"Does that open the *seventh seal?*" she asked.

"Yes, it activates the light of the seventh chakra in the crown of the head--the *thousand-pedaled lotus*-- once the other six candles are lit through sacred meditation. Then we are *one* with the Father and need not *go out*, suffer *second death*, or reincarnate into another physical body; we are eternally free."

She was speechless.

"And here's the kicker, Madi: The letters to the seven churches in Revelations talk about *two witnesses*. Scholars can't agree what they represent, but they're also called *two olive trees*, *two lamp stands* and *two prophets killed* then *resurrected*."

"Benevolent beings or forces, maybe?" she asked.

"More likely a very specific encoded message: Have you ever noticed how the revolving trunk of an olive tree resembles the twist of a strand of DNA? Or how the 1111 number sequence looks like the four ladder-like steps in a loop of DNA? *Killed* and *resurrected* doesn't mean physically, Madi; it means the deactivation or *death* of our old DNA and the activation or *resurrection* of our new DNA in preparation for the shift!"

"How many times can a person say *whoa, amazing, incredible, spectacular,* before they sound like a complete idiot?"

"I've got one more brain blender for you," I responded.

"The silver bullet?" she asked.

"Indeed it is; Revelations has twenty-two chapters, right? What is twenty-two divided by two?"

"Ugh! What's the use of answering anymore?" she succumbed.

"I guess it would be overkill to tell you what chapter these so-called witnesses are *killed* and *raised* in, wouldn't it?"

"I'll humor you," she replied. "Eleven."

"Bull's-eye!" I answered.

"The bottom line is," I said as I handed the ventilated good book back to her while she sat in a pool of cool drool, "In Revelations, Madi, Yochanan is literally handing us the spiritual key codes to the mother ship of post-shift earth!"

Another ringtone went off.

"We just got that chat request, twenty minutes," she said.

"Confirm it and let's go get a room," I replied.

"Yee haw, Lone Ranger," she said as she twirled her invisible lasso.

{ 25 }

Prophetiae de Septum Utres

NOTHING SAYS VACATION LIKE HOTEL SHEETS," I said and collapsed on the comfy air condition-chilled bed.

"You like strange hotels?" Madi asked playfully. Suddenly, the tablet began to vibrate noisily on the dresser.

"Screen name's the *Librarian*," she said as she retrieved it. "It's from--no way--the Vatican!"

I flung off the sheets.

"Bonjour, Monsieur Avery Cole?"

"Yes...who are you?"

"I should not say my name."

"I recognize that face," Madi said.

Her finger went into search overtime.

"How may I help you?" I asked.

"It is I who wish to help *you*."

"Your name is *The Librarian*. What books do you keep?"

"Those men would kill for. Surely I will be killed for the one I am about to give you," he replied.

"What is this book you would die for?"

"It is a great secret, Monsieur."

"Why share it with us?"

"I believe your technology is named in it," he replied.

"If true your life *is* in danger," I warned.

"If true*?"* he laughed. "I am the administrator of the Library of Secret Archives. I am *Cardinal De La Montreaux.* In light of recent events I must take action now by contacting you directly. I would not do so if there were any doubt."

"Is this another *Fatima* secret?"

"Fatima is a nursery rhyme in comparison," he replied. "In the Book of Revelations there is a chapter, ten."

"Verse?" I asked.

"Four," he answered. "*I heard a voice from heaven saying unto me, seal up those things which the seven thunders uttered, and write them not,*" he recited.

"I know the verse."

"There is a prophecy," he went on, "a lost document which has been locked in an obscure vault for centuries. It is called *Prophetiae de Septum Utres.*"

"My Latin's non-existent...is that *seven utterances?*" Madi asked.

"No," I answered.

"John wrote what he heard," His Holiness said, "but it was not by *uttered* by seven *thunders*. What he experienced in the divine vision was altered at Nicaea in the fourth century."

The *First Council of Nicaea* was assembled in AD 325 by the Roman Emperor Constantine; it was the first meeting of Christian leadership to decide the meaning of early scripture, which would shape Christianity for generations to come as the New Testament. Any church leader who would not endorse the *Nicaean Creed* was exiled, while those who openly challenged it were executed—a policy that represented the first formal politically sanctioned contradiction of Christ's true teachings of tolerance and non-violence.

"What does *utres* mean?" she asked.

"Madi, what comes with thunder?"

"Lightening? Prophecy of seven *lightenings?*" she asked.

I sighed dramatically.

"What's the saying, Madi? Lightening in a--?" I hinted.

Her expression turned pallid.

"You mean..."

"Yes, *utres* means *bottle*. *Prophecy of the Seven Bottles.*"

Her mouth dropped open.

"When I read of the strange carafes and the reported miracles I myself took note of the similarities," the Cardinal said. "The recent sensation reignited my interest and I downloaded your software application; I am certain it is of the prophecy."

"Why wasn't the document destroyed like others?" I asked.

"For the same reason the moth cannot avoid the flame," he answered. "It is the church's most cherished and feared secret."

The Cardinal's webcam began to cut in and out, and then died.

"Cardinal, are you there? *Cardinal De Le Montreaux*? He's offline...we've lost him," I said.

Madi nudged me with her forearm, as I had become immobile as I tried to connect with any available spiritual guidance on the sudden interruption.

"We need some music," I said.

"I have some Gregorian chants of the Benedictine Monks on my player pod," she said

"Perfect," I replied.

I began to pray to summon Christ and the masters. "Lord Jesus and great saints and souls of the ages please guide and protect us," I spoke. "Let us feel your holy presence."

Tears began to well in Madi's eyes.

"I feel such sadness and pain right now; I can't explain it."

"Madi, you're sensing souls persecuted and killed for their mystical beliefs against the dogma forced upon people in the name of religion in those dark times. They are drawn here because of the holy nature of what is unfolding and seeking closure."

Suddenly there was a brilliant white light, and a voice spoke:

"My children, if you have an ear hear me," it began.

Madi's neck swiveled as she scanned the room for the source.

"The Pharisees and the scholars have taken the keys of knowledge and have hidden them," it continued. "They have not entered nor have they allowed those who want to enter to do so. As for you, be sly as snakes and simple as doves."

"What's going on?" she asked as the source-less light faded.

"That was from the banned Gnostic *Gospel of Thomas.*"

"Ugh," she uttered in frustration. "Why can't they just come out and say, *yo, keep this on the down low but...*"

"Words could get you killed back then, Madi."

"What are the *Pharisees and scholars?*" she asked.

"Factions aligned with the darks maybe," I answered. "Some in the church no doubt."

"*Keys to knowledge* could be the document the Cardinal talked about," she suggested. "*Sly as snakes*...a foxy lizard maybe? Nah, that sounds like a pickup bar."

"What about *simple as doves*?" I asked.

She furrowed her brow and went deep in thought.

"That's it!" she exclaimed. "Doves, the Vatican! The Church's symbol is a dove!" She began typing wildly.

"The Vatican website, look," she said, "There's our dove!"

"You think he hid the document there? Where?" I queried.

"Where else?—The Secret Archives!"

"Could it be that easy?" I asked.

As she scrolled down, the words almost flew off the screen:

PROPHETIAE DE SEPTUM UTRES.DOC

"Score!" she hooted and clicked *download*. "Oh, is *he* fired."

A voice said seal up these things uttered in seven bottles until the red dragon returns in the seven of thirteen, and the prophesied mystery of seven becomes eight, no beginning and no end.

From the first bottle poured wine of PROSPERITY; *the seed, fruit, and press of all creative power, labor and increase. Seek the enriching Source first in all tilling, sowing and tending, the voice spoke. Empires will be lush vineyards of dreams for the united spiritual growth and benefit of all, not desolate soul-scorching deserts of ego, greed, lust and power to usurp, exclude and divide. Every ambition should nourish and increase the crop of all humanity, or be abandoned. Kindness, fairness, trust, true caring, compassion and love must be the sustenance circulating in the branches of all worthy endeavors of trade and commerce.*

From the second bottle flowed the ochre ambrosia of HEALING. *In the churning bowels of hurts, the translucent soul-cleansing milk of forgiveness, understanding, and acceptance neutralizes the bitterness of anger, guilt, shame and judgment; may the sweet honey of creative delight fill the basket of your soul-joy to overflowing. Remove the spirit-sapping habit of idle gossip, complaining and blame, and substitute self-control, gratitude and responsibility. Only through wisdompurified unconditional love free from impurities of hostility, misunderstanding, control, expectation, betrayal and possessiveness, will one receive.*

From the third bottle shone golden rays of inner POWER. *Inextinguishable light of courage illuminates dark chasms of unfounded fear and worry. A new confidence born of true purpose driven by Divine Light empowers you to take risks in service of others. May your lion-strong heart inspire the weak, and your sense of justice bring respect, admiration and cooperation. Let the roar of your indomitable divinely charged will clear all obstacles in your path as you fearlessly pursue and conquer in the name of love.*

As the fourth bottle unsealed, living waters of LOVE *filled the infertile valleys of thirsty hearts. Soul-suffocating obstructions of ignorance, anger, fear, resentment and hatred dissolve and wash away. New emerald forests of wisdom, self-love, and forgiveness take root and flourish, releasing the combustible ether of omniscience, fueling the Divine Spark in the sacred heart to light the kindle of all hearts. The way is now clear, the ultimate goal within reach.*

Freed from the fifth bottle were billowing light vapors of TRUTH *that dissolve dark storm clouds of mute inner-conflict. Trumpeters of clear, blue, resonant authenticity proclaim the grand opus. Stirring melodies of true heart's strings play in perfect time with the rhythmic thoughts of the in-tune heart and mind, as our symphony reaches the blissful crescendo of neverending refrain.*

From the sixth bottle poured the liquid indigo potion of starry-eye mystical dreams. In the magical keyhole are the secrets of time and space unlocked, revealed and dissolved into dust at eternity's silent feet. All KNOWLEDGE *and sight is restored and distant universes of possibility brought within reach of the telescopic lens of the infinite stargazer's singular eye.*

In the seventh do the contents of all other bottles combine to open the sacred soul flower of ENLIGHTEN-

MENT. *It is finished, as the Helper, Mary, and I come again to finish the work of the Master. I returned in flesh in the one, nine and the seven of six and one, Mary to come after as we reunite at the meeting place of sea and sand. Placed within each bottle was a key to a great abacus of stone with many libraries written on the flesh of the master returned, to make one true book.*

I sealed the seven bottles and tossed them to the sea.

As the red dragon drew nigh the earth shook with fear. A voice said: IF ONE OF SEVEN SEES THE TRUE BOOK, *those with the* LIGHT OF GOD IN THEIR HEADS WILL NOT SUFFER *the wrath of purification in the time of ten times three-hundred sixty and the return of the dragon. These true things did the voice speak and show unto me.*

I finished the reading and turned to see Madi curled up in a ball on the floor, as she rocked back and forth. Her complexion was white as the sheets.

"I don't feel so good," she said.

"You're not going to wig out on me now are you? You can't be a rock one minute and a wreck the next."

"What if I make a mistake? People have a strange habit of dying or disappearing around me," she replied anxiously.

I sensed a presence downloading into my brain. I spoke what I was receiving, though it made no sense at first...

"It wasn't your fault, Madi; there was nothing you could do."

"What did you say?" she looked at me, confused.

"You are The Helper, Madi; it's *your* name."

"My name?"

"Madelyn is *Magdala* in Hebrew, a village in Galilee; it means *Mary of Magdala*. There's a reason Madelyn is your middle name in this incarnation...and you chose to use it as your first name."

"This incarnation?" she asked, still disoriented.

"Look at the document, Madi: *I returned in flesh in the one, nine and the seven of six and one...Mary to come after at the meeting of sea and sand.* Nineteen Sixty-one is the year of my birth, remember? *I sealed seven bottles and tossed them to the sea.* Come on, Madi, it's undeniable...you know what this means!"

"No, no, no!" she waved off my assertion.

"It's true, Madi...in this banned document John the Apostle is describing future incarnations. Of all the disciples I've always felt oddly close to him; now I know why: Yochanan, *John*, was describing his future life--as me! Madi, the fact is I *was* John and you were Mary, Mary Magdalene! We were there when it happened!"

"When what happened?"

"You followed as he dragged the cross to Calvary," I answered. "You were at the tomb when ET's said he had gone."

"I was raised hard core Catholic, Avery; this is hard to wrap my head around," she resisted.

"Madi, those weren't *angels* at Jesus' tomb. They were star people. They had come to take something from his body."

"What did they take?" she replied.

I tapped my finger on the computer tablet screen.

"Read it," I answered: *Many libraries written on the flesh of the master, returned to make one true book.*

"The true book is *Jinni*," I said. "And what are the *many libraries* written on, Miryam?"

The sound of her past life name in Hebrew struck a chord in her soul memory, as she grudgingly entered in and out of a spell-like trance.

"It's okay Madi, go there," I encouraged.

She began to tremble.

"What's happening to me?" she mumbled.

"It's a regression. As Miryam, you never recovered from the horrible crucifixion of your beloved teacher, Madi."

"I don't understand," she mumbled.

"As Mary Magdalene you saw in him hopes for a terribly cruel world you didn't belong in. You never left his side, until he left you--when he was crucified." She began to weep from a deep unconscious wound.

"In this life you are unconsciously repeating the past with the early loss of your father to a stroke, then your husband--and finally--the disappearance of your child," I associated.

"No, stop, please!" she cried.

She began to ramble in broken Hebrew and English.

"He was so still, peaceful. Please wake rabbi, don't leave me," she wept deliriously. "I whispered *Amen* in his ear, but I couldn't rouse him, I couldn't," she sobbed. Speaking the sound of vibratory creation--Aum, Om, or Amen--into the ear can recall the advanced yogi from deep, death-defying samadhi, and help return their consciousness to the earth plane.

"It's alright Madi." I held her as she came out of it.

"It's not your fault," I said.

"But he died; he died for us, for me, all of us!" she cried.

"Jesus didn't die, Madi. The body was a meaningless shell to him. He could leave it or pick it up at will."

"What about our sins?" she implored.

"He didn't take the rap for anyone. Jesus came to shock the wicked and wretched into decency. If he could forgive and love those who murdered him, surely *we* could begin to forgive and love each other and ourselves, and someday even accept the real teaching he came to impart. That *someday* is now, Madi."

"This isn't the second coming most envisioned. We'll be called antichrists," she said.

"*Anyone* who denies Christ's return *in the flesh* is an antichrist according to the scripture, Madi."

"It is *his* flesh, isn't it? Jesus Christ's flesh?"

"Yes, that's what the ET's were doing at Christ's tomb while he was in nirbikalpa samadhi. There were two more unaccounted for wounds besides the holy five...those two were from samples taken. Those who reject that his DNA--*Jesus Christ's flesh*--is inside Jinni's hard drive, they are the real *anti-*Christs!"

"The ones who think they're going aren't, are they?"

"Not on this trip," I answered. She covered her mouth. "It's their lesson for narrow inflexibility in this life, and not seeking the true kingdom of heaven *within*," I added, as I gazed at the digitized relic on the computer screen. "Imagine...the answer to the world's greatest mystery, locked away in a clay jar in a church vault for centuries."

"The inscription on the front of the jar: Is there a translation?" she asked.

"Yes, here," I answered, and pointed to the screen.

A cure from a seed unplanted, the final answer written in stone, and two must become one. The seventh found, it will be done when the father returns for the son.

"Let me help you up, Madi."

"I'm okay, let's go."

I took her hand. The long hug we shared next was closure, 2,000 years in the waiting. They were already standing there when we opened the door.

{ 26 }

The Second Coming

"VIK, WHAT THE HECK IS THAT?" I asked.
"I don't know Señor; I found it by your door."
"Be careful," Madi cautioned as I opened it.
"It's some kind of intel briefing," I said.

FOR IMMEDIATE RELEASE:
Recent unexplained plane crashes linked to electro-magnetic grid pulses are due to Incoming X. Do not fly unless absolutely necessary. Massive underground fortresses and FEMA survivor internment camps are now active. Do not get within 500 yards or risk permanent capture or death. The purpose of ET/human cooperative bases and reason for lower water levels in Great Lakes has been uncovered: Precious fresh water is being pipelined via diamond thread pump hoses suspended from the ground in orbit to orbiting tankers and moon colony transports.

"Señor, this report is sent to all opposition agents upon *imminent event* status; this means the shift could happen at any time!"

"There's more." I continued reading.

Three Dark Star personnel levels are now on the move: Tier one leadership being extracted to cloaked ET ships, while top technology professionals, engineers, scientists, middle managers and select population reporting for transport to moon. Lower-level operatives remain planetary for post-shift 'reorganization.'

A public announcement of International Emergency Communications Testing has been made. Under the guise of testing a so-called back-up system, cellular networks will be intermittently interrupted, temporarily at first. The purpose is to reduce psychological impact and panic of planned longer and permanent shut-offs and to neutralize the antagonist 'inner peace' technology.

"They're talking about Jinni," Madi noted.

"We have something else to show you, Vik," I said.

He studied the photos and translation absorbedly.

"Hijole' Señor, where did you get this?"

"A Cardinal at the Vatican," Madi replied.

"Was it Cardinal De La Montreaux?" he asked.

"How did you know?" I inquired.

"He was found dead an hour ago, an apparent suicide."

"We just video chatted with him," I said.

"It's a noble death, Señor; he will be remembered as a great martyr, but what now?"

"We have to prevent the network shutdowns," I answered. "If what this is saying is true and Internet in twenty-one major cities is going to be shut down for one hour starting tonight...that could seriously hurt our cause," I added.

"Let's have another look at that church document," Viktor requested. "This talks about one of seven seeing the true book..."

"That means we need a billion Jinni addicts," Madi said.

"I agree; Viktor, it's saying the sudden change of consciousness of a billion people *is* the catalyst needed to initiate the shift," I concurred.

"Sí, but what does *the final answer written in stone* mean? "Viktor inquired.

"Maybe it's the Tiponi," Madi suggested. "We only got a few words as the computer was crashing."

"Sí, Señorita," Viktor said. "That's it--there must be more!"

"We'll have to go back to Varuna to re-run the analysis," I said.

"A bad storm is coming, Señor. You don't want to be caught out there in a dingy. Can you access Jinni remotely?"

"More bad news guys," Madi broke in. "Says here Mexico City and vicinity is one of the first on the blackout list; the network is going down in thirty minutes."

"Our tablet is cellular wireless, so remote is out," I informed. "Madi, you stay here with Viktor; I'll make a run for *Varuna* with the Tiponi. Since Jinni accesses the Internet with the NASA array, I can run the analysis now directly--without interference."

"Oh no, not without me...you're not going anywhere in this." Her expression was final.

"Madi look at me...nothing is going to happen, okay, I'll be fine. I just have to use the bathroom first."

"Alright, whatever," she relented.

When I returned she had gone.

"Vik, where's Madi?"

"I don't know, she said she had to get something."

"Where is the Tiponi--and the controller for *Varuna*?"

"I'm sorry, I do not know Señor."

"She's going for the raft, Vik, let's go, we have to stop her!"

Madi was already in the water when we arrived on the beach.

"That last wave almost capsized her. I'm going in, Vik."

"No, it's too rough," he yelled, as wind blew him off balance. I made a dash for the churning surf as a big set rolled in.

"Madi!" I yelled, but she couldn't hear me.

She went up the face of the wave near vertical. The engine whined like a buzz saw as the prop left the water. She scarcely made it over the foaming crest when a twenty-foot monster prepared to break me. I went under to avoid the onslaught as the wave smashed me and nearly crushed the air out of my lungs. I made it to the surface but the undertow dragged me out toward the next wall bigger than the last. All of a sudden a raft came zipping over the top of the swelling upsurge and spun a circle around me. I grabbed on to the side.

"Hold on!" she yelled and floored it to avoid the break. Another huge wave barreled in as I pulled myself aboard. She shrieked into the face of the wrath of Poseidon, as the Zodiac climbed straight up the monster wall. I looked back and saw horror on Viktor's face. The boat began tipping back then went straight up. Everything was in slow motion. I knew our chances if we flipped over. I had all but resigned to our fate when suddenly it seemed a giant hand had grabbed the boat, lifted us up and pulled us over the wave. We slapped down in the water well past the kelp-crushing killer that nearly claimed us, and raced beyond the big breakers to safety. Madi loosened her death-grip on the motor handle.

"If I wasn't so happy to see you alive, I'd kill you!" I yelled.

"Nice to see you too, Mr. Non-violence."

"How'd you know I was there?"

"Dude with the long hair and orange robe," she answered.

"Yogananda?"

"I felt this tap on my shoulder and he was sitting behind me; he said: *Turn around, your crazy boyfriend is going to drown trying to save you*," she imitated.

"Nice impression," I said.

She tapped on the watch controller. Varuna surfaced and we pulled alongside. I was nearly washed off by a rolling swell as I secured the raft. I quickly opened the hatch and we climbed down.

"Gotta get these wet clothes off," she said as she began to strip. "Hurry, you too or you'll get hypothermia," she warned emphatically. I obliged, though I knew it was near eighty-degree water.

"That was exciting," she said as she flung her top.

"A cup of tea and a good book would have substituted quite nicely for me," I came back.

"You risked your life for me," she said as we stood there naked, dripping wet, and panting.

"You did the same for me," I replied and threw her a dry towel. "Come on, we've got work to do," I said.

Madi sauntered up behind me on the bridge in a robe. She reshuffled the towel wrapped in her hair.

"We're getting something," I said, as the analysis progressed.

"I just realized something odd," she said, as we waited for the translation. "We've been riding around in this tin can with DNA from the actual body of Jesus Christ."

"First of all *Varuna* is not a tin can," I pretend scolded. "But it's pretty cool when you realize each tiny bit of information gets a special cyber-blessing from one of the most revered spiritual figures of the last 2,000 years."

"Who saw *that* coming," she quipped.

"John, err, *me*, apparently," I replied. "*He who eats my flesh and drinks my blood has eternal life and I will raise him up on the last day,*" I quoted the scripture.

"More code?" she asked.

"*Eat* and *drink*s are forms of nourishment, Madi, spiritual nourishment."

"Flesh could be Jinni's hardware, but what about blood?"

"What flows through the hardware?" I hinted.

"Data?"

"Cha ching, spiritualized data. Jesus' *flesh* would almost certainly have a holy vibration that would raise the frequency of everything it contacts physically--and electronically," I proposed.

"Wow," she said as she bit her apple. "No wonder this apple is so good; did *Varuna* make this in her food replicator?"

"No, Madi: *Total Foods Market.*"

"Oh."

"Speaking of data," I said, "How do the outreach metrics look?"

She opened a browser on the tablet, but a headline story stopped her cold.

"Whoa!" she gasped. "Look at these pics!"

"That's it, everyone can see it now," I said soberly.

"Looks like a tiny rust moon with a red tail," she noted.

"It's the Red Star of the Mayan prophecy; the Purifier of the Hopi, Red Dragon of scripture, Madi; there's no denying it now." As we looked at each other, we realized the ante had just been raised and the game was on; there was no turning back, and whatever happened we knew we were going to be center stage."

"We're halfway there," she disclosed reservedly. "Almost half a billion people have downloaded Jinni."

"That's good, but not enough, and we're running out of time," I said. "And now they're cutting Internet."

"We've got another problem," Madi said. "Shares, ads, comments, likes, and other posts have fallen below previous counts."

"How?" I asked.

"Only one way," she answered. "They are being erased. That's not all: Jinni's app has been deleted from several major stores."

"Sabotage," I said.

Suddenly, an ominous dialogue box appeared on the monitor. I took the pen from my mouth and tossed it down. "God sure likes to make things interesting," I quipped.

"What's wrong?" she asked.

"Add another chunk of lead to our Zeppelin...I'm getting more error codes. Jinni's been corked, I can't run the analysis."

"So much for those tiny cyber-blessings," she gibed. "Can Jinni whip up a hack to stop this?"

"Not with all these errors and glitches. This is a major offensive, Madi; they're throwing the farm at us," I replied.

"Wait a minute!" she interjected. "The inscription on the cardinal's jar said a *cure from a seed unplanted*, remember?"

"What are you thinking?" I asked.

"There were two folders on that USB drive in the sixth bottle," she answered. "What was the other one for?" she asked.

"I don't know, I forgot to check it," I answered sheepishly. I re-opened the folder and hurriedly installed the mystery files.

"By the way, when this is over you're fired," she ragged.

"Good, I need a vacation!"

All at once, an eerie glow began to come from Jinni's CPU enclosure. Translucent white swirls and tiny silvery sparkles began to move throughout the entire bridge. Windows popped up and vanished on the monitor at extraordinary speed.

"What was that?" she asked, "the divine-intervention file?"

"Those tiny cyber-blessings," I came back.

Gradually, the bizarre light dimmed. The screen was blank. Each second it remained black was like a thousand lifetimes without air. Suddenly, the monitor came back to life and the analysis appeared! I read the decoded translation:

Go to the place where men become gods.

"Of course...I get it!" I exclaimed. "Madi, text Viktor and tell him to search helicopter rentals!"

"I don't get it," she said.

"You will--soon enough."

"Cellular is down, remember?" she reminded.

All of a sudden, *Varuna* pitched violently.

Master, incoming rogue wave, impact in sixty seconds.

"Here we go again," Madi grumbled.

"Jinni, dive to safe depth, stationary!" I ordered.

Propulsion system unresponsive, Master.

"I should have bought the extended warranty," I cracked. "Madi, get in the seat and strap in now!"

Protective cushions inflated on our seats just as a huge wave lifted *Varuna* like a bath toy. I could almost smell the hot burning grind of roller coaster wheels and feel the wind in my hair as we went up and careened back down. The massive surge pinned us back and we hurled forward toward shore like a torpedo.

I flipped on the sea cam.

"Hold tight, we're gonna hit the beach," I announced.

"There's the hotel!" She yelled.

Foaming brown water and debris stirred violently as the cam gave us a washing machine-lid view of the churning milieu.

"Pool chairs!" Madi shouted.

"I think we just hit the tiki bar," I yelled.

"Talk about getting smashed," she bantered.

"The rip is pulling us back out," I said. Suddenly we stopped dead as if we hit a brick wall.

"We're stuck in the pool...let's get out before another wave comes, Madi. I'll get Jinni's hard drive, you take the Tiponi!"

As we climbed out of the beached sub, passersby offered no more than a quick puzzled glance as they rushed inland to safety.

"Señor!" A familiar voice sounded. The others were wading through debris with chair cushions as floats.

"I've been waiting for my ship to come in, but this is ridiculous!" he joked.

"We might not be so lucky with the next one, Vik."

"Follow me, Señor, our sky cab is waiting!"

Where Men Become Gods

THE NETWORK HAD BEEN RESTORED, AND Viktor received our unusual transportation request.

"We're going up in this?" Madi asked apprehensively.

"She's not pretty, Señorita, but she'll fly," the charter pilot assured.

"It's not the flying part that worries me," Madi retorted.

"Clear," the pilot said. The motor popped and coughed ominously, but smoothed out as the blades began to rotate.

"Where are we going, Señor?" Viktor asked.

"He won't tell us," Madi replied.

"It's a surprise--about thirty miles east," I disclosed.

"Seventeen major quakes in the last six hours have been reported, guys—it's gettin' real," Madi informed as she read the online reports. "Los Angeles, Tokyo, Buenos Aires, the Philippines, London..."

When was the last quake in London?" Kelly asked.

"Mexico City just got hit by an 8.0!" Madi stated.

"Maria and Oswaldo—I sent them back last night!" Viktor cried.

"I'm getting they're fine, Vik," I consoled him.

"Mira, down there!" he shouted.

Suddenly, the ground began to split open on the desert floor beneath us.

"That poor car almost fell in!" Kelly shouted.

"*Hijole!* That looks like Maria's car, and they're heading for another fissure! Señor, take us down!" Viktor told the pilot.

We quickly descended from five-hundred feet and pulled alongside the stricken car.

"Maria, stop, pull over!" Viktor yelled.

"I can't, the accelerator is stuck!" she answered.

"Pull the emergency brake," he shouted.

She held up the broken brake handle.

"Oh jeez," Madi said.

"Oswaldo, grab my arm!" he yelled to the child in the back seat. Maria gasped helplessly as Viktor pulled him out of the doomed vehicle at over sixty miles per hour.

"Viktor, make it fast, the crevice is coming," I warned, as he lifted the child in safely.

"Maria, do you have a belt?" Viktor yelled.

"No—Why?" she shouted back.

"Then take off your *sostén* and use it to tie the wheel to the door handle," he instructed. "Then climb out the window and give me your hand."

"I can't...just go!" she yelled.

"What's a sostén?" Madi asked me.

"Her brassiere, Madi."

"Oye vey," she said. "I hope it's a double D."

"Madi, this is no time to joke," I rebuked.

"I'm just saying."

"Do it woman!" Viktor roared.

Maria removed her bra and tied the wheel to the door handle. She got out to her waist and reached for Viktor's hand. Just as their hands locked, the vehicle fell into the chasm below. She shrieked in terror as her body dangled above the bottomless pit below, Viktor's tiring hand her only hope for survival. Suddenly, a rapid burst of adrenaline shot into Maria's bloodstream. Like an Olympian gymnast, she grabbed the helicopter skid and catapulted herself in.

"Going my way?" Viktor joked as she flailed in his lap and hyperventilated like a fish in a dry boat. She began tongue-lashing him in a peppery vernacular. The next few moments were silent with reflection on the near brush with disaster.

"Down there," I announced. "Ladies and gentlemen I present our next and final destination: *Teotihuacan.*"

"I knew you would come!" Oswaldo cried. "I knew it!"

"The name means: *The place where men become gods*," I said.

The scope of the ancient metropolis was striking. An avenue stretched two and a half miles through the middle. Situated along the barren pre-historic boulevard were three main structures: The Temple of Quetzalcoatl, Pyramid of the Sun and the Pyramid of the Moon.

"We were on our way," Maria disclosed. "Oswaldo wouldn't leave me alone until I promised to bring him."

Madi snapped a photo of the complex with her smartphone. As we neared touchdown I saw an astral imprint of the city's ancient inhabitants gathered below. At the end of the third world these survivors witnessed a similar but more spectacular descent of the Aztec sky god *Quetzalcoatl:* the space being with whose direction this vast complex was built.

The huge dust cloud stirred up by our rotors began to clear. We landed in the courtyard where a hundred thousand Aztecs or more would have gathered to worship their enigmatic star teacher. Only dancing tumbleweeds and the whistling wind were left to pay homage to his silent memory now. Like Chichen Itza, the site was oddly vacant.

"Look, the Pyramid of Quetzalcoatl!" Oswaldo exclaimed.

"Sí, the Aztec's *plumed serpent god*," Viktor said.

"I read it was built by a race of *gigantes* thousands of years before the Aztecs!" The boy exclaimed.

"Nobody really knows for sure who built it and when," Viktor replied. "But Aztec legends say the sky god would return."

"Will he come today, Señor Avery?" Oswaldo asked.

I was suddenly preoccupied as resident specters encircled us.

"What are you picking up?" Madi asked.

"Many spirits are here," I replied.

As I looked at the worn down red, white and yellow thunderbird motif painted on the helicopter, the realization came to me that it was not the great white god Quetzalcoatl himself, but *us*, his re-embodied envoys, who had returned to fulfill the prophecy. Clad in period tribal garb their etheric tan faces seemed to gleam starry, content that the long-awaited purpose for this great stone mystery might finally be fulfilled. Madi stared at the pic she had snapped before we landed.

"Check this out," she said. "What does this place look like to you from the air?"

"Yes, I know," I answered. "It's a big computer chip. Placement of these structures is almost an exact copy of a modern computer circuit. Those three largest buildings," I pointed out, "That's where the microprocessors would be. The layout is the same as X-rays of

Jinni's circuitry showed in that lab back in 1985," I revealed.

"Whoa," she emoted.

"And guess what coordinates this structure is aligned with?" I asked.

"The Pleiades and Orion," Stone Bear answered.

"That's right, star brother central, folks! I said.

"The whole place is layered in sheets of mica," Kelly observed.

"What's mica for?" Madi asked.

"Insulation for electronics," I answered.

Madi's face could have been cast for a mask of irony. "Earth is just a solder point on some giant cosmic computer mother board!"

"Surely this structure is more than a solder point, Señorita," Viktor said. "It is a *communications* point!"

Abruptly the earth shuddered violently. A few loose bricks tumbled off nearby monuments.

"Mira!" Maria exclaimed and pointed up to the sky.

Hundreds of red streaks showered across the sky like Independence Day fireworks.

"Meteors!" Oswaldo shrieked, clinging to Maria.

"We better move fast, Señor; we don't have much time," Viktor advised.

Our helicopter pilot fidgeted nervously.

"Señors, I, um..." He stuttered and pointed to the copter as if seeking permission to leave.

"My friend, do you have children or a wife?" Viktor asked. He shook his head no.

"Then you better stay."

"But the quakes and comets," he replied fearfully.

"Where will you go?" Viktor inquired. "Mexico City is devastated and surely you will die from what is coming next."

"Do you believe in God?" I asked.

"Yes, very much," he replied meekly.

"Our chariot driver's good karma has invited him to witness history as an immortal!" I announced, as I put my arm around him. The young pilot smiled tenuously.

"Where to now, Señor?" Viktor asked.

"Pyramid of the Sun; there's a cave," I answered.

"That's a mile walk," our pilot said. "I will take us there." We re-boarded the tin thunderbird.

"Clear."

{ 28 }

Friend in the End

OUR FLASHLIGHT BEAMS CRISSCROSSED the stone walls of the ancient Mexican passage.

"Where does this lead?" Kelly asked.

"To the center of a cloverleaf-shaped cave," I answered. "The Aztecs believed these caves were the shape of the cosmos," I added.

"Pictures from space prove it," Viktor said. "Where would the Azteca's get that idea, eh?" he kidded.

I think we're at the center," I announced.

"Stone, more stone," Maria whined. "Waste of time."

"In one of these corridors there's a cave discovered in a recent excavation; isn't that right, Oswaldo?"

"Sí, Señor Avery."

"*Ahi!*" The child led us to a spot in one of the passages.

"It's blocked," Kelly said. "I wonder what's so secret that they needed to put in a vault door?" she added.

"The secret is the reason you are here," a voice suddenly spoke from the darkness.

"Who is there? Show yourself!" Maria dared with rock in hand.

"That voice!" Madi exclaimed.

A mysterious form slowly emerged from the dank shadows; a pale man with black hair parted to one side, round lensed wire-framed glasses and a thin homely face with tired red-rimmed eyes.

Madi covered her mouth in shock.

"Oh my god is it...?" she asked.

"Yes, Madi, it's me...what's left of me."

She nearly collapsed from shock.

"I'm sorry this deception was necessary," he said.

"Necessary, Bob?" She asked furiously.

"Yes, to protect you and Jehsi. I was a working on secret government programs, Madi. I couldn't tell anyone--not even you--what I did and knew."

"E Pluribus Unum? You are The Friend?" I asked him.

"*Out of the many, one,* yes, but in reverse: *Over the many, one.* Once I realized the truth I couldn't go on. I joined the resistance against the Establishment. They've also known about the alien drive and the prophecies for quite some time. I asked to be assigned to the case—for obvious reasons."

"Why didn't you just quit, Bob?" She entreated.

"You don't leave," he answered, "or you're good as..."

Suddenly he keeled over in agony.

"Bob are you alright?" she implored, as he doubled over.

"I'm fine," he answered as he agonizingly returned to his feet.

"Jehsi is gone, Bob."

"I know."

"You know where he is, don't you?" Madi railed.

"Yes, I took him, Madi. I'm sorry...they were going to kidnap him. They knew I was alive and helping the two of you."

"Couldn't you have said something in one of those damn letters of yours?"

"And risk discovery? It took everything I had to block the remote viewers assigned to probe my mind. Who would prevent them from reading yours?"

"Where is my son, Bob?" she demanded.

"A nearby village, with members of the opposition, he's safe."

"Safe?" she cried. "The planet is going to split in two, Bob!"

"Sweetheart, please calm down..."

"Don't tell me to calm down...I want my child back now, Bob!" she fired back as she brushed away his outstretched hand.

"Madi, trust me...I am--err at least I *was*--your husband!"

"I buried you over a year ago, Bobby Blake," she cried. "Everything has changed...*everything*."

"You love *him* now don't you?" He asked.

"Use your psychic stuff to figure it out."

"It doesn't work on those you love," he replied.

"You left me, Bob. You pretended you were dead, for Christ's sake," she cried. "What was I supposed to do?"

"Your lives were in danger because of me! I had no other choice except suicide, would you have preferred that?"

He collapsed again.

"What's happening to him?" Madi asked.

"Psychic attacks," I told her.

"Uncle Sam is a very bitter former employer," Viktor added.

"This is what I've endured daily, hourly, since the moment I went underground," Bob revealed. "Even in my sleep they torture me."

"Bob, this is going to seem a little off topic...maybe even a little deluded," I interjected, but I'm getting some strong impressions...something I think you should know. I don't know any other way except to just say it...you were *Judas*."

"What?" he asked incredulously.

"Judas, you know, *Judas Iscariot*? I can't explain all the detail now, but it's *your* betrayal of Jesus that led to the crucifixion; that's why you're here now. You were Judas in a past life."

"Now *that* is a heavy cross to bear," Maria quipped.

"Maria, please!" Viktor rebuked.

"Sorry," she retracted.

"That's strange...his middle name happens to be *Jude*," Madi revealed. "Robert Jude Blake."

"The pain you've endured through helping us has been your penance, Bob. Your agony is now over," I reassured him.

Straightaway his discomfort ceased.

"The pain--it's gone!" he marveled.

"Tell us what's going on out there," I asked him.

"Level red, evacuations are in full swing," he said feeling anew his long-tortured body. "The highest ranks are now off the planet."

"Have the people been told?" I inquired.

"The president disclosed everything and he'll be left behind for it. Communications have all but been cut off, except for some global elements of the Internet and power grids that strangely the darks have been unable to override or shut down."

"Jinni, the *seed* unplanted," Madi uttered and looked at me.

"Yeah, tiny little cyber-blessings," I replied with a faint smile.

"I wonder if we made it," she asked.

"I think we're about to find out," I replied.

The ground shook again as pieces of the cave began to fall.

"Cha-cha-cha!" Maria chirped clapping. "Let's get going or we are going to die in here."

"She's right; this geology can't take much more," Kelly warned. "We'd better go or this cave will be our tomb."

"Mira!" Viktor exclaimed. "The quake loosened the stones by the door to the cave!" We removed the shattered pieces and squeezed in through the narrow passage to its terminus.

"What, another door?" Maria kvetched.

"There's a thin crack down the middle; it must open somehow," I said, and began feeling for a release.

"Look at these walls," Bob noted. "The cut angles and the focal point at the door; they're not for decoration."

"*Sonido*! It opens with sound!" Viktor hypothesized.

Everyone began making sounds, clapping, yelling, whooping, hollering, but nothing happened. Suddenly, a deep low-pitched hum emerged from behind us. Stone Bear was standing in two foot-shaped wells carved into the rock floor.

"Om, Om, Om," he chanted.

Amazingly, the slab began to retract. We were in disbelief.

"How did you know, Stone Bear?" I asked him.

"Just my shoe size, I guess."

"Señor, the Greek insignia for the word *Omega* is carved in stone between the feet!" Viktor observed.

As we entered the sacred chamber, we were awestruck by its splendor. The room was pyramid-shaped, fifty feet from floor to apex. The entire interior surface was beautiful glass-smooth mica. Arrays of flawlessly polished mirrors were arranged in a pattern of clusters that suggested a purpose beyond mere decor. A solid quartz crystal pedestal stood in the center of the chamber embellished with copper, gold and huge multi-colored cut gems.

"It's lovely," Kelly gaped. "But what is it for?"

"The mirrors look to be positioned to reflect something from the apex into those channels on each side of the pyramid," I answered.

"Something is missing from the pedestal," Viktor observed.

The ground resumed shaking like a mad trampoline. We were tossed to the hard floor. Though longer in duration and intensity, the shuddering finally stopped. Amidst a refrain of moans and groans we returned to our feet.

"Time to end this before we turn to Jell-O," Madi declared. "Give me the Tiponi and get out Jinni's hard drive," she directed.

Stone Bear removed the Tiponi from his backpack. I opened the safe box and removed Jinni's drive.

"The inscription on the Cardinal's jar said *two must become one*," Madi said. "Somehow this drive goes inside this Tiponi, which then goes on *that* pedestal," she added decisively.

"Question is how," I asked. "The thin rectangular outline on the Tiponi seems to have no visible external means of removal."

"I know," Oswaldo said. "Put the Tiponi on the *plataforma* and maybe it will open."

We were flabbergasted by the obviousness.

"Stone Bear, please do the honors for your people and put the Tiponi on the pedestal," I said.

"I do it for *all* people!" he replied as he set it in place.

"Fits like a ruby slipper," Madi remarked.

Seconds turned into a minute, then two, still nothing. A few restless sighs and grumbles came from the group.

Finally, Viktor let out a deep, long exasperated *ugh*. A quick rattling noise came from the pedestal.

"Did you hear that?" Madi asked. "He made that sound and that thing did something," she added.

Viktor repeated the sound and the noise repeated.

"Is anyone thinking what I'm thinking?" Madi asked.

"Sí," Vik replied. "Quickly, everyone start chanting Om!"

After a muddled intro that sounded like dying cows, rich choruses of *Oms* echoed and vibrated the chamber with increasing intensity. On the seventh repetition it happened, like tumblers in a lock, and with a cadre of clicks, pops and grinding noises.

"It's opening," Madi cried, "the Tiponi is open! Hurry," she urged me. "Put the hard drive inside of it!

"I wouldn't do that if I were you," a voice suddenly spoke up.

Two men had entered the chamber; one with a gun and the other carried a small toddler.

"Jehsi!" Madi cried.

"Put the hard drive down and step aside," one man ordered.

"Give me my son!" she roared like a protective lioness.

"Relax, lady; do what you're told and somebody might not get hurt."

"What are *you* looking at?" the other asked as they advanced.

"He's just a boy; leave him alone," Stone Bear replied.

"Shut up, totem pole," the intruder snapped and hit him with his pistol. "Everyone line up against the wall," the man ordered, as he waved his pistol threateningly.

"Do I look familiar, *rock star?*" one crook asked me.

"Sorry, all sewer slugs look alike to me," I replied.

"I told you you'd fail Mr. Jesus, didn't I?" he shot back.

Abruptly, the earth buckled again more intensely, and that was our opportunity. In the milieu Madi grabbed Jehsi from the stumbling rogue while I recovered Jinni's drive. Bob accosted the man with the weapon. A tussle ensued, but more intense tremors prevented our reaching him.

Suddenly, gunshots rang out and Bob fell to the ground.

"Oh my god, Bob, no!" Madi shrieked.

Viktor went to him, felt his pulse and shook his head.

"I'm sorry, he's gone," he pronounced.

"Alright, cut, this scene is all wrong!" a strident voice rang out.

Nobody noticed how the man in an ocher robe--who earlier defied physical law by floating above the waves--had entered the temple.

"Master!" I called out exuberantly.

"Where did *you* come from towel head?" the slick-tongued offender that had earlier crashed the One Nation event asked.

"I come from *Mars*," the swami turned and replied facetiously with a contorted, ghoulish face and wiggling fingers.

"Oh, you don't like fire do you?" he asked in a shrill Hindi accent. All of a sudden the man dropped to the floor.

"Fire, I'm burning!" he yelled.

Viktor grabbed the gun and threw it.

"You," he said to the other, his eyes shining like a thousand sun-charged diamonds, "is it spiders or bees you hate; I cannot recall," he added, pinching his chin inquisitively.

"Bees, why?" he answered.

"Ah, thank you!" the master replied.

Spontaneously, the man began to sprint around the temple as a swarm of unseen winged pollinators chased and stung him. He fell to the floor passed out from fear.

"Okay," the master said. "Places everyone, then action!"

"Master, what about him," I said and pointed to Bob's bleeding, lifeless form.

"What about him?" he replied nonchalantly.

"Can you help him?" I asked.

"God can, through one who believes in life over the dream. Will he live or die? I guess we won't know until the next scene!" he said with contrived enthusiasm, as he rubbed his hands together.

"Master, please," I said.

"What?" he asked and dropped the act. "You could have done this all yourself," he went on quietly smiling. "You are like the big dog who does not know his own size, cowering before miniatures. Those are the best kind though," he laughed, "because they don't know God has made them big. God likes that because ego is gone, and that's the only thing that keeps us from him. *You* are a master now," he said as he beamed silent approving rays of the Infinite at me, and put his astral-produced hand on my shoulder. "You always were— and now...you have *realized* it.

"I will come when you need me, but not always when you call me. *Lazarus* lives," he added with a wink and vanished.

To our astonishment Bob began to stir then rise. The gaping bloody bullet hole had totally vanished.

"What happened?" he said holding his head.

"You dreamed you died," Stone Bear replied.

Again the earth heaved, as mica dust fell on our heads.

"Now is the time, Señor," Viktor nodded hastily.

"This device," I began to speak as I held up the drive, "was willed to me on a deserted highway by mysterious benefactors long ago. Unknown to me at the time, its memory was constructed of the precious DNA of Jesus Christ obtained by extraterrestrials after the crucifixion. Today it is joined by the vibratory essence of the enlightened thoughts of millions of like-minded souls, written upon it for the purpose of fulfilling a Divine compact planned for millennia by a committee of spiritual superstars and advanced celestial and inter-dimensional beings. Who would have known we had such a big family!" I chuckled.

"Avery, now, please!" Madi urged, as the shaking continued.

"I know I'm rambling. Let me say it's been an honor to have played in this drama with you all," I said as I beamed at my co-starring cast. "The Second Coming says that *what Jesus and the Masters achieved we can all achieve;* we must, for this is the only reason we keep coming back, and we will continue to return in suffering and disillusionment until we realize this. Through the spiritual star-science behind all true religions, and through the masters, saints and sages of all religions and ages, including the now *true Gospel of Jesus Christ;* our Maker has given us the original and sure means to return to Him. Nothing else will ever satisfy the longing in our hearts and souls, nothing.

"Blessed are you all in Christ and the Eternal Cosmic Masters of the Supreme Realization. I thank you from my heart in Him,"

Amidst strengthening tremors, I inserted Jinni's drive into the Tiponi.

{ 29 }

Cosmic Overdrive

A N INTENSE LIGHT BEGAN TO GLOW AROUND the pedestal, yet we could stare at it; we had to; it was irresistible. Rays shot up in succession at seven hanging mirror and gem-like clusters. Radiant beams began to multiply like dominoes, as spectacular holograms of geodesic patterns and mandalas unraveled within our own infinite perception.

I was aware of distant galaxies, star systems and their planets. I could count their moons and the beings that inhabited them. I knew their stories; their knowledge was my own. The history and future of countless dimensions flashed before my omniscient awareness. I experienced the complete cycle of life of every plant, mineral, object, each speck of dust, cell, molecule and atom on every level of vibration--from gross material to causal idea, from birth to death and renewal--and then the absolute insight:

It is all me, all God, all now.

Scott Troy Kovarik

Then, like a plunge into an icy bath, my awareness returned to the cold hard walls of the pyramid in time for the next scene.

A six-inch wide beam shot up from a metallic and crystal canopy above the Tiponi to the apex. Simultaneous beams fired at the sides of the pyramid into four channels that presumably led to other parts of the complex. A peaceful, soothing hum undulated throughout the sanctum. I was in the midst of a portal that could slurp my awareness back into eternity at any moment.

Each member of our party knew intuitively that everyone on earth who made the shift was having the exact same experience. We were all one mind, body and soul: We were CHRIST CONSCIOUSNESS, the only begotten SON of GOD manifest in the world. Truly, we knew we *had* all been given power to become Sons and Daughters of God.

Directed by silent command, we left the pyramid. No words were spoken, or needed. It was night, but the entire complex was enveloped in light. Suddenly, seven beams shot from the top Pyramid of the Sun toward the Pleiades stars. At the same time, shafts of light from presumably pyramids all over the world, converged with the others in a singular point in the sky. The same luminous geometry we witnessed inside now began to infuse the entire horizon and sky. Then, all at once, it stopped. The cosmic grand finale had ended and all was still.

A few token creatures called out rhythmically from the wilds, yet something integral had changed, like when you were a kid and you came back from vacation; you knew you were home but everything seemed a little less familiar. Old smells were new again. You couldn't wait to jump on your own bed, bury your face in your pillow, use your own toilet, run next door and scream *we're home*. It was kind of like that. We were home but it was all new.

Who would speak first? You felt like recording it, writing everything down. This was history prime time; we all knew. Thoughts seemed louder, more dimensional with texture. Perhaps words had taken a back seat to thoughts in the shift; fine with me.

There was no script now. In a thousand years people would probably debate every word, or maybe not because the world was different, more transparent, less self-serving and materially focused. But what changed? Who was left behind? What structures and businesses remained? Was there power and communications? Who was in charge? These questions would soon be answered.

"Are we dead or something?" Maria broke the ice and spoke.

"In a way," I answered. "Death is just change from one consciousness to another," I added. "In each moment we are dying toward realization of the Infinite or dying into more delusion."

"Beautiful," Kelly said looking up. "The stars are like glowing plums you could almost pick out of the sky."

"Earth Spirit is breathing easy under my feet again," Stone Bear shared.

"I could stay here for a day, a week, no hurry, no feeling I have to do something or be somewhere," Madi spoke.

"That's the *flow*," I said. "The planet is now free from the dense material vibrations of ignorance and greed."

"So what's next, Avy-ji?"

"What do you *want* to be next?" I asked.

"Mexico City," he answered.

"Feels right to me," I replied.

Viktor opened the copter's gas cap and put his nose to it.

"Sí, refined gasoline Señor, we *are* alive!" he cackled.

We rose in the air to witness the first dawn, as the sun's astral twin fired up the newborn sky in swashes of red, yellow, amber, and violet. Light is one of those few words for which there is no synonym, as everything is already one in it.

In the distance a few columns of smoke arose from the city.

"The only destruction here was what occurred up to the moment of the shift," I stated in anticipation of their thoughts.

"What are those big silver things in the air?" Maria asked.

"Ships," I answered over the sound of chopper blades.

"Como?" she replied skeptically.

"*Cosmic Red Cross*," Madi replied.

"Aliens are real!" Oswaldo exclaimed.

"They will help teach the old ways," Stone Bear said, "Like they did for our brothers at the end of the last world."

"Except this time we have photographic evidence!" Madi quipped as she took a shot with her phone.

"They will tell the survivors what happened," I replied.

Some residents drifted by, confused, while others more aware reached out to help others.

"Don't worry, there are many here to help ease the anxiety and sadness," I said as we walked.

"Look, a camp," Madi said.

Tents and rows of tables and chairs filled the compound. People were being lovingly escorted to seats with plates of food, drinks and other items. Family members made tearful reunions. Huge monitors on poles featured presentations of people calmly explaining things in English and Spanish.

"They look like us," Madi said.

"They can assume any physical form they like," I replied.

"Better than little green men, eh?" Viktor joked.

"Hey, I got a cell signal," Madi said. "But most of my contacts are gone." Frantically, she skimmed through her phone book. "My mom...she's gone too!" she cried.

"I'm sorry, Madi," I responded. "The details of reality are conforming to those who made the shift." Bob awkwardly tried to console her. Others began checking their contacts.

"Everyone, I know we are all concerned about our friends and loved ones; know that no matter what they are safe," I solaced. "I have to return to the Manzanilla Hotel now," I added.

"I will fly you there, Señor," our pilot said.

"Going back to California, Avy-ji?"

I nodded.

"I could use a ride if you don't mind," Bob said.

"Sure," I answered.

Madi tried to conceal her uneasiness.

"Stone Bear, Kelly, I'm sure you're both more than ready to begin your journey home to Arizona," I said.

"Wherever my feet are is home now," Stone Bear answered. "But the ancestors are calling. We will find a way north; the Great Spirit will guide us."

Just then a car pulled up. The anonymous driver gazed at Stone bear and nodded cheerfully, then spoke.

"I'm heading to Arizona, need a ride?" he asked.

"See," Stone Bear said.

Stone Bear and I hugged as our watery eyes met on a beam of mutual respect and blessings.

"I will never forget," he said reverently.

"Of course you won't...we saved the world together!" I replied. All waved and smiled as the car pulled away.

"You know I must stay, Avy-ji," Viktor said.

"Yes, and I'll miss you most of all," I replied warmly.

"Me too scarecrow," Madi joked.

"Okay, okay, let's get on with it. I'm sure we'll see you all *somewhere over the rainbow*," Maria chimed in. "Muchas gracias, Señor Avery," she added sincerely and hugged me. "You have awakened me and given me a new life."

"El gusto es mio. Adios," I said, as the three of them walked away hand in hand.

We touched down at Manzanilla.

"Where's the hotel," Madi asked.

"There have been a few adjustments," I answered. "Some things aren't needed for the *new way*," I replied. "They're all just programs, Madi, props divinely placed, sustained, or dissolved according to Supreme Will."

"Well this is one heck of a reboot," she noted.

Varuna was where we had left her, less the pool. As the tide came up she slowly drifted off the beach into the belly of the new Pacific blue. On deck I scribbled notes between glances at the sky. Madi came up from below.

"What are you doing?" she asked.

"Navigating," I answered. "Old school, no GPS, apparently."

"What about homes, cars and stuff?" She asked.

"I don't think we'll see ownership quite like before."

"What about jobs? I think I'm about out of PTO."

"People will be encouraged to do what they do best, Madi. Artists will paint, musicians will sing, actors will entertain, farmers will farm, caregivers will care for others. We'll be supported to live simply, creatively and spiritually. I know it's tough to envision, but there won't be any resistance or difficult survival issues like before when we followed our delusions about happiness. Like you saw with the sudden appearance of Stone Bear's ride, as long as you are growing on the path and living authentically what you need will show up without struggle."

"Level with me...we *are* dead aren't we?" Madi quipped.

"Yes, Madi, and I am Saint Peter; of course we're not dead! The only thing dead is the old way that brought misery."

She looked out to sea nostalgically.

"What does all this mean for you and me?" she asked.

"I'm not sure," I answered.

"You *are* the love of my life, Avery Cole."

"I love you, Madi, as God appearing to me in your form; in that way we are one. But I know that as soon as I separate you from that oneness mentally I must suffer some form of delusion and upset. You're still attached to the untrue drama of the dream--and conflicted within. You feel guilt over him, but memories won't be enough anymore."

"He risked his life; maybe that deserves a chance," she replied.

"A rose blooms for you to see and adore then it dies and falls away. You can't resurrect the old leaves and paste them back on the living plant, Madi."

She slinked below in tears. Faint sobs came from her bunk throughout the night as *Varuna* cut through the saline strata of the new sea.

Bob went to her door. I intercepted him.

"Leave her alone," I said. "She is going with you, but against her heart."

"Then why?" he asked.

"She thinks it's the right thing to do," I answered.

"She loves you," he said.

"She loves the *idea* of me, but I love God, Robert, the one in all, so how could I confine my love to just one, selfishly? She knows that. The temptations could destroy us both spiritually if she stayed; she's saving us both," I told him. "Love her no matter what."

"I will," he replied.

"Thank you for all you did," I said.

"It is I who should be thanking you," he replied.

{ 30 }

Time Aftertime

MARINA DEL REY WAS A THROWBACK to black and white. At least fifty years of so-called progress had vanished. As we cruised in the quiet harbor, ET ships buzzed in and out like the set of a sci-fi movie. I found a vacant slip in the made-over port and pulled in. I called down to the passengers and slipped into the forward berth.

"Where's Avery?" Madi asked. "I have to say good-bye."

"It's best you don't," Bob said. "Let's just go."

I could hear resistance, then a quiet shuffling out. A short spear of sadness overcame me, an upstart surge of self-pity even. Once I was sure they had gone I left the boat. As I wondered, I spotted a transition camp near what was Venice Boulevard.

I got a text from Madi.

I love you always, it read.

I pondered a reply when two men approached.

"Are you Avery Cole?" one asked.

"Yes," I answered.

"Will you please come with us?" one asked politely. I nodded. We entered a house-sized tent with a metallic door cloaked by canvass flaps. In a nearby room a man sat behind a desk clerk-like with office supplies and papers scattered on the desk. I sensed they were props and that he wasn't exactly from earth, and he knew I knew. Suddenly all three got up and performed an unfamiliar ritual of movements. I bowed in return. His lips never moved, but I heard him speak.

"You are the awakened one here."

"How may I serve?" I projected back.

"The Supreme Master seeks volunteers," he replied.

"Volunteers?"

"The other world is in need of teachers," he said.

"If I'm needed to help my brothers and sisters, then His will is spoken through you," I transmitted my reply in thought.

"There is much destruction, no land will be familiar, there will be few conveniences and those in power before will return. You will be alone and your views unpopular. You will be persecuted."

"Sounds like my last day job. How long will I stay?" I asked.

"Fifteen earth years."

"Whoa," I reacted.

"Do you decline?" he asked.

"Considering the source, it's an offer I don't think I can refuse." Suddenly, the desk and occupants disappeared. The room turned white, much as my old Pinto did that night long ago on a dark, lonely Seattle highway. I awoke in a cave by a fire, with a huge body of water just outside the entrance.

"Who are you?" a startled man in torn clothing said bellicosely.

"Name's Cole," I answered.

"Didn't see you come in; whaddya want?"

"I'm a friend," I replied.

"Nobody's a friend now," he said. "It's every man for himself."

"We need friends now more than ever. We'll survive better if we work together," I retorted. He grumbled and poked the fire.

"What is that out there?"

"My front door," he replied.

"I mean the water; is it a lake?" I asked.

"Don't think it has a name yet...was Yellowstone."

"Yellowstone National Park, *Wyoming*?"

"No, Beverly Hills," he replied sarcastically. "Of course it's Wyoming! Prime beachfront property now, though. Welcome to the new coastline of the northwest United States of America!" He declared.

"Are there other survivors?" I asked.

"If there are I haven't seen any yet."

"Nice," I muttered. "I could have been in a nice warm alien transitional camp in Socal sipping hot synthesized cider."

"Huh?"

"Forget it."

"Where you from, mister?" he asked.

"Long story."

"Got nothin' but time," he replied.

"You probably wouldn't believe me," I said.

"After what I've just been through, you could tell me Jesus Christ himself *sentchya* and I might believe it."

"Funny thing about that," I responded. "You might want to sit down."

{ 31 }

A Thousand Words

OUR ASHRAM WAS IN THE HILLS OF WHAT WAS Ohio. I had found my way there with travelling bands along one of the few remaining interstates. What remained was mostly dirt and gravel, as the quakes and shifting earth had damaged most beyond usefulness, but there were paths for foot and rarer vehicle traffic. I made a few friends and even recruited a few students along the way.

Parts of the former buckeye state were now submerged as the Great Lakes had emptied during the shift making a new system of rivers and smaller lakes. Old exposed lakebeds formed a muddy life-devoid land bridge all the way to Canada. Debris, old tires and the occasional shipwreck marked the transfigured marine wasteland, while in other places new mountains sprang up in the geological reboot.

Small communes began to form within months of the shift, some run by surviving elites and their horded technology. Violent crime and power struggles were commonplace. I sat chatting with students in the relative safety of the tranquil foothill retreat.

"Master," one young student spoke, "the more I study the more I see even the simplest things are lessons."

"Do you have an example?" I asked.

"No matter how hot our ashram gets in the day, when exposed to the long hours of night, it gradually becomes cool again."

"What is your insight?"

"When we expose ourselves to conditions long enough we become like them," he answered. "I feel my willpower and good habits deteriorate when I'm in extended company with miscreants in town."

"I think you just took the pebble from my hand," I replied. "I had another student do that once." I laughed reminiscently.

"The chameleon can blend with its surroundings, yet always remains a chameleon," I said. "Put on the adaptable, indestructible skin of wisdom through relentless self-study. Make self-improvement your permanent soul-pattern and meditate on God, incessantly," I told him. "With your thoughts fully centered on the Infinite you can walk safely through the roasting fires of Hades."

The silent wind gave sudden dance to the green troupe of leaves in the trees above as birds called and sang in applause.

"Everything is God," I went on. "He dreams Himself as us all both ignorant and wise. You are his lit candle lighting the candle souls of all others with His flame. But when the ego thinks it is doing it the flame goes out and you fall back into darkness."

"Yes, Master," he replied.

Suddenly, the room began to slip away.

"Master, are you alright?" the student asked.

"If God is safe, so am I!" I replied with one last truth nugget. Everything turned white and my body went weightless: It had been fifteen years to the day. I dematerialized before my astonished followers and awoke seated sitting in sermon on a sunny hill before the congregation of the vast blue Pacific Ocean: My beloved Latigo Canyon! Dirt had replaced the once-paved road, yet the location was familiar. I followed the trail to the top and there was the shack! Clothing hung on a cord flapping in the sea breeze. There was a garden and a rusted old swing in the back. Someone lived here, I thought. I couldn't leave without knocking.

"Hi," I said. "Do you live here?"

"Who are you?" a startled teenage boy replied.

"I lived here once a long time ago," I replied. "Just curious, sorry to bother you."

"No problem," he replied.

I turned to walk away.

"Wait," he said as he eyed me carefully. "You look like the man in the pictures," he said.

"What pictures?" I asked.

"Sweetie, who's at the door," an unseen voice called.

"A man says he used to live here, mom," he answered. I heard footsteps shuffling toward the door.

"Oh god!" the female voice exclaimed.

As our eyes met the glass jar she'd been holding fell to the floor and exploded into a thousand tiny pieces.

"Hello Madi...you look well."

It was as if each shard had shot from our bursting hearts, sharp tokens of crystal-clear memories and lost years now restored.

"Is it really you or am I seeing things? I had seen you many times in my room in meditation," she said.

"Yes, it's me in the flesh. At least I seemed to have made the trip back with my physical body intact," I joked wryly. Many times I tried to project my form to you from the other world, so you'd know I was all right. I'm happy you got the message." Her smile was like an endless field of blooming daisies. She rushed into my arms and squeezed me breathless.

"I thought I had lost you," she cried, "but eventually I found your soul within my own...in God."

"I see you've been practicing the methods; you've come far," I praised her.

"Yes," she replied. "But I've done nothing; it's all Him *and you.*"

"Even further than I thought then!"

She blushed humbly.

"Who is this handsome young man? Jehsi? Boy, you've grown!" I said.

"Sweetie," she told the child. "Could we be alone for a moment? Please go clean your room."

"Aw, momma," he protested. She gave him *the look* and he acquiesced.

"I came to look for you, Avery. I changed my mind. I knew I couldn't live in the past, but I couldn't find you. Eventually, I had to tell Bob the truth about *Avi* and that was just the reason he needed to set me free. Jehsi went to stay with him."

"Tell Bob what about whom? And who is Avi?" I asked.

"Please--sit down," she said.

"Madi, what's going on? Is he...?"

"Yes, Avery," she said beaming, "I was pregnant with a child...with your child; he is *your* son!"

"What's his name?" I asked in shock.

"Avari, of course!"

"What you do to good English names!" I joked. "Who does he think his father is?"

"Bob was the only father he ever knew," she answered. "Would you like to go talk with him?"

I knocked on the door.

"Come in."

"Hey," he said.

"Hope I'm not interrupting anything."

"So are you like one of mom's old boyfriends or something?"

"Why do you say that?"

"I can tell by the way you look at each other," he replied.

"Yes, we were lovers once."

"Whoa, too much information!" the boy came back.

"What did you mean I look like *the guy* in the pictures?"

"Some pictures I found down by the beach," he replied.

"What beach?"

"Malibu Road. Mom said she used to live there when Jehsi was born. I found it buried in sand there--with the pics on it."

"It?"

He reached down for something under his bed.

"I found them in this," he said.

"May I see that please?"

"Sure," he replied.

"Have you shown this to your mom?" I asked.

"No. I found *this* inside with the pictures on it," he answered.

"Can you show them to me?" I asked.

"Sure and there's some other files on here too," he said.

"What do you think the other files are for?" I asked.

"They kind of look like an early version of *Ekajnana*."

"What is Ekajnana?" I asked.

"Our teacher."

"Teacher?" I asked.

"Yeah, this." He handed me a beat up smart phone.

"We go to school on Eka, ask her questions and she answers; Eka is the source of all our knowledge and teaching."

"Eka and jnana mean *one knowledge* in Hindi," I told him.

"Eka says the *First Father* helped create it at the beginning of the fifth world," he replied.

"Who's this *first father?*" I asked him.

"His name was Avery Cole. He made a computer from a chip given to him by star people that helped bring peace after the shift; that's *Ekajnana*. Our writings say seven bottles went to sea, but only six returned."

"Ah, so you think this might be one of *those* bottles," I questioned.

"If so it could be priceless!" he replied. "The other six are at the sacred shrine. This one's probably fake though."

"So this *Ekajnana*...How did it save the world again?" I asked.

"It taught people to live in peace and know God through the One Religion, the *Kriya* of Ekajnana."

I sensed Madi by the door.

The boy clicked on the folder and opened it.

"I feel like I know the people in these photos," he said, "but the pictures look so old."

"Madi come in," I said.

She came in beaming.

"Look how you've grown in Spirit," I praised and took her hand. "You even dress in a *sari*, which you look beautiful in."

"Thank you *Master*," she replied. "I made it myself."

"Master? What's going on here?" the child asked.

"Avari, we have something to tell you," Madi began. "The man who threw those bottles into the sea..."

"It was me...I'm Avery Cole, son."

"What?" the child exclaimed. "Mom, is this one of your pranks?"

"He knows you well!" I cracked.

"No, it's true Avi," she replied.

"Wait, if your name is Avery and my name is *Avari* and you guys, were, well you know, and you just called me son, then are you my..."

"Yes, Avi, he, Avery, is your father," Madi confirmed.

"Avari, those pictures were taken when I was about your age and lived in your mom's old place on the beach years before she did. That's how we met. She came down on the beach as I was about to release the bottles. I must have accidentally left the photos on the USB drive I placed in the seventh bottle."

"No wonder they're familiar," Madi said. "He looks like you, so handsome," she added proudly.

"But that place I found them," the boy said, "something happened there, but I can't remember what."

"And I think I *know* what that thing was," I responded. "Remember the inscription, Madi, the last line of the prophecy?"

"I think I know where you're going with this; a past life?"

"You still got that prophecy-cracking thing don't you?"

"It's like riding a bike. Do you think he's ready?" she asked.

"What are you guys talking about? Who's past life and ready for what?" The child asked with his confusion at a fevered pitch.

"Before you were born, Avari, your mother and I helped solve the prophecy that enabled many to survive the shift.

"Mom, you were the *Helper*?" he asked excitedly.

"Yes, baby...most of the time," she replied.

"A line of text on an old church relic uttered a final but until now unfulfilled prediction, Avari," I said.

"*The seventh found, it will be done when the father returns for the son.*"

"You found the seventh bottle, Avari!" Madi exclaimed.

"Whoa, seriously?" he asked, his eyes afire.

"Yes, and you have fulfilled the final prophecy, the Prophecy of the Seven Bottles!"

"Wow, and it said you'd come back for me, cool!" Avari said.

"Well, actually it's not saying that *I* came back for *you.*"

"What? I don't understand," the boy replied.

"You see, Avari, the picture you found on that drive that seems so familiar to you is a picture of me, yes, but with *my* father.

"I'm totally confused now," he said.

"Avi, what the prophecy was really saying," I began, "was not that I came back for you, but that you actually came back--for me."

The shell, the body had changed, but not his eyes, the windows of the soul. As I looked at him the years of separation melted away. He was still unable to remember, but at least he was here.

"It's good to see you again, Dad."

Prophecy of the Seven Bottles

ABOUT THE AUTHOR

Scott Troy Kovarik is an author, musician, and songwriter with music on film and television. He has studied and practiced spiritual, self-help and Kriya Yoga methods for over thirty years. Scott is also a health and wellness consultant in the medical field. He has a Bachelor's in Science degree in Political Science, was born, and currently lives in Cleveland, Ohio USA

CPSIA information can be obtained at www.ICGtesting.com
Printed in the USA
LVOW10s0057290715

447962LV00001B/70/P